WESTON FIELDS

The Weather Belt

Book Two of the Guardians of Kawts Trilogy

First published by Lumen Books 2025

Copyright © 2025 by Weston Fields

All rights reserved. No part of this publication may be reproduced, stored or transmitted in any form or by any means, electronic, mechanical, photocopying, recording, scanning, or otherwise without written permission from the publisher. It is illegal to copy this book, post it to a website, or distribute it by any other means without permission.

This novel is entirely a work of fiction. The names, characters and incidents portrayed in it are the work of the author's imagination. Any resemblance to actual persons, living or dead, events or localities is entirely coincidental.

The theological beliefs expressed by characters in this book do not necessarily reflect the theological opinions of the author. All acts of God are purely fictional, although they have been based off of similar real-life accounts whenever possible.

First edition

ISBN (paperback): 979-8-9867921-4-9
ISBN (hardcover): 979-8-9867921-5-6

This book was professionally typeset on Reedsy.
Find out more at reedsy.com

Sign up for my newsletter at weston-fields.com to receive regular updates on future titles and get a free copy of the previously unreleased short story "The Smugglers."

Chapter 1

"According to the map, we should only be a few hours out," Howard said, the tips of his mustache fluttering in the wind. Timothy nodded and studied the horizon, one hand shielding his eyes from the late afternoon sunlight. "We might as well set up camp here for the night. We want to make sure we have plenty of daylight when we get to the site of the attack."

Howard nodded and glanced down at his tablet. "I'll send the drone on a reconnaissance run," he said, directing the reprogrammed attack drone hovering overhead to scout out the intervening terrain. The dome-shaped robot zipped off, the familiar buzzing sound dying away as it disappeared over the hills.

Timothy flinched as the drone flew past him, instinctively reaching for a shuriken. Then he stopped himself, shaking his head.

"No matter how many times you use that thing, it still makes me nervous. It's hard to get used to having an attack drone that's not shooting at us."

Howard laughed. "It's definitely a bit of an adjustment. But these drones really are quite versatile. It's easy to see why the Council favored them."

At the mention of the Council, Timothy stiffened. Although the rebellion had succeeded in overthrowing the Council, the Council members themselves had managed to escape in the confusion. Among them was Timothy's friend Aksell, who had sided with his father, the Councilman Ethos, in the battle.

If I'd just been a little faster, Ethos wouldn't have gotten away. I had the chance to attack him, but instead, I froze.

He shook his head, forcing himself to focus on something other than the Council. His mind drifted to his present mission, he looked up toward the horizon.

He and Howard had spent the last week hiking to the place where Timothy's brother Maurice had been last seen. Maurice had vanished from Kawts during the Council's reign, along with his fiancée and best friend. At Timothy's request, Gearwire eventually tracked them as far as the camp of one of the nomadic tribes in the area. Unfortunately, the camp had been attacked by the Council, and Maurice and his companions had vanished once more. They were presumed dead, but their bodies were never found.

A frown flickered across Timothy's face.

If Maurice is still alive, surely he would have come back to Kawts by now. He sighed. *I wish Jewel was with me for this. I was hoping she would be out of the hospital by now.*

He glanced at his companion.

I suppose Howard is probably the better choice, anyway, he consoled himself. *With those inventions of his, he'll be able to help me track down and identify any... remains we find at the campsite.*

"Thanks again for agreeing to come out here with me," Timothy said to Howard.

Howard nodded. "Of course. If it wasn't for you, most of my family would still be Blanks. It's only right that I should help you try to locate your brother."

Timothy shook his head. "I think we all already know what happened to him. But it would be nice to know for sure. At least for Mom and Dad's sake." He trailed off, lost in thought. "It's hard to believe it's been over a year now."

Howard smiled sympathetically. "I'm sorry that it's taken so long for this mission to get put together."

Timothy sighed. "Yeah. But Samuel needed our help. Undoing the Council's crimes is more than a full-time job."

Which is yet another reason I was hoping Jewel and I could do this together, he added silently. *It would have been nice to hang out for a few days somewhere away from all the chaos. We both could have used a break.*

Howard's tablet beeped twice, interrupting Timothy's reflections. The scientist squinted down at the device, a puzzled frown on his face.

"What is it?" Timothy asked, surprised by the surge of anxiety he felt. "Did the drone find them?"

Howard shook his head slowly. "It found something. I'm not quite sure what. The radar footage almost makes it look like a ship."

"A ship? Like a boat? Or like Gearwire's ship?"

"Like Gearwire's."

"I didn't know anyone else had a ship around here."

Howard's frown deepened. "Me neither. Of course, for all we know, it could be nothing more than an oddly shaped boulder. All I'm really getting is the general outline of the thing." He looked up at Timothy. "It's pretty close to the camp. We can check it out tomorrow after we've examined the site."

Timothy nodded. "Sounds like a plan."

There was silence for a moment, and Timothy became aware of a low humming sound in the distance. He froze, listening intently.

"Do you hear that?"

Howard paused, cocking his head to one side. "Maybe I just have airships on the brain, but that almost sounds like Gearwire's ship."

Timothy nodded. "That's what I was thinking, too." He turned back toward the direction they had come, watching the horizon. A distant speck hurtled towards them, growing larger by the second. As the speck drew closer, Timothy realized that their initial hunch was correct. It was, in fact, Gearwire's ship.

The ship touched down a few meters away from where they stood, flattening the grass in a wide radius around it. Timothy and Howard started towards it, reaching the vessel just as Dr. Maddium emerged from the cockpit. The time-traveling scientist looked unusually serious, and Timothy knew at once that something big had happened.

"What is it?" he asked with a growing sense of dread.

"Samuel's called an emergency meeting of the Guardians of Kawts," Dr. Maddium said, looking between Timothy and Howard. "I know this trip you're on is important, but I think you're going to have to postpone it for a few weeks longer."

"It's that serious?" Howard asked. "What's this meeting about?"

"Samuel's been rather tight-lipped about the details, but Gearwire's certain it has something to do with the Council."

Howard glanced over at Timothy. "It sounds like we'd better go. If it really is the Council, Gearwire's going to need all hands on deck."

Timothy nodded, trying to quash the slight feeling of resentment that arose within him.

"Taking care of the Council once and for all is the top priority," he agreed, sighing.

Dr. Maddium smiled sympathetically. "I wouldn't be here if it wasn't important," he said. "I'll lower the hatch to the cargo hold so you can get Snipps onboard," he added, disappearing back into the ship.

Timothy turned and made his way over to Snipps, who had been snacking on the grass a few feet away. He led the horse-sized raccoon up the ramp and into the cargo hold, making sure she was safely secured before ducking into the cabin.

He took a seat next to Howard, staring out the window as the ship lifted into the air.

"As soon as the Council is under lock and key, we'll continue the search," Howard said. "I promise."

Timothy sighed and sank down in his seat. "What's the point? Even if we actually capture the Council this time, there will always be another crisis that the Guardians of Kawts need to deal with. First, it was taking care of the Blanks. Then it was dealing with the Council loyalists in Aria and Johnson's Clearing. Then it was rebuilding Kawts' infrastructure. And now this."

Howard nodded sympathetically. "I know what you mean. It's a lot. A bit more than I signed up for, if I'm being honest." He sighed, scratching his chin. "I'll admit, I've been considering retiring myself. But not until the Council has been dealt with. I joined up with Gearwire to free Kawts and defeat the Council. I need to see it through to the end."

"We'll arrive in Kawts in just a few minutes," Dr. Maddium said over the ship's loudspeaker, interrupting their conversation. "Samuel's waiting for us in the old library. There have been some delays with the construction of the new building."

Dr. Maddium's voice died away, leaving the cabin silent. Timothy sighed and turned toward the window.

Here we go again.

Chapter 2

Dr. Maddium brought the ship down just outside of Kawts, near the main gate.

"I'll get to the library as quickly as I can," Timothy said, leading Snipps out of the cargo hold. "I have to drop Snipps off at the stables first."

Dr. Maddium nodded. "I'll tell Samuel. We'll see you there."

Timothy leapt up onto Snipps' back, riding the genetically modified raccoon into the city.

Everything's been changing so fast, he thought as he rode through the streets, noting the skeletons of several new buildings that had popped up in his absence. *It's hard to believe this is the same city that the Council chased me out of last year.*

Snipps chuffed softly, and Timothy realized that he had almost ridden right past the stables.

"Thanks for the warning," he said with a smile. He slid off the raccoon's back, leading her into the building.

The attendant looked up as Timothy entered. "Timothy! We didn't expect you back so soon!"

"Something came up," Timothy said, trying to avoid giving away too much information. The stable attendant, he was reasonably sure, was a direct informant for the *Kawts Tribune,* and bitter experience had taught him to be wary of how much he said about active cases.

If the Tribune announces that we've found the Council, who knows how the people will react? Assuming that's what this meeting is about.

Timothy smiled wryly as a thought occurred to him.

Which is probably why Samuel is keeping this so close to his chest. He doesn't want whatever it is to get out before we have a chance to figure out what to do about it.

"I'll be back later today to pick Snipps up," Timothy told the attendant. "I don't know how long it'll take."

The man straightened up to his full height. "I'll be waiting," he said with a little salute.

Timothy turned and left the stables, trying to conceal his discomfort over his new celebrity status. He dashed over to the library, which was all the way on the other side of town. He ducked inside, scanning the room for an empty seat.

The rest of the Guardians of Kawts were already there, seated around a long table they had taken from the house of the head Councilman, Ethos. In the far corner of the room, Timothy spotted Idalbo and Adalbo, Alpen's emissaries to Kawts, whispering frantically to each other. Beside them sat Quill, who had been Timothy's best friend before the Council had captured and brainwashed him. Seeing no open chairs on that side of the room, Timothy turned his attention elsewhere, finally finding a spot between the Golden Knight and Jewel.

"It's good to have you back," Jewel said with a smile as Timothy took his seat.

"I was just about to say the same thing to you," Timothy said, his own smile widening. "I take it you're feeling better?"

Jewel nodded. "The doctors released me a couple days after you left. My fighting skills are a bit rusty still, but other than that, I'm pretty much back to normal."

"That's good to hear," Timothy said. "Maybe we can have a training session after-"

"Thank you all for coming on such short notice," Samuel said, calling the meeting to order. The elderly former librarian had been a respected figure in the community before his capture by the Council, which had been a major factor in Gearwire's decision to appoint him as the ruler of Kawts.

Samuel waited for the idle chatter to fizzle out before he continued. "I received a concerning message earlier today from Draagetsew - the president of the Koalition der Alpen," he explained with a glance at Quill and Volker, the Council's former head of security. "It seems that the Council has taken over Alpen, and he and those still loyal to him have been forced into hiding. He says that he suspects they're after the Weather Belt. He's asking us to come as quickly as possible to help."

Gearwire frowned, a steely look coming into his blue eyes. "So having lost one of the fail-safe devices, they intend to go after another." The former rebel general exhaled heavily, running his hand over his long, grey beard. "I should have expected they would try something of the sort."

Timothy frowned. *What does he mean by 'the fail-safe devices?'* he wondered. *And why does it sound like the Council already had one of those?*

"If these 'fail-safe devices' are something that the Council wants, it might help if we actually knew what they were," Crystal said from her seat beside Jewel. Crystal and Jewel were twins, sharing the same blue eyes and jet-black hair - though Crystal's was dyed bright red.

"The fail-safe devices were created in the wake of the Robot War," Gearwire said after a moment's pause. "Suffice it to say that they are extremely powerful - especially the ones kept by Kawts and Alpen."

"And the Weather Belt was one of these weapons?" Quill breathed, leaning forward in his chair.

Gearwire nodded. "And so was the device that the Council modified to turn people into Blanks. But the Weather Belt was arguably the strongest of them all."

"Even if we prevent the Council from getting their hands on this Weather Belt, what's to stop them from tracking down the rest of these superweapons?" the Mysterious Man asked, his battered fedora pulled down low over his eyes. "They seem to have a remarkable aptitude for finding things like that."

"After the fail-safe project broke down, the devices were scattered in secure locations around the world," Dr. Maddium said. "There's no way the Council could track all of them down before we catch up to them."

"In the meantime, it seems the situation in Alpen is rather urgent," Samuel said, taking control of the conversation once more. "What should I tell Draagetsew?"

"We can't let them take over Alpen without a fight!" Idalbo said, his porcupine-like quills bristling with anger.

"We have to stop them," Adalbo said at the same moment, rising. "We've been away from Alpen too long," he added, shaking his head.

"Then stop them, we shall," Gearwire said. "You two have stood by us throughout our fight with the Council. It's only right that we return the favor now that Alpen is the one threatened." He turned toward Samuel. "Did Draagetsew say anything else? Any signs of what he might be planning?"

Samuel shook his head. "All he said was that he wanted us to come over there as soon as we got the message. Given the state of his handwriting, it seems he was in a bit of a hurry when he wrote this. He probably didn't have time to write much else."

"Even if he had, he wouldn't want to risk a message with his battle plans falling into the Council's hands," Idalbo said. "President Draagetsew may be more gifted in brawn than in brains, but he's no fool."

"He's going to want to go after the Weather Belt himself," Adalbo said. Idalbo gave his brother a quizzical look, but Adalbo waved it off. "Penn Echse is his greatest hero. He'd jump at any excuse to follow in his footsteps. And besides, Draagetsew has never been one to wait around for diplomatic work."

"Let's hope you're mistaken," the Golden Knight said, breaking his customary silence. "The trap-filled complex that houses the Weather Belt has already been the doom of some of Alpen's finest. Any attempt to retrieve it is almost certain to end in disaster."

"Not to mention the fact that it's probably safer in the complex than it would be with us," Dr. Maddium said.

"So what's the plan, sir?" Volker asked, turning to Gearwire.

"If we're going to have any hope of taking down the Council, we're going to need every man we can get," Gearwire said after a momentary pause.

"With all due respect, we can't abandon Kawts to chase the Council across the continent! No offense," Volker added, glancing at Idalbo and Adalbo.

"Idalbo and I are going regardless of whether anyone else is joining us," Adalbo said. "Someone has to stop the Council before they get too firmly entrenched. We can't let what happened to Kawts happen to Alpen."

"Volker, you and Samuel should stay behind to watch over Kawts. Cedar should do the same for Grimshaw," Gearwire said, glancing over at the Prime Minister of the tree people. "I don't think our cities can afford to be without them right now. And if they run into any trouble, they can radio us and we can have a team back here within a few hours. My crew and I will take my ship over to Alpen to meet with Draagetsew. We'll take a look at the situation and figure out where to go from there once we have a better sense of what's going on."

"I'm coming, too," Quill said, interrupting Gearwire's planning.

"I'm not sure that's the best idea," Gearwire said. "Going head to head with the Council is not something to take lightly. It's a lot more dangerous than basic recon missions."

Quill straightened himself up to his full height. "I have a weapon," he said. "And I've been practicing almost every day since the battle. I can be useful. I was the one who first discovered what was really going on with the Blanks, remember?"

"And for that, we owe you," Gearwire said. "But this isn't the mission for people who have no real combat experience."

"If Quill's willing to join us, let him come," Madison chimed in. At sixteen, she was the youngest of the Guardians of Kawts, beating out Quill by just a few months. Unlike Quill, however, she had been a member of Gearwire's crew before the Battle of Kawts. "Most of us didn't have more than a few missions under our belts before we joined your crew."

Gearwire glanced over at the twins, but Crystal just shrugged. "Don't look at me. I'm with Madison on this one. The first time I had a run-in with the Council, I had only known about my powers for less than a day. You have to start sometime."

"Please?" Quill said. "I got turned into a Blank to make sure we could defeat the Council. I deserve the chance to be there when we do."

For a long time, Gearwire said nothing. Then he nodded slowly. "Okay. You can come. If you are willing to take that risk, and you truly believe you can hold your own, you may join us."

Quill nodded solemnly, but Timothy could see the smile breaking out over his face the second Gearwire looked away. A determined look came into his eyes, and Timothy knew his friend was relishing the opportunity to take part in finishing the fight that he had played such a vital role in. But in spite of Quill's optimism, Timothy couldn't help but frown.

He's not ready. He's going to get himself killed.

He shook his head, trying to push the thoughts aside.

Quill's probably more equipped for this than you were when you joined Gearwire, he reminded himself.

Even so, he couldn't quite shake his anxiety.

"You won't regret this," Quill said to Gearwire, no longer trying to conceal his smile.

Gearwire studied him for a moment. "No, I don't think I will," he agreed.

"Now that we've gotten that out of the way, shouldn't we get back to planning the trip?" the Mysterious Man remarked drily. "We are on a bit of a tight schedule, it would seem."

"Right," Gearwire said, nodding. "Thomas, how long do you think it will take us to load up the ship?"

"It depends," Dr. Maddium replied, staring up at the ceiling as he ran the numbers. "If we're doing the standard long-term mission gear, we should be able to have everything ready by late afternoon."

Gearwire nodded. "Good. We'll take off at first light tomorrow. That should be enough time for everyone to prepare." He turned to Samuel and Cedar. "I'm going to leave you each with a radio beacon. Make sure you send us a report every day. If we don't hear from you, we'll know something has gone wrong."

"That sounds like a plan," Samuel said. "Any questions?"

He glanced around the room, and Timothy shook his head. Samuel let the silence linger for a few moments longer before he said, "Alright then. Meeting adjourned. I'll see you all at the hangar tomorrow morning."

Chapter 3

The idle chatter returned, and Timothy pushed back his chair. As he stood up, Gearwire came over to him.

"I appreciate you coming back on such short notice," the former rebel leader said. "I know how important that mission was to you."

"It isn't more important than preventing the Council from ruining more people's lives," Timothy replied, shaking his head.

Gearwire smiled sympathetically. "I hope you know that we're all praying for your brother's return."

"Thanks," Timothy said, without much conviction.

After everything that we've been through, how does he still believe in all that? he wondered as Gearwire walked off to speak to Samuel. *After everything the Council has done, he still thinks there's an omnipotent being who cares about what happens to us.*

He sighed. *But Maurice believed it too. And there was a time when I almost did, myself.*

Wrapped up in his thoughts, he left the room, weaving among the haphazardly stacked piles of books that littered the library floor. As he passed one particularly large pile, he felt someone tapping him on his left shoulder. He twisted around to see who it was, but saw no one. He heard laughter coming from his right and he groaned.

"Really? I can't believe I fell for that old trick!" he said, turning towards Quill, who made no effort to hide his mile-wide grin.

"What old trick?" Quill asked with an air of innocence. "Maybe I've just spent so much time around you that I've become an expert in stealth by osmosis."

Timothy shook his head, laughing. "Quill, you are about as stealthy as a half-blind bear. I seriously doubt you managed to sneak around me that fast."

"Hey - I infiltrated the Council Records room on multiple occasions," Quill protested, feigning indignation. "That sounds pretty stealthy to me!"

"Yeah," Timothy agreed. "Only the Council knew you had been there the whole time!"

"Like you did any better on your first try," Quill replied. "I bet that if we'd had a contest back before any of this happened, I'd-"

"You both would have been pretty awful at it," Madison interjected, coming up behind them. She looked from one to the other, a bemused smile on her face. "Don't you two have mission prep to do?"

Quill brightened at once, his smile growing even wider. "Yes! The mission! I can't believe I'm finally going to get the chance to strike back against the Council!"

"This isn't all fun and games," Timothy said. An image of Henry's death at the Council's hands flashed before him. "The Council is dangerous, Quill. Someone might die."

"I know it's dangerous," Quill said. "I got turned into a Blank, remember? But you have to admit, it's pretty exciting."

Timothy shook his head. "No. I don't."

An awkward silence settled over the pair. Finally, Quill cleared his throat.

"Well. I guess I'll see you tomorrow, Tim."

"Yeah," Timothy repeated as Quill headed off towards his house. "See you tomorrow."

"What was that all about?" Jewel asked, coming up alongside Timothy.

Timothy sighed. "It's nothing. I was just thinking about Henry."

Jewel nodded sympathetically. "He was a good man. He spent most of his time around the base, so I never really got to know him that well. But I still remember the first time I met him. He was the second member of Gearwire's crew Crystal and I ever met."

Timothy nodded absently, memories of their fallen crewmember filling his head. Henry had been killed by Ethos a few months before the Council's defeat, meeting his demise during the Battle of Garrington.

They reached a fork in the road, and Timothy shook off the memories of his late friend. "Do you want some help packing for the mission?" he asked. "I mean, with your injury and everything…"

"I'll be fine," Jewel said. "The doctors said that I'm fully recovered. And if I need anything, I can always ask Crystal."

Timothy nodded. "Right. Of course." He smiled. "I'll see you tomorrow."

"See you tomorrow," Jewel repeated, then disappeared deeper into Kawts.

Timothy turned and went the opposite direction, making his way to Gearwire's Cave.

His family had moved into the Cave shortly after the Battle of Kawts, wanting to be closer to the epicenter of the new teachings and knowledge. Timothy's mother, along with many other teachers from the old Kawts, were taking classes from the people of Gearwire's Cave, rediscovering lost knowledge that they hadn't known was missing. Many people from Kawts' Science Guild also attended these classes, though there were a few who refused, insisting that they already knew everything they needed to know.

Riding on Snipps, it took Timothy only half an hour to get back to the former rebel base. He spent most of that time deep in thought, mentally rehearsing the speech he would give to his parents when they inevitably asked why he was packing for a trip.

They had responded surprisingly well to the idea of him being part of Gearwire's crew, and they were more than a little proud of the fact that he was now a member of the Guardians of Kawts. But Timothy knew that they still had reservations about him continuing to go on missions, disliking how his stealth training meant that he always seemed to be assigned the most dangerous of tasks.

As he neared the cave, he slid off of Snipps' back, walking beside the giant raccoon the rest of the way to the base. Out of habit, he stopped for a moment to wait for the sentry's challenge before remembering that the entrance was no longer guarded.

It feels so weird to just be able to walk in here, he reflected as he led Snipps into the cave. *A side effect of spending so long working for the resistance, I suppose.*

He dropped Snipps off at the stables, then circled back to his house, a sturdy wooden building that had once served as one of the resistance's barracks. Neither of his parents were home when he arrived, so he set to work packing clothes and gear for the coming expedition. He was nearly finished by the time they returned, his mother excitedly trying to explain cell division to his father.

Timothy heard their voices as they entered the house and came down to greet them, one of his shurikens still in his hand. They stopped their conversation when they saw him, concern flashing across their faces when they noticed the weapon.

"You're back already?" his mother said. "Does that mean you found…" She trailed off, her voice catching.

Timothy shook his head. "We never made it to the site. Samuel summoned us back for an emergency meeting."

"Another mission?"

Timothy nodded. "And this one might take a while."

"How long?" his father asked, his frown deepening.

"We're not sure," Timothy replied. "Somehow, the Council took over the nation of Alpen. We're going over there to defeat them once and for all."

"Alpen is its own country!" his father protested. "They're ten, if not one hundred times bigger than Kawts is! Why can't they fight the Council themselves!"

"Draagetsew didn't say," Timothy said, shaking his head. "But regardless of their size, it's pretty clear from the message he sent that they're in trouble. We've fought the Council before. We know how best to defeat them."

And it's the only way I have a chance of ever seeing Aksell again, he added silently, thoughts of his brainwashed friend creeping unbidden to his mind.

"But they have an entire army!" his father protested, throwing his hands up in exasperation. "A couple dozen more people aren't going to make that much of a difference!"

"It's not just that," Timothy said. He hesitated, not sure how much he should tell them. "Gearwire thinks that the Council is looking for something," he said at last. "If they find it before we can, they might become too powerful for us to stop them."

"Do what you have to do," his mother said suddenly, cutting off another protest from Timothy's father. He looked at her in surprise, a betrayed look in his eyes. "You're almost an adult," she continued, ignoring him. "You can make that decision for yourself. Just promise me that you'll be careful?"

Timothy nodded. "I will. Don't worry." He turned to his father, who said nothing for a long time.

"Fine," he sighed at last. "I suppose the Council needs to be stopped. But don't do anything foolish. I - we don't want to lose you a second time. Not like Maurice."

"Thanks, Dad," Timothy said, wincing inwardly as he thought of what it must have been like for his parents after he'd been chased out of Kawts. The Council had told them that he had been executed for treason.

Timothy lingered in the entryway for a few minutes longer, feeling slightly guilty for putting his parents through this again. Eventually, he excused himself to his bedroom to finish packing before slipping out the back door to arrange for someone to take care of Snipps while he was gone.

He took Snipps for a lap around the corral, a million thoughts and emotions swirling in his mind. Finally, he brought her back to her pen, forgetting in his distraction to make sure that the gate was properly latched. He started toward the hangar, taking a roundabout route to give himself time to think. Lost in thought, he hardly realized when he arrived. He stared up at Gearwire's ship, oblivious to everything else around him.

"Is everything alright?" Samuel asked, appearing next to Timothy.

Timothy looked up at him, startled. "Samuel! What are you doing here?"

"I came over so I could see you guys off tomorrow. And get a good look at this ship of Gearwire's. I've never actually seen it up close before, you know."

Timothy nodded. "It's pretty cool. And fast, too. Faster than anything I've ever seen."

He fell silent, and Samuel said, "Are you sure you're okay? You don't seem like yourself."

Timothy sighed. "I'm not sure," he said. He hesitated for a moment, then went on. "When we were fighting the Council, all I thought about was freeing you and Quill and defeating the Council. I always expected things to go back to normal after we won. But they didn't. Kawts has changed. I've changed. Aksell's gone." He shook his head. "And yet, Quill is exactly the same as he was the day the Council captured him. He doesn't understand what it's like to go head-to-head with the Council."

Samuel smiled sympathetically. "I get what you mean. There are some days where I want nothing more than to get back to putting the Kawts Library in order. Especially now that we have all the Council's old records to go through, too. But right now, Kawts needs me at the helm."

"It's not just that," Timothy said. "Ever since we defeated the Council, we've been dealing with one crisis after another. Don't get me wrong, I'm honored to be part of Gearwire's crew and a member of the Guardians of Kawts. But I just want to live my life like a normal person. I don't want to be a full-time hero."

Samuel nodded, staring up at Gearwire's ship. Finally, he said, "Did I ever tell you about how I became a Christian?"

Timothy narrowed his eyes, shaking his head slowly. "No. Why?"

"I know I've told you the story of Jane being Blanked. After she was gone, I was so bitter. I became cynical, depressed. I hated the Council with every fiber of my being. I spent every day focused on what happened the day of that Race. Wishing I had done something differently. Mourning the loss of all the things that might have been. But there was nothing I could do about it."

Samuel sighed, staring off into space. "I was like that for almost twenty years. Stuck trying to get back to a future that no longer existed. My mentor, Elijah, tried to coax me out of it, but I pushed him away. Then one day, he was killed by the Council while on a mission with Gearwire. He left me a note and a Bible, to be delivered in the event of his death. That letter made me realize that something had to change. He'd always been trying to convince me to read through the Bible, but it wasn't until then that I took him up on his offer. It showed me an omnipotent being that saw the evil in the world, acknowledged it, even came down and suffered under it. He didn't downplay the pain, but he didn't stay in it either. He was always pointing and working toward the future, a future where all the pains of the present are transformed into joys."

Samuel paused, turning to look at Timothy. "My point is, the things that are done are done. There's nothing anyone can do to go back to the way things were. No amount of wishing was going to bring Jane back - or put Kawts back the way it used to be. All you can do is to keep moving forwards. Find new dreams, new goals. New hopes."

Timothy was silent for a moment, taking in everything that Samuel had said. "I don't even know what that would look like," he said. "I've been so busy the last few months that I've hardly had any time to think."

"I suspect you'll have plenty of time for reflection on this mission," Samuel said with a smile. "There's bound to be a good amount of downtime while Gearwire gets a feel for the lay of the land."

"And what about Quill? If you listen to him talk about what we're about to do, you'd almost think we're going on a vacation!"

"Give him time," Samuel said. "You were right when you said that he hasn't changed a bit since he was Blanked. He's effectively been in a coma for the last few years. Once he gets some more experience, he'll understand. Just be patient."

Timothy nodded. "I'll try. Thanks, Samuel."

"Anytime."

Chapter 4

When Timothy returned to the hangar the next morning, he was surprised to see that a sizable crowd had gathered to see them off. Samuel and the remaining Guardians of Kawts were at the front of the group, but there were several dozen others present as well, a combination of friends, reporters, and curious pedestrians.

As Timothy climbed the stairs to the entrance of the ship, he saw Samuel standing a couple of feet in front of the crowd. Samuel gave him a knowing smile, and Timothy smiled back, giving him a little wave before turning and stepping onto the cold metal floor of the ship. He walked past the door to the cockpit, sitting down in an empty spot on one of the benches that lined the interior walls of the cabin.

Quill slid into place next to him, his blue eyes shining with excitement. "I can't believe we get to fly to Alpen!" he whispered.

"Just in order to fight the Council," Timothy said. "We're not there to go sightseeing."

"I know," Quill said. He sighed, his smile growing even wider. "I've been training for something like this ever since the Battle of Kawts."

"It's not all fun and games," Timothy said. "The Council means business."

Quill was silent for a moment, eager to avoid a repeat of their conversation from the previous afternoon.

"What's it like?" he asked at last. "Alpen, I mean. You've been there once before, right?"

Timothy nodded. "It's pretty cool, I suppose," he said. "I was really only there for a few hours. But their capital city, Blancstadt, is beautiful. And the castle…" he trailed off, searching for the perfect word. He shook his head. "It's the most impressive building I've ever seen. I guess it's one of those things you just need to see for yourself."

Quill opened his mouth to ask another question, but at that moment, Gearwire's voice came on over the ship's intercom.

"Make sure you strap yourselves in," he said as the cabin door sealed itself shut. "Takeoffs can sometimes be a bit rough. Once we're in the air, it'll be safe for you to move around the cabin. If we run into any turbulence, I'll let you know." Timothy felt a dull rumble as the ship came to life, its engines causing the entire ship to vibrate slightly. After a few seconds, the vibrations stopped, although the muted rumblings of the engines did not.

"It feels good to be back in the field again," Jewel said, turning to him as the ship took flight.

"I suppose it would," Timothy said, trying to keep his voice cheerful.

There was silence for a moment, then Jewel added, "You never told me how your mission went. Did you find your brother?"

"Maurice is still MIA," Timothy said, shaking his head. "I know he's probably dead, but I just wish Howard and I would have had the chance to find out for sure."

"I'm sure you'll find him some day. Now that I'm recovered, maybe I could help you look. After we take care of the Council, of course."

"Thanks," Timothy said. "That means a lot."

Jewel smiled, then turned to talk to Madison, leaving Timothy alone with his thoughts.

* * *

As the novelty of flying wore off, Gearwire's crew settled in for a long trip, knowing that it would still be several hours before they arrived.

Gearwire was holed up inside the cockpit, manning the controls. Dr. Maddium was with him, acting as his co-pilot and navigator. Near the door to the cargo hold, the Mysterious Man and the Golden Knight were fencing, their blades ringing as they crashed together again and again. Idalbo watched them, ready to step in if something went wrong. Adalbo strummed idly on his lute, mumbling what sounded like an old Alpenite love song. Quill stared out the window, watching the ground far below.

Timothy watched the duel for a few minutes, then turned away, double-checking to make sure that his suit and weapons were still in good working order.

After the Battle of Kawts, he had spent a lot of time upgrading his armor with the help of Dr. Maddium and Howard Kolt. The entire suit had been painted a mottled shade of dark grey, making it sleeker and even more suited for stealth missions.

Cosmetic differences aside, the upgraded suit had been redesigned to be much more efficient than it had been previously. After spending countless hours puzzling over the issue, Dr. Maddium had finally succeeded in installing a miniature Infini-case into the chest plate of the armor, allowing Timothy to have several spare shurikens on hand in just a few seconds, not to mention anything else he might need.

He had discarded his satchel altogether, which was cumbersome in both battle and stealth. Now, four shurikens ran down the outside of each leg of his suit, popping off into his hand with the press of a button. Timothy inspected this mechanism next, making sure that it was still working smoothly. After making sure that all of his shurikens were intact and accounted for, he began a meticulous examination of the wind chime staff, checking for any damage it might have acquired since he had last used it. This accomplished, he tested out the staff's silencer, a sound-cancelling device that Howard Kolt had made for him to avoid the wind chimes blowing Timothy's cover.

It really is kind of a strange thing to put on the end of a staff, he realized, glancing over at the Mysterious Man. Not for the first time, he found himself wondering where the staff had come from and who had wielded it before him.

All the Mysterious Man said when he gave it to me was that it had belonged to a friend of his. Which probably means that whoever it was is dead now. But who was it? Were they a member of Gearwire's crew? Or were they someone the Mysterious Man knew before he joined the rebellion? For a brief moment, he considered asking the Mysterious Man about the staff's origins, but he quickly dismissed the notion.

If he wanted to tell me, he would have. If he doesn't want to tell me, he won't answer, anyway. There's a reason he goes by 'Mysterious Man.'

They had been traveling for just over an hour when the ship lurched suddenly to one side. Timothy was thrown from the bench, hitting his head on the Golden Knight's armored knee. A sharp pain blossomed from the back of his head where they had collided. Timothy blinked in confusion, his vision swimming. Slowly, he staggered to his feet, struggling to find his balance on a floor that appeared to be slanted. As the pain shifted to a dull throbbing, Gearwire's voice came on over the speakers.

"We've lost control of our port side engine," Gearwire announced, as calmly as if he were stating the weather. "The Council apparently left someone behind on that mountain over there to cover their tracks. They launched a small missile at us when we flew by, and it hit our engine. Dr. Maddium and I are going to try to land us in that valley so we can assess the damage."

Just as he finished speaking, Dr. Maddium's voice rang out from the cockpit. "Hold on!" he shouted as the ship began to spin, spiraling out of control. Timothy grabbed a handle mounted on the ceiling by his head and clung to it, using all of his strength to avoid being tossed around the cabin.

There was a jarring crash as the ship collided with the ground, and the lights went out, plunging the interior of the ship into near-total darkness. They skidded along for a few yards before coming to stop, the ship carving a deep furrow into the ground. For a moment, Timothy had the terrifying thought that he was dead. Then the throbbing pain in his head returned, and he quickly dismissed that fear.

I'm pretty sure being dead wouldn't hurt this much.

Chapter 5

A low humming noise filled the air, and the lights flickered back on. Gearwire emerged from the cockpit, a worried frown on his face. "Is everyone all right?" he asked, looking out over the tangle of bodies on the floor.

"I'm fine, I think," Howard's muffled voice called from the bottom of the pile. "Just a little squashed."

As if spurred into action by his comment, the rest of the Guardians of Kawts quickly disentangled themselves, checking themselves for any serious injuries.

"We should probably get outside," Gearwire said, coughing as a trickle of smoke drifted out from the cockpit. "Part of the ship is definitely on fire. I don't want any of us in here on the off chance that something explodes."

Timothy nodded, moving carefully to the door of the cabin. He tried to push it open, but it remained tightly sealed. His breathing grew more frantic as he realized that they were trapped.

"Let me try," Gearwire said, gently pushing Timothy aside. He examined the door for a moment, then swiftly kicked the bottom panel. A metallic clang echoed throughout the ship, making Timothy wince. Gearwire, however, seemed unaffected by the noise and kicked the door again. This time, it slid open a crack, creaking in protest. Gearwire hooked his fingers in the opening and pulled, forcing the door open.

The bright morning sunlight shone into the ship, and Timothy put his hand up to shield his eyes. He blinked rapidly as his eyes adjusted to the light. Then, seeing that Gearwire had already climbed outside, Timothy followed suit, letting himself slide down the outside of the ship to reach the ground. One by one, the rest of the Guardians of Kawts emerged, battered and disoriented.

As Timothy looked at the ship from the outside, he could tell right away that they were in trouble. The ship was leaning slightly to one side, its starboard engine buried in the dirt. The port-side engine was slightly elevated and on fire, the rising smoke a clear giveaway of their location. Timothy grabbed a shuriken from the socket on his leg, throwing it over the fire. It spun through the air, releasing a steady stream of water as it did. The fire shrank down to a fraction of its original size. Timothy reached for another shuriken of the same type, but Jewel stopped him.

"Let me," she said, raising her hands toward the engine. A film of crystal appeared around it, choking out what remained of the fire.

Gearwire knelt down to inspect the engine, careful not to touch it. Now that the fire was out, the extent of the damage became more evident. A large portion of the casing had been blown away by the blast, and parts of the inside had fused together in a mess of half-melted slag. The pain in Timothy's head beat the time as Gearwire examined the smoking engine more closely. The tense silence stretched on, interrupted only by occasional ominous creaking sounds from the ship. Finally, Gearwire stood, his face grave.

"It's pretty badly damaged," he said, shaking his head slightly. "But with a little luck, I might be able to rig something up to keep us in the air long enough to get back to Kawts for more extensive repairs. Assuming that the other engine isn't damaged too badly."

"How long do you think it'll take?" the Mysterious Man asked. To

Timothy's surprise, he realized he could clearly see the top half of his face, his trademark fedora having fallen off somewhere inside the ship.

Gearwire's face scrunched up as he ran the numbers. "A few hours, at least," he replied at last. "And that's with Howard and Dr. Maddium's help."

He opened the hatch to the cargo hold to retrieve the tools he would need to repair the engine. Suddenly, Snipps tumbled out of the hold, staggering past Gearwire before coming to a stop in front of Timothy. She shook her head vigorously, then wagged her tail. She seemed to be a bit disoriented by the crash, but otherwise unharmed, the crates of supplies that filled the cargo hold having somewhat cushioned her fall. Everyone stared at her, shocked into silence.

It was Timothy who found his tongue first. "Well," he said, looking around at the others. "Since it looks like we're going to be here awhile, why don't I go scout out the area?" he asked. "See if I can find who or whatever tried to shoot us down?"

"Good thinking," Gearwire said with a nod. "Why don't you bring Quill with you. Two sets of eyes are better than one." With that, he disappeared into the cargo hold, searching the debris for his toolbox.

Ignoring the pain in his head, Timothy swung up onto Snipps' back. He reached out his hand and pulled Quill up after him. Then, with one last glance back at the fallen ship, Timothy rode off in the direction they came.

They rode up into the rocky hills, the camp quickly vanishing behind them. As they climbed higher, Quill said, "That was intense! Does this kind of thing happen a lot?"

"What kind of thing?" Timothy asked, his focus on the path in front of him.

"We just got shot out of the sky! And now we're going on a top-secret mission in search of the culprit."

"We've been through worse than that," Timothy said, turning to face Quill. In spite of himself, a smile flickered across his face. "And this is hardly a top-secret mission. Everyone knows where we're going."

"Not whoever the Council left behind to cover their tracks," Quill said with a grin. He fell silent for a moment, then said, "You know, I've really missed this. Reconnaissance missions and all that. Knowing that you're doing your part to take down the Council."

"It's not nearly as much fun when you're up against the Council themselves," Timothy said. "But I get what you mean. Those first few days when I was starting to uncover what the Council was up to were exhilarating."

"I know, right? And then when you realize that someone else that you know has already been down the same path? It just feels like nothing can stop you from finding the truth."

"Well, we certainly found it," Timothy said. "Honestly, sometimes it amazes me how many people I knew were wrapped up in all of this."

Quill laughed. "Yeah. I think just about the only person we know who wasn't involved is Aksell."

Timothy's smile faded at the mention of his friend.

"I'm sure Aksell will realize something is up sooner or later," Quill said, noticing Timothy's discomfort. "He's no fool. I bet he's already having second thoughts about Ethos."

Timothy shook his head. "He was in Kawts during those last few days. Even Volker realized the Council was evil at that point. How could Aksell have missed it?"

"To be fair, he thought you were dead. Finding out that your dead friend is not only not dead, but also fighting alongside the dangerous anarchists is a lot to take in all at once."

Timothy glanced back at Quill, searching for any signs of sarcasm. But Quill seemed completely serious, and Timothy couldn't help but nod, remembering the day he had discovered the same things about

Quill.

"He'll come around eventually," Quill said. "Once we defeat the Council once and for all, we can explain everything to him."

Timothy opened his mouth to reply when a footprint on the edge of the path caught his eye. Motioning for Quill to be quiet, he slid off of Snipps' back, dropping to the ground and rolling behind a pair of large boulders. Quill stayed where he was, readying his stun rifle, a gadget he had created with Howard's help after the Battle of Kawts.

Slowly, Timothy edged his way around the boulder, his head beginning to throb once more. As he neared the corner, he paused for a moment to steady himself, taking a deep breath to expel the pain. He shrugged his staff free of its sheath and slipped around the side of the boulder. Sitting near the edge of a cliff with his back turned toward him was one of the Councilmen, a high-strung man named Ray. Mounted on the boulder beside him was the rocket launcher that he had used on Gearwire's ship.

If Ray had gotten a direct hit, we'd all be dead right now, Timothy realized, noticing the size of the missiles still loaded into the machine. *If one of those had hit us head-on, the ship probably would have exploded mid-air.*

Returning his attention to the Councilman, Timothy silently crept up behind him, raising his staff to knock him unconscious. But before he could strike, Ray spasmed and crumpled to the ground. Timothy knelt down beside him, feeling for a pulse.

He's still alive, he thought, standing up again. *Then what...* He straightened up as he realized what had happened. He turned around to see Quill perched atop the boulder. He grinned, waving his stun rifle.

"Really," Timothy said, feigning indignation. "You couldn't have let me handle him?"

Quill shrugged, still grinning. "You were taking too long," he said.

"Besides, you've already had a turn to fight the Council."

"Okay then, Mr. Sharpshooter. Would you care to help me carry him out of here?"

Quill's smile grew wider as he slid down from his perch, stepping nimbly over the rocks that littered the ground. Re-holstering his rifle, he helped Timothy carry Ray's unconscious form back around the boulders, draping him over Snipps' back. Timothy tied him down with a bit of rope from his Infini-case, then turned and rode back to the wreckage of the ship.

* * *

Gearwire and Dr. Maddium were still working on the engine when they returned, assisted by Howard and the twins. Gearwire stood up as they approached, wiping his hands off on a grease-stained apron he wore around his neck. "Did you find anything?" he asked, looking up at him.

"We found the rocket launcher," Timothy replied, carefully lowering himself to the ground. "And we found him too," he added, untying Ray and letting him fall to the ground at Gearwire's feet.

Gearwire bent over the still-unconscious form of the Councilman, turning him over so he could see his face. "Councilman Ray," he said, his voice neutral. "He would be the logical choice to leave behind, I suppose. Did you see anyone else there?"

Timothy shook his head. "He was all by himself with the rocket-launcher on the edge of a cliff."

"Did you find where he's been staying?" Gearwire asked. "If our information about the Council's movements is correct, he would have had to have been here for at least a few weeks."

"We… didn't look," Timothy said. "We were mostly just focused on getting Ray back here."

"Why don't you go back and see what you can find. There might be something there that will tell us more about what the Council's planning. It'll be another few hours before the ship is flight-worthy again, anyway."

"What about the rocket launcher?" Quill asked. "Do you want us to bring it back here?"

Gearwire thought for a moment. "No," he said at last. "Without the right equipment, it would be too much of a risk to try to fly it back to Kawts. The best we can do is to destroy it. Stash any remaining missiles somewhere safe and then push it off the cliff. The Golden Knight can help you with that."

He waved the Golden Knight over, explaining to him what he had told Timothy and Quill. The Golden Knight nodded and followed them back to where the rocket launcher was, his gold-painted armor glinting in the sunlight.

As they drew nearer to the site, Quill turned around to face the Golden Knight. "I don't think we've ever officially met," Quill said, extending a hand. "I'm Quill."

The Golden Knight hesitated a moment, then shook Quill's hand. "I'm the Golden Knight."

Quill smiled. "I know that. But what's your *real* name?" Timothy elbowed him, but Quill ignored the hint.

"I don't know."

Quill looked skeptical of this, but he didn't press the matter further. "Well, how did you get your armor, then?" he asked. "And why does your shield have a golden gear on it?"

"I can't remember."

Something in his tone made Timothy pause.

He's lying, he realized. *That's weird. I never thought the Golden Knight had anything to hide.*

"He's not very talkative, is he?" Quill whispered to Timothy, turning back towards the front.

"Not really," Timothy said in a low tone. Then, in a louder voice, he added, "We're almost there. The rocket launcher is just on the other side of those boulders."

The Golden Knight nodded and set to work disarming the device. Timothy and Quill searched for Ray's campsite, scouring the area for any signs of recent habitation. They had been looking for several fruitless minutes when Quill's voice suddenly rang through the air.

"I think I found something!" he shouted. Timothy jogged over to his friend, who was standing in the mouth of a medium-sized cave. As Timothy drew closer, he could see what Quill meant. Inside the cave were several crates of supplies, along with a makeshift desk, chair, and sleeping bag. A book lay open on the desk, and Timothy slowly walked towards it, scanning the room for traps as he did. Only when he was sure it was safe did he pick up the book.

"It looks like a journal of some kind," he said, paging through it. "It seems to be fairly recent, too. None of the entries go back further than a month ago."

"Poor guy," Quill said, nodding sympathetically. "There wasn't much else he could do way out here. He must've been bored out of his mind."

Timothy raised an eyebrow at him. "You aren't seriously feeling bad about a Councilman?" he asked incredulously. "You do remember the part where they turned you into a mindless zombie for several years, right?"

"That was Ethos," Quill said, his face souring. "I'm not convinced Ray ever enjoyed being a part of it. The Council has other ways of brainwashing people without turning them into Blanks."

Like Aksell, Timothy thought, the thought springing into his head before he could stop it.

"I guess you're right," he said, snapping the book closed. "We'll bring this back to Gearwire and see if he finds anything useful in it."

A great crash interrupted their conversation. Timothy hurried outside, his staff in his hand. The Golden Knight straightened himself up, dusting off his palms. Timothy breathed a sigh of relief. "I think that takes care of that rocket launcher," the Golden Knight said, a smirk playing at the corners of his mouth. "Did you and Quill find that snake's hole?"

Timothy nodded. "We haven't had much time to explore it yet. We'll just be a few minutes longer."

The Golden Knight nodded. "Take all the time you need. We can't go anywhere until the ship is fixed, anyway."

Surprised and a little alarmed at the Golden Knight's uncharacteristic chattiness, Timothy hurried back into the cave. With Quill's help, it only took them fifteen minutes to do a complete search of the area. But in the end, they didn't find anything more of interest except for Ray's weapon, an artfully decorated pistol. Quill slipped this into his pocket as they left the cave, returning to the Golden Knight, who was waiting peacefully outside. The trio rode back to where they had left the ship, arriving at about an hour before noon.

Gearwire was just packing up his tools by the time they arrived, having repaired the engine to the best of his ability. He straightened up when he saw Timothy approaching. "What did you find?" he asked, leaving his toolbox behind.

"He was holed up in a cave a little ways from where we found him," Timothy said. "Nothing fancy. It was pretty bare except for this," he added, handing Gearwire the journal.

Gearwire inspected it thoughtfully. "Very good," he said, nodding approvingly. "I'll leave this with Samuel and Volker when we get back to Kawts. They can take a closer look at it while we get our engine fixed."

"Are we going to make it back to Kawts?" Timothy asked, eyeing the improvised patch on the engine.

Gearwire hesitated. "The repairs should hold until we get there. And I should be able to replace the engine once we're back in the hangar. I had some spares made up a while ago for just such an occasion."

After a quick meal prepared by Madison, Idalbo, and Adalbo, the group loaded everything back onto the ship, tying a still-unconscious Ray to one of the benches. As they took off once more, Timothy soon fell asleep, the soothing vibrations of the ship making it all but impossible for him to stay awake.

He woke up just as they reached Gearwire's Cave and was pleased to note that his headache was gone. As the hangar doors opened below them, he could see the tiny figures of Volker and Samuel staring up at them, having been radioed in advance about their arrival by Dr. Maddium. The ship landed awkwardly on the stone floor, the landing gear buckling under the strain. Ray and the journal were left in the care of Volker, who was tasked with questioning him about the Council's activities.

Timothy led Snipps off the ship and back to the stables, this time making sure that the gate was properly latched. While he was gone, Gearwire was hard at work, swapping out the damaged parts of the ship for new ones. After only an hour of work, the repairs were complete, and the ship was ready to fly once more. The Guardians of Kawts re-boarded the ship and took off, reaching Alpen a few hours later with no further problems.

They landed quietly at the coordinates that Draagetsew had given them, a place just outside of Blancstadt, hidden from sight by a large stone outcropping. A small wooden house stood a few yards off, scarcely more than a shed. Standing in the doorway awaiting their arrival were Draagetsew and Alpen's Prime Minister, Suorotiart.

Chapter 6

"You're here!" Draagetsew exclaimed, throwing his four massive arms up in relief. His voice was deep and booming, yet cheerful, as though he somehow found the situation comical, despite the danger. He grabbed Gearwire and embraced him in a massive bear hug.

"That's… enough… Draagetsew," Gearwire gasped. Draagetsew abruptly released him, and the former rebel general staggered backwards, taking a moment to make sure he was still in one piece.

"Idalbo! Adalbo! So good to see your faces again! It's been far too long!"

Idalbo snapped to attention, giving Draagetsew a stiff salute. Adalbo dropped into a goofy bow, grinning ear to ear.

"I wish we were here under better circumstances, sir," Idalbo said.

Draagetsew waved his words off. "But you're here. That's what really matters." He turned to Adalbo. "And how have you been holding up? Meet anyone special while you were over there?"

"I think you already know the answer to that question."

Draagetsew chuckled. "Yes, I suppose I do." He turned toward Timothy. "Nice to see you again, too, Timothy. Any other daring adventures you'd like to share?"

Timothy opened his mouth to reply, then stopped, at a complete loss for what to say. Before he could make up his mind, Suorotiart spoke.

"Come inside," he said in a vaguely snakelike voice. "You can catch up later. If the Council's nearby, they'll have seen you land for sure." The short, squat mutant's papery, bat-like wings twitched as he spoke.

"Suorotiart is right," Draagetsew boomed, thumping his advisor on the back with enough force to stagger the smaller mutant. Suorotiart glared at him, but said nothing.

Draagetsew evidently doesn't know his own strength, Timothy noted, adding this fact to his running list of the Alpenite president's unusual traits.

As the Guardians of Kawts filed into the dilapidated building, Suorotiart flew up into the sky, circling overhead to make sure that no one had noticed their arrival. Only once the last person had stepped inside did he come down, closing the door behind the little group.

"Thank you for coming," Draagetsew said, squeezing his massive build into a rickety old chair that had evidently been built for a much smaller person. His voice was more subdued now, his concern for Alpen overtaking his natural joviality. "As we said in our message, we desperately need your help."

"We came as quickly as we could," Gearwire said. "We actually had a run-in with the Council on our way over," he added, briefly outlining what had happened.

"Good," Draagetsew said, nodding appreciatively. "That's one less of them we'll have on our tails."

"What do you mean, 'on our tails?'" Dr. Maddium asked, raising an eyebrow.

"Suorotiart and I have been discussing what to do for the last few weeks. We've decided that the only thing we can do is to get to the Weather Belt before the Council does. If we can pull it off, we'll be powerful enough to defeat them once and for all."

The room fell deathly silent. Timothy glanced over at Gearwire and

Dr. Maddium, remembering how strongly they had opposed that idea the day before.

I guess Adalbo was right. Draagetsew really does want to go after the Weather Belt.

"I'm not sure that's the best idea," Gearwire said slowly. "The Weather Belt is a lot safer right where it is than it would be with us. The risk of the Council getting a hold of it is just too great."

"And we can fight them off even without the Weather Belt," the Mysterious Man said. "We've done it before, and we can do it again. Especially now that they don't have the Blanks and attack drones to back them up."

"So you say. And yet somehow, the Council still got away from you, didn't they?" Suorotiart said. "No matter how hard you try, the Council always seems to evade you. As long as they're still on the loose, they're free to go after the Weather Belt. Whoever let them escape ought to be court-martialed!"

Timothy stood up abruptly, his chair grating against the floor. "That would be me," he said, feeling his face flush. Then, before anyone could say anything, he turned and left the building, sitting down on the rickety old porch. He exhaled heavily, staring off into the distance. He heard the door creak behind him, and a few seconds later, Quill sat down beside him, followed shortly after by Madison, Crystal, and Jewel. For a long time, no one spoke.

"You know it's not your fault that the Council got away," Jewel said at last. "None of the rest of us could stop them, either."

"Yeah," Madison said. "I didn't even *get* to the Council Building until after the battle was over."

"But I actually *had* a chance to stop Ethos," Timothy said. "I hesitated. And I let Aksell catch me off guard. If I had just attacked when I had the chance, we wouldn't even be here right now. Alpen would be free, and we'd all be safely back in Kawts."

"Timothy, if you'd attacked him, he would have taken you out in a heartbeat," Crystal said. "Besides, this way we all get to visit Alpen and listen to a grumpy bat complain about the people whose assistance he specifically requested."

In spite of himself, Timothy couldn't help but smile at Crystal's unflattering description of Suorotiart.

"And besides," Quill said. "Now we have a chance to all go on a mission together. We've all pretty much been flying solo so far."

Timothy winced inwardly at Quill's excitement, but Samuel's advice from the previous day kept him from speaking.

There's no universe where it's a good thing that the Council escaped. But I guess it might be possible that it might have some positive side effects. Maybe this mission is just what I needed.

"I suppose you're right," Timothy said at last.

Crystal smirked. "Of course we are."

The door creaked again, and the Mysterious Man stepped out onto the porch.

"Are they still arguing about going after the Weather Belt?" Quill asked as he passed by.

The Mysterious Man nodded. "Once Draagetsew gets an idea into his head, he refuses to listen to any reasoning to the contrary. He's as stubborn as an ox, and every bit as strong." He shook his head. "But I hope that Gearwire and Dr. Maddium will be able to talk him out of it this time. Going after the Weather Belt is a suicide mission."

The Mysterious Man disappeared onto the ship, leaving Timothy and his friends alone outside once more. After a few minutes, other members of the crew began to trickle out of the building, until finally, only Gearwire and Dr. Maddium remained inside. Another half hour passed before Suorotiart poked his head out the door.

"I think we've reached an understanding," he said, the look on his face making it plain that he was displeased with the outcome. "You'd all better come inside."

Timothy stood and followed the others back into the building, forcing himself to focus on what Gearwire would say.

I don't have time to feel sorry for myself, he thought. *No matter what's happening, Gearwire is going to need my help.*

"We've all agreed on our best course of action now, I believe," Gearwire said as they crowded around the small table. He looked weary, as if the debate had taken a lot out of him. "We're going to try to set up a resistance movement here in Blancstadt. We'll spend some time keeping an eye on the Council's movements. They haven't been here long enough to get too firmly entrenched. They'll have weaknesses - places they've left unprotected. It is our mission to find those weaknesses and to exploit them to the best of our ability."

"The Kriegerhelden could help with that," Adalbo said. "Regardless of what's happened since we left, they'll still want to protect Alpen."

Gearwire shook his head. "I'd prefer to leave the Kriegerhelden out of it. If you can find a way to let them know that we're in the area without being spotted, that's fine, but we can't risk telling them anything else. Ethos will have them under heavy surveillance as soon as he realizes they were heroes of Alpen. We can't take the risk that they would accidentally reveal something to the Council."

"A man cannot reveal what he does not know," the Mysterious Man added grimly. "Even under torture."

"I think you're underestimating the Kriegerhelden!" Adalbo said. "We're Alpen's best warriors - none of us would ever betray Alpen - even if we had to die a horrible death!"

"There is another reason we don't want them to be involved in this first fight," Dr. Maddium said. "If things go wrong, we need to know that there's still hope for Alpen and for Kawts. The situation is too precarious for us to put all of our eggs in one basket."

"We're your contingency plan," Idalbo said. He stared at the wall, considering the proposal. "That's smart," he said at last, nodding. Adalbo sighed and took his seat again, although Timothy could see his beetle-like wings twitching.

"Thomas, you and the Mysterious Man will spend the next few days scouting out a location for a permanent base of operations," Gearwire said. "With luck, we won't be here long enough to need it, but it's always good to have a fallback."

The Mysterious Man nodded. "We'll find a place."

"Idalbo, Adalbo, and Timothy - it's going to be up to you three to figure out what the Council's up to," Gearwire said, turning to face them. "Find out what they're planning. Where their strengths and weaknesses are."

"I'll go with them," Quill said. "In case they run into trouble."

Gearwire frowned. "No, you will not. Not only do you have no real combat experience, but you'd stick out like a sore thumb in Blancstadt."

"And Timothy wouldn't?"

"Timothy is a stealth expert who has been to Alpen once before," Gearwire said. "I trust him to keep a low profile. But if word gets out that a bunch of people from beyond Alpen showed up and started asking questions, the Council is going to put two and two together."

Quill opened his mouth to argue his point further, but Timothy elbowed him in the ribs. When Quill turned to look at him, he shook his head.

Not now, he mouthed. Quill hesitated for a moment, then sighed and sat back down.

Gearwire nodded approvingly. "There's not much else we can do until we have more information," he said. "Timothy, if you're up for it, I'd like you to infiltrate the castle tonight. See if you can discover anything useful."

Timothy sat up straighter in his chair. "I'm ready," he said.

"Good. Draagetsew and Suorotiart will tell you everything you need to know about the layout of the castle." Gearwire looked around at the group. "We need to put a stop to the Council's trail of destruction before things get any worse. If we lose Alpen, or worse, the Weather Belt, we might not get another shot."

* * *

Timothy ducked behind an abandoned storefront, being careful to stay out of the light given off by the streetlamps that lined the capital city's main street. He had been steadily working his way towards the castle for the last several hours, starting out as soon as the sun went down.

The magnificent building looked very different in the dark, its blue turrets looking almost black against the starless sky. Timothy heard footsteps at the top of the wall and ducked out of sight once more, listening intently. The footsteps grew louder, then suddenly stopped altogether. The seconds seemed to stretch into hours as he waited, straining his ears for any indication that the guard had noticed that something was amiss. Finally, the footsteps resumed, gradually fading to nothingness.

Timothy let out a sigh of relief as he stepped around the corner and inspected the wall. It was tall and wide, the gate reinforced by horizontal iron bars. Draagetsew had bragged on his last visit that the castle walls had never been breached.

Let's hope that doesn't mean it can't be done, Timothy thought, removing a coil of rope from his chest plate. He glanced around the abandoned square to make sure there were no witnesses, then twirled the rope over his head, sending one end sailing up onto the wall. The hook on the end clattered onto the stone floor of the walkway, and

Timothy froze, waiting to see if the guard had heard.

Several seconds passed with no signs of the footsteps returning, and Timothy slowly pulled the rope taut. The grappling hook grated noisily across the stones, making him wince. But he continued to pull until the head snagged on the edge of the battlement, making sure that it had caught before allowing himself to check for guards. The silence stretched on, and Timothy began his climb up the rope. When he reached the top, he lowered it down the other side, making sure to anchor it in a spot that wouldn't be clearly visible to any guards who might walk by.

Timothy dropped lightly down onto the grass below, making almost no sound as he crept towards the castle keep. The darkness made finding his way difficult, and even despite his vague recollections of the castle layout from his last visit and the instructions given to him by Draagetsew and Suorotiart, he lost his way several times before arriving at the entrance.

He stooped down to examine the lock on the door.

Mechanical, he thought with a frown. *That means I won't be able to use my shuriken to get in.*

Gently, he tugged on the handle, hoping that somehow it would be unlocked. The door refused to budge, and he stepped back from the wall, considering his options. As he stared up at the building in front of him, his eyes came to rest on a window a few stories up. It looked to be open, although he couldn't tell for sure at this distance.

He examined the wall thoughtfully, paying special attention to the gaps between the stones. He popped one of his shurikens off into his hand and wedged it into one of these gaps a few feet off the ground. The shuriken stuck fast, and Timothy gave it a preliminary shove, testing if it could hold his weight. The shuriken wobbled a little, but Timothy ignored it.

That'll have to do, he thought, reaching into the compartment in his chest plate. He pulled out several more shurikens and began to climb, sticking one into the wall wherever he needed a foothold.

As he neared the top, he was relieved to find that the window was, in fact, open. He clung to the wall, listening intently for any signs of life on the other side. Nothing but silence greeted him, and he cautiously stepped inside, his eyes darting around the room. A single bed lay up against the outer wall, only a few feet from where Timothy was standing. For one brief, terrifying second, Timothy worried that he had unwittingly walked directly into one of the Councilmen's bedrooms. He took one tentative step closer and breathed a sigh of relief. The bed was empty. Satisfied that he was alone, Timothy looked around the room, checking for anything that would be of use to the rebellion.

The room was completely devoid of any signs of the Council's presence, containing only a dusty portrait of a regal-looking mutant in a hood and a few books arranged haphazardly on a shelf. Overcome with curiosity, Timothy examined the titles. To his disappointment, most of them seemed to be biographies about a mutant named Swehpen and his impact on Alpen. Timothy tore himself away from the books, forcing himself to focus on the task at hand. He crept over to the door and pressed his ear against it, listening hard.

There was silence from the other side, and after a moment's hesitation, Timothy eased the door open. The door opened soundlessly, allowing the light of the hallway to shine into the darkened bedroom. Timothy carefully shut the door behind him, noting the plaque on the wall beside him.

Looks like that was Draagetsew's bedroom, he thought with a smile. *I'm sure he'll get a kick out of that.*

Committing the room number to memory, he ventured out further down the hall. Several times, he was forced to duck into a nearby room as a mutant approached, hoping that they hadn't heard him moving around. Finally, as he neared the Great Hall, he began to hear voices. One of them, loud and scornful, rose louder than the others.

Ethos.

"Don't be a fool!" he shouted, his voice echoing throughout the vast stone room. "We can't just charge them head-on! We need to bide our time. You heard what he said about those blasted rebels! The pieces are not yet in place."

He's talking about Ray, Timothy realized. *He must have told them we were coming.*

"Nonetheless," Simms' high, nervous voice piped up. "As long as we continue to employ those who are loyal to Draagetsew, we are putting ourselves at risk of invasion or assassination!"

"Stick to the plan," Ethos said. "They outfought us back in Kawts. Our best chance to come out of this on top is by out-thinking them. We can't afford to get dragged into another all-out war. Not yet."

As Simms started to reply, Timothy heard footsteps coming down the corridor behind him. For a split second, he froze, weighing the risk of being spotted against the value of hearing more of the Council's plans. As the footsteps grew louder, he came to a decision, slipping away from the Great Hall in the direction he had come.

As he hurried back to the presidential suite, he ran over the Council's conversation in his mind, trying to make sense of what he had heard.

The Council's planning something big, he realized. *Something that our arrival has interrupted. They aren't ready for us yet. If we strike now, we might still be able to-*

As Timothy rounded the corner of the hallway, he almost collided with a person heading in the opposite direction. He scrambled backwards, his pulse racing. A million thoughts ran through his head as he tried to figure out how to respond.

"Tim? What are you doing here?"

Timothy's panic abruptly shut down as he recognised the voice.

"Aksell?"

"Why are you here? Haven't you guys done enough damage already?"

Timothy shook his head, quickly regaining control of his emotions. "I'm saving Alpen from your dad and the rest of the Council."

Aksell shook his head. When he spoke, his voice was full of betrayal. "You really are one of them, aren't you? I was hoping I was just misunderstanding what happened back in Kawts." He looked up at Timothy, looking directly into his eyes. "What happened to you, Tim? The Council was the only thing protecting Kawts from total anarchy. Why would you betray your city?"

"I'm not the one who betrayed Kawts," Timothy said. "The Council weren't the city's protectors. They were the ones keeping us all living in fear."

"Timothy, listen to yourself! The Council has always tried to do what's best for Kawts!"

"How is enslaving everyone in the town what's best for Kawts?" Timothy shot back, a bit more sharply than he'd intended.

"My dad did what had to be done. His methods might be a little harsh sometimes, but he has Kawts' best interest at heart," Aksell said, but Timothy could tell he wasn't quite as confident as he had been before.

"Do you really believe that?"

Aksell was silent, and Timothy added, "It's not too late to change sides. I'm sure Gearwire would let you join us. You could help set Alpen free."

Aksell shook his head, his resolve returning. "No. Timothy, this is *your* last chance. I can smooth things over with my dad. I could get him to pardon you. But if you leave, I can't guarantee you'll make it out of this alive. Please, Tim. You're still my friend. I don't want you to die. Like Quill."

"I can't do that," Timothy said, shaking his head. "Tell Ethos about me if you have to. If he catches me and kills me, I can accept that. But I can't let him keep oppressing people. He and the rest of the Council need to be brought to justice."

Before Aksell could respond, Timothy ran past him, losing himself in the twisting corridors of the castle. He made his way back to the presidential suite, sealing himself inside. Without missing a beat, he scrambled out the window and slipped away from the castle, making it back to the little ramshackle house outside of town in record time.

Chapter 7

"The Council is planning something," Timothy said, pacing the little room where the leaders of Alpen and the Guardians of Kawts were holding court. "But whatever it is, it isn't ready yet. They weren't expecting us to show up this soon."

"I knew it! They're after the Weather Belt!" Draagetsew exclaimed, slamming one of his massive fists down on the table.

"We don't know that for sure," Gearwire said. "It could be anything." He turned to Timothy. "Did you hear anything about the Weather Belt specifically?"

Timothy shook his head. "Ethos just said something about the pieces not being in place yet and that they couldn't afford to attack us outright."

"We'll have to make our move soon, then," Gearwire said. "Good work, Timothy."

Timothy swallowed hard. "Actually, it's a little more complicated than that." Gearwire raised an eyebrow, and Timothy continued, "While I was over there, I ran into Aksell."

"Ran into as in…?"

"I almost collided with him. He recognised me."

Gearwire exhaled slowly, running his hand over his long, grey beard. "So the Council knows for sure that we're here. And that you were in the castle last night."

Timothy nodded. "Probably. It's always possible that Aksell kept it a secret from Ethos, but I don't think we can count on it."

"That certainly complicates things," Dr. Maddium agreed.

"If we strike now, we can push them out before they have a chance to react!" Draagetsew said. "We'll call in the Kriegerhelden and storm the castle!"

"If the Council knows Timothy was spying on them last night, they'll probably expect us to try something like that," Gearwire said. "Or at the very least, they'll alter their plans a bit."

"And don't forget about their evaporation cannon," Suorotiart said. "They've told us they can and will use it on civilian buildings if we try anything. They'll be waiting for us if we try a direct attack."

"What if I sneak back into the castle?" Timothy suggested. "I could find where they're storing this cannon and disable it. Just like in the Battle of Kawts."

"We need more information," Gearwire said, shaking his head. "You know I trust you, Timothy. But I don't trust the Council. I can't justify such a risky expedition without knowing how much they know."

"With all due respect, I think I'm with Draagetsew on this one, Gearwire," Timothy said. "I can't say for sure what Aksell will tell the rest of the Council, but it's not something he's going to take lightly. If we strike today, it's possible that he hasn't made up his mind yet."

"And even if he has, the Council won't have had time to prepare!" Draagetsew added.

"And neither will we," Gearwire said. "We only got here yesterday. We don't have a secure base, we know next to nothing about the situation in Blancstadt, and we have yet to make contact with the Kriegerhelden. I'm sorry, but we aren't ready for an all-out attack."

Timothy sighed. *He has a point,* he realized. *Although I can't shake the feeling that we're wasting a perfect opportunity to end this once and for all.*

"Is there anything else you'd like to report?" Gearwire asked.

"That's all I can think of."

"In that case, you're free to leave. Send Idalbo and Adalbo in here on your way out. Hopefully, they'll be able to help us discover exactly what the Council is planning."

Timothy nodded, excusing himself from the war room. He stepped out of the building, walking past Quill, who had been standing near the door.

"Gearwire wants to talk to you two," Timothy said, turning to Adalbo and Idalbo. "I think he's going to send you on a reconnaissance mission."

Idalbo nodded stiffly. "We'll be right there."

As soon as the door had shut behind them, Quill spoke. "Did you really see Aksell last night?"

Timothy stopped and looked at him. "What gave you that idea?"

Quill grinned. "Let's just say I've been doing a little reconnaissance of my own."

"You were listening at the door, weren't you?"

"I can neither confirm nor deny that statement," Quill said, his grin growing wider.

Timothy smiled, shaking his head. "I'm afraid you just did." His smile faded a little as he considered Quill's question. "Yes, I did see Aksell last night. We even had a conversation."

"How is he?" Quill asked.

"He seemed fine," Timothy said. "But he's bought Ethos' act hook, line, and sinker. He thought *I* was the one who had gone to the dark side. There was a moment when I thought I was getting through to him, but then he just gave me the same old pack of lies the Council has been feeding everyone for years."

Quill's face fell a little. "He'll figure it out eventually," he insisted. "Did he say anything else?"

"Only that if I surrendered now, he could get me a pardon from the

Council," Timothy said with a wry smile. "And that if I stayed with Gearwire, he couldn't guarantee my safety."

"I hate to say it, but I'm not sure Aksell's coming back," Crystal said, coming up to the pair. "If the Council's behavior just before the battle didn't convince him that he's on the wrong side, I'm not sure what would."

"He's probably just in denial," Jewel said, joining her sister. "Even if he's seen what the Council is doing, he doesn't want to believe that his father is a terrorist. It'll just take him longer to accept it."

"Well, he'd better accept it soon," Timothy said. "The Council is planning something big, and I don't want to fight him."

* * *

"Left! Left! Right! Center! Right!" the Mysterious Man shouted, calling out the targets at a rapid pace. Timothy whipped a shuriken toward one of the makeshift targets, nailing it about an inch from the center. He risked a quick glance over at Jewel and saw that she had likewise hit her target.

"Right! Center! Right! Stop!" the Mysterious Man called. Timothy dropped his arms to his side, breathing heavily. The training session had been going on for nearly half an hour, the Mysterious Man maintaining the same breakneck pace throughout.

The Mysterious Man walked up to the targets, inspecting their aim. "Pretty good," he said at last. "I'd say you've gotten back in practice, Jewel. You too, Timothy. Although you could benefit from taking just a split second longer to line up your throws."

Timothy flushed slightly, glancing over at Jewel. If she had heard the Mysterious Man's criticism, however, she gave no indication of it.

"Once you guys have had a chance to rest a bit, we should set up some sparring matches," the Golden Knight said, leaning up against Gearwire's ship.

Timothy quickly shook his head, remembering the last time he and the Golden Knight sparred. The Golden Knight was an expert swordsman, and it had taken all of Timothy's energy just to avoid his attacks. "No, I think we're good," he said. "We've had enough training for today."

The Golden Knight frowned, as if to say that one could never have too much training. He opened his mouth to respond, when something at the edge of the camp drew his attention.

Timothy turned to see what was causing the commotion. The rest of the Guardians of Kawts were clustered together outside their temporary base, surrounding two people who had just arrived.

It's Idalbo and Adalbo, Timothy realized. *They're back from their mission.*

"Any sparring matches or lack thereof will have to wait, I think," the Mysterious Man said. "If they're back after only two days, it's got to mean they've found something."

Timothy turned back toward the targets, recalling his shurikens to his hand and stashing them in their proper places. Beside him, Jewel did the same, dissolving the crystal darts that were embedded in her targets. The four of them walked over to the rest of the group, where their suspicions were quickly confirmed. Idalbo and Adalbo had discovered more information about the Council's plans, confirming that they were, in fact, planning to go after the Weather Belt. It was all the confirmation that Gearwire needed, and mere minutes later, the Guardians of Kawts were once again crammed into the tiny house as Gearwire laid out their plan of attack.

* * *

Timothy stood partway up a skyscraper with Idalbo and Adalbo, the sun barely peeking out over the tops of the hills. The building was currently empty, the city still fast asleep. From here, they had a clear view of the area where the battle for Alpen was soon to play out.

Timothy hid a yawn as he left Idalbo and Adalbo by the open window.

Next time we fight the Council, we should pick a time that still gives us a chance to get a good night's sleep, he thought wryly, rubbing his eyes. He moved to the other side of the building, coming to a stop in front of another window. Timothy pried the window open and crept onto the ledge. He gauged the distance between this building and the next, studiously avoiding looking at the street far below. He slipped his staff into its sheath and leapt across the gap. He slammed into the opposite wall, scrabbling desperately for a handhold. For one brief, horrifying moment, he was in a free fall. Then his hand caught on the edge of the windowsill and he pulled himself up, his arms shaking.

He stood stock-still on the ledge for a few minutes, trying to bring his racing heartbeat back to normal. Finally, he turned to face the window, smashing it open with one of the heavy, blunted shurikens he had designed for knocking out Blanks.

Timothy grabbed the top of the window and swung himself into the room, shards of glass crunching under his armored feet. He weaved his way through the offices to the staircase and sprinted up it, emerging onto the roof a few minutes later. He crouched down near the edge of the building, watching the castle courtyard below.

"I'm in position," he whispered into his radio beacon.

"Good. We're on our way," Gearwire said. Timothy switched the radio off and looked down at the castle, waiting.

It only took a few minutes before the rest of the Guardians of Kawts began to arrive, appearing one by one on the edges of the street. Gearwire walked into the center of the street, taking the guise of a mutant with a horse's hooves for feet. A guard marched up to him, his spear raised. They exchanged words, and Timothy wished he could hear what was being said. Taking his eyes off the castle for a brief moment, he pulled out a shuriken from his chest plate and threw it towards the wall, embedding it between the stones only a couple of yards away from the guards.

Timothy removed a small box from his chest plate and switched it on. Seconds later, Gearwire's voice came out of the speaker.

"-need to see the Council right away. Ray sent me with an important message for Ethos."

"If this is official business, what are all your friends doing hiding in the shadows?" the guard asked, his voice sounding almost amused.

Timothy saw Gearwire turn his head. "My friends? I don't know-" Without even finishing his sentence, he turned and grabbed the guard, hitting him in the face with a short punch. The guard sagged to the ground, and Gearwire gently lowered him to the pavement. As he motioned for the others to join him, Timothy saw movement from the courtyard below. He pulled out Henry's old pair of field binoculars and peered through them. A shudder ran through him as he saw who it was.

"Gearwire. Ethos is already on his way to the wall," he said into the radio, speaking quickly. He put the binoculars up to his eyes again, watching the Councilman's approach. "You have maybe two minutes before he reaches you - if that."

"Thanks for the warning, Timothy," Gearwire replied. With the guard incapacitated, he had returned to his normal form, deactivating the disguise mechanism in his robotic legs. He waved Madison forward, and she produced a grappling hook from her tool belt, swinging it over her head several times before sending it sailing over the edge of the wall. She gave the rope a tug, then handed it over to Gearwire.

"We're going to have to move fast," Gearwire's voice came through Timothy's speaker. "Ethos is on his way. We only have a few minutes to get inside and take out the Council before they realize what's happening." He turned back towards the wall and gave the rope a tug himself. He was about to begin his climb when Ethos appeared at the top of the wall.

"I wouldn't do that if I were you, Milkop," Ethos sneered.

Gearwire stiffened and froze, one foot still pressed against the wall.

Milkop? As in Milkop Quawz? The man who led a rebellion against the Council a hundred years ago? What is Ethos-

Ethos' laugh echoed across the square. "Oh yes. I know all about you. I've done my research this time. It took the Baron weeks, but he finally discovered your true identity. I know exactly who you are."

Gearwire slowly turned to face the smug Councilman. Even through the speaker, Timothy could hear the steely tone in his voice. "You know nothing about me," he said, his hand drifting to the hilt of his glue gun.

"Oh, I think I do," Ethos said, a patronizing smirk on his face. "Milkop Quawz: general, politician, revolutionary. You thought you'd covered your tracks well. You thought you hadn't left behind anything that might tell me who you truly are." Ethos laughed. "You'd be amazed what you can find in the ancient archives."

"You have five seconds to come down here and hand over your sword," Gearwire said, pointing his glue gun at the Councilman. "If not, you have a very high chance of ending up dead."

"Oh, I don't think I do," Ethos said. He took his hand out of his pocket, balled into a fist. "You're a military man, *Milkop*," he said, stepping closer to the edge of the wall. "Tell me, do you recognise this?" He pulled his fingers back from the device in his hand, holding it between his index finger and his thumb.

"It's a dead-man's trigger," Gearwire said warily.

"That's right," Ethos said. "Would you like to explain to your band of rabble what that means?" Gearwire was silent, his eyes darting around as he tried to come up with a way to redeem the situation. "That's alright," Ethos said. "I'll do it. If I die or take my hand off of this trigger, all of Blancstadt will evaporate."

"You're bluffing," Gearwire said, although Timothy could still detect a note of fear in his voice.

"Am I?" Ethos asked. He nodded to someone outside of Timothy's field of vision. Across the street, a building blinked out of existence, leaving behind only a steaming crater. "I'm sure that fool of a president Draagetsew told you about our new toy. It's currently set up to vaporize the entire city with a press of a button." Grinning like a madman, Ethos slowly peeled his fingers off of the trigger, one by one.

Gearwire stared him down, unwavering. But by the time Ethos reached two fingers, it was clear the Councilman was serious. "Stop!" Gearwire shouted, defeated. "What do you want, Ethos?"

Ethos closed his fist once more, looking immensely pleased with himself. Timothy felt a surge of anger, which he quickly pushed aside.

Not now. I need to stay focused.

"I'll tell you what, Milkop," Ethos said. "In light of all you've done for the Council over the years, I'll cut you a deal. Leave Alpen. You will never come back here, nor will you send anyone else to disrupt our rule. Take the four-armed freak and the bat-man with you. In exchange, I will spare your lives."

Gearwire hesitated, and Ethos added, "There's one other thing I forgot to mention. As we speak, the rest of the Council is waiting outside the city limits. If they see the city evaporate, they have orders to march on Kawts. If you leave right now, I promise you that neither

I nor any other member of the Council will ever again set foot in Kawts."

Timothy fingered a shuriken as Gearwire considered Ethos' offer.

I can't believe that I used to think Ethos was a nice guy, he thought, shaking his head. *If he didn't have that detonator in his hand, he'd have half a dozen shurikens heading his way by now.*

"Fall back!" Gearwire shouted, his voice breaking. The Guardians of Kawts looked at each other in confusion. Then, slowly, they backed away from the castle, keeping one wary eye on Ethos until he was out of sight. His head spinning, Timothy followed suit, meeting up with them again just outside the city limits. Melancholy silence filled the air as the group returned to the house, filing inside.

For a long moment, no one spoke. Then Quill said, "Is anyone else wondering why Ethos kept calling Gearwire Milkop Quawz?"

Timothy elbowed his friend, shaking his head. *This is not the time,* he mouthed.

Gearwire stared off into space, the look on his face the closest thing to an expression of anger Timothy had ever seen him display. Quill, ignoring Timothy's warning, repeated his question a second time.

Gearwire looked up at him, his face stern. "Do you trust me?"

Quill's eyes scanned the room. The awkward silence stretched on as he tried to figure out where Gearwire was going with this question. "Yes..." he said at last.

"Then we will leave the question at that," Gearwire said, his face hardening. "You were right, Timothy. It seems we've waited too long to make our move," he continued, beginning to pace the length of the room. "The Council has already spun their web." He turned to face the group, a look of grim resignation on his face. "As much as I hate to say it, our only chance now is to go after the Weather Belt ourselves."

"I don't like it," the Mysterious Man said, shaking his head. "I see Ethos' meddling written all over this." He looked Gearwire in the eyes. "I request your permission to remain here for the duration of this mission."

The Mysterious Man's words rippled through the room like a shockwave. Timothy felt his stomach drop.

The Mysterious Man never sits these things out. What are we getting ourselves into?

Gearwire nodded slowly. "I grant your request. Is there anyone else who would prefer to remain behind?"

"I'll stay," Howard said. "My skills will be of more use to you out here, anyway."

"If it's alright with you, Idalbo and I would like to stay as well," Adalbo said, exchanging a glance with his brother. "We can keep an eye on the Council and try to get the Kriegerhelden back together. Maybe we'll be able to find a way to beat them without using the Weather Belt."

"You have my permission," Gearwire said. "The rest of us will leave early tomorrow morning. The Weather Belt is hidden in an ancient compound atop a mountain a few miles from here. We'll take the ship as high up the mountain as we can, but I suspect we'll still have a bit of climbing to do."

"We won't be able to retrieve the Weather Belt in just one day," Draagetsew said. "The complex is massive and stuffed full of traps. We'll need food and supplies for a fortnight at least - maybe a month to be safe."

Gearwire nodded. "Idalbo and Adalbo, could you two sneak back into town to get the supplies we'll need?"

"You can count on us, sir," Idalbo said. "We'll do whatever it takes to get the Council out of Alpen."

"Draagetsew and I will write up a list of things we might need," Dr. Maddium said. "I assume you hid the map of the complex in a safe place?"

Draagetsew grinned. "There's no way I would have left that where the Council could find it," he said. From his back pocket, he pulled out a tattered old map, unrolling it on the table. "It's been passed down from president to president for centuries in case Alpen ever needed to retrieve the Weather Belt again."

"Good," Gearwire said. "Everyone else, gather your gear and get ready. We leave for the complex first thing tomorrow."

* * *

It was dusk by the time Idalbo and Adalbo returned with the supplies, dragging them behind them on an improvised sledge. The rest of the team gathered around, helping to organize the supplies into smaller bundles. They were about halfway done when Samuel's voice squawked over the radio.

"Samuel to Gearwire, Samuel to Gearwire," he said. "Do you read me?"

Gearwire set down the crate of food he was carrying and picked up the radio. "I hear you, Samuel," he replied. "Anything new to report?"

"There's no sign of the Council in Kawts or Gearwire's Cave," Samuel said. "Cedar says that all is well in Grimshaw, too."

"Keep us posted," Gearwire said. "What about Ray?" he asked. "Have you gotten anything out of him yet?"

"Not yet," Samuel replied. "There wasn't really anything in his journal that we didn't already know. It seems like he mostly just wrote to give himself something to do. Volker's been questioning him, but he refuses to talk. He's planning on bringing Crofton along with him next time."

"Smart move. They were friends once, as I recall."

"That's what Volker's banking on," Samuel said. "I take it that the attack on the castle didn't go according to plan. Is everyone okay?"

"We're all fine. Nothing wounded but our pride. Ethos rigged the entire city to evaporate if we killed him. He forced us into agreeing to leave Alpen and stay in Kawts. We're leaving for the Weather Belt complex in the morning."

There was silence for a while as Samuel digested this fresh development. "I'll be praying for you," he said at last.

"Thanks," Gearwire replied. "We're going to need it. Let us know if anything new comes up with Ray," he added. "He could be the key to our victory."

"I will," Samuel assured him. "Good luck."

Chapter 8

As the sun peeked out above the horizon, Timothy climbed up the stairs to Gearwire's ship, taking a seat on the side of the cabin opposite to the door. Dr. Maddium sat on the bench beside him, Draagetsew taking the scientist's place in the cockpit as Gearwire's navigator. As the ship lifted into the air, Timothy waved out the window to the four members of their team who remained behind.

As the camp disappeared behind them, Timothy stared off into space, thinking about everything that had happened over the last several days.

Less than a week ago, I was hiking through the mountains with Howard, trying to learn what happened to Maurice. Now I'm on my way to a several-week long mission in one of the most dangerous places on earth. He sighed. *There's always another crisis.*

His mind went to what Howard had said on their ride back to Kawts.

Howard's planning on resigning from the Guardians of Kawts after this mission. Maybe I should, too.

He heard the rustle of fabric beside him, bringing him back to the present. He turned to see Quill slide onto the bench beside him. Dropping his voice to a conspiratorial whisper, Quill said, "We need to talk about what Ethos said yesterday."

"About Gearwire?"

Quill nodded. "Why did he keep calling him Milkop?"

"I don't know, Quill."

"Come on! You've been a part of his crew for almost a year now. You must have heard something!"

Timothy shook his head. "All I know is that he's not from this time. He and Dr. Maddium and Henry came from the past to help defeat the Council." He glanced over at Dr. Maddium, then added in a lower tone, "And… the night of the battle, Gearwire told me that he was the one who put the Council in power."

Quill frowned, his forehead furrowing. "That doesn't add up. The Council's been in charge since Kawts' founding. And Milkop Quawz' rebellion wasn't until a couple hundred years later."

"As I said, I don't know much," Timothy said. "To be honest, I think Dr. Maddium might be the only person left besides Gearwire who knows what Ethos meant."

"Maybe I should ask him, then."

"If Gearwire wanted us to know, he would have told us."

"Come on. Aren't you just a little curious? I mean, if we're going to be spending the next few weeks with him in a building full of traps, shouldn't we know what we're getting ourselves into? And remember, Ethos thanked Gearwire for helping them, too. That sounds like something that we need to know about."

Without waiting for Timothy to respond, Quill turned to Dr. Maddium. "Dr. Maddium, we have a question," he said, loud enough for the entire cabin to hear.

"Go on."

"What was Ethos talking about yesterday? Was he telling the truth? And who is Gearwire, really?"

"That sounds like three questions," Dr. Maddium said with a slight smile. "But I'm afraid I'm not at liberty to answer any of them."

"We need to know the person who's leading us into danger," Quill said.

"Gearwire's secrets are his own to keep," Dr. Maddium said. "Do you trust him to do what's best for Kawts?"

"Well, yeah, but-"

"Then that should be good enough," Dr. Maddium said. "Gearwire can tell you about his own history if and when he feels it's necessary."

"I'm afraid you're going to have to do better than that, Doc," Suorotiart said. "You all might trust Gearwire to do what's best for Kawts, but we're not fighting for Kawts. And I've only met the man twice. How do you know he really is who he says he is? How do you know he won't betray Alpen to save Kawts? How do you know he isn't working with the Council?"

"I'd go easy on the accusations if I were you," the Golden Knight said, slowly getting to his feet. "Gearwire's a good man. And his first priority is protecting all lives, not just those who live in Kawts. Anyone who says otherwise will have to contend with me."

"There's no need to resort to violence," Dr. Maddium said. "I'm sure every one of us can produce sufficient testimony to Gearwire's character to support what the Golden Knight has said. You're not going to get better evidence than that for any of the rest of us."

"And as a matter of fact, *we* know much less about *you* than we know about Gearwire," Crystal said. "So why don't you tell us *your* whole life's story?"

Suorotiart took his seat again, grumbling under his breath.

"So much for just asking," Quill muttered, shaking his head. For a moment, Timothy thought he was going to protest further, but he let the subject drop.

Timothy turned toward the widow, staring absently at the pine forests which lined the foothills below. As they approached the mountaintop, the ground grew steeper, giving way to towering grey peaks liberally dusted with snow. Despite the danger they were soon to be in, Timothy found himself marveling at the majestic beauty of the mountains.

If we weren't in such a hurry, it might be fun to climb it by foot, he thought as the ship flew between two spires of rock.

"Is that the complex?" Madison asked, pointing at something ahead of them.

Timothy craned his neck to get a better look at what she was talking about. Off in the distance, a huge old building sat, perched atop the tallest peak in the area. A clear dome arched over the building and the dense forest that surrounded it. Running around the forest was a series of concentric walls, one of which stretched to over thirty feet tall.

As they drew closer, Timothy realized for the first time how truly massive the compound was. It completely dwarfed Gearwire's ship, looming over the entire mountain range. But despite its almost impossible size, the building looked like it had been meticulously crafted, bearing more than a slight resemblance to an ancient Greek temple. The edges of the marble building were trimmed with gold, arranged into elaborate swirls.

"If we are all about to die, at least we'll be buried in a really cool mausoleum," Crystal said, taking in the sight of the massive building.

"The Weather Belt is hidden somewhere in there?" Quill asked in disbelief. "This is going to be a lot harder than I thought."

Dr. Maddium nodded. "Right in the middle of a complex stuffed full of nearly every kind of trap known to man. Plus a few new ones for good measure. It's one of Alpen's greatest feats of engineering."

"How do you know so much about the Weather Belt complex?" Suorotiart challenged, evidently still irritated by Dr. Maddium's response to his earlier objection.

"I may have had a hand in inventing some of the more novel aspects," Dr. Maddium admitted. "The first ruler of Alpen hired me to work on a few portions of the complex."

"So if we all die, we have you to blame," Suorotiart said. "Now at least I'll know who to curse in my dying breath."

"Give it a break, Suorotiart," Madison said. "We're never going to get to the Weather Belt if we're already at each other's throats before we even get inside."

"We're beginning our descent now," Gearwire announced over the loudspeaker. "Everyone, take your seats and buckle in."

Gearwire flew the ship in a lazy circle around the building, searching for a suitable place to land. After several fruitless minutes of searching, the ship began to descend, landing on a medium-sized ledge a relatively short distance away from the top of the mountain. As the humming of the engines slowly died away, Gearwire emerged from the cockpit, Draagetsew right behind him. They made an odd contrast - Gearwire's face was set in a look of grim determination, while Draagetsew was practically bouncing with excitement.

"Make sure you have all your assigned gear in your pack," Gearwire said, shouldering the backpack that contained his bedroll and some basic camping gear. "And make sure you have your climbing equipment out. We're going to need it."

The rest of the Guardians of Kawts followed suit, getting their packs in order. Timothy stood and walked towards the exit of the ship, waiting for the others to finish. Of all of them, only he and Dr. Maddium did not have a pack of their own, carrying the bulk of the group's supplies in Timothy's chest plate and the Infini-case. Timothy had suggested that the two of them carry all the supplies, but Gearwire had vetoed the idea, wanting to make sure that everyone had access to at least basic supplies on the chance that they got separated from the group or the Infini-case malfunctioned.

As the rest of the Guardians of Kawts got ready to disembark, Timothy climbed out of the ship, sinking up to his ankles in powdery snow. He struggled to the side of the ship to make room for the others to disembark. As the others climbed out after him, he slowly craned his neck upward, taking in the height of the mountain they now had to climb.

This is not going to be nearly as much fun as I thought, is it?

"Gah!" came a voice from behind him, and Timothy turned to see Quill standing beside him, likewise up to his ankles in snow.

A smile tugged at the corner of Timothy's mouth. "Colder than you expected?"

"A little," Quill agreed, walking over to Timothy. "Mostly, I just didn't think the snow would be this deep."

"Should've brought boots then," Crystal said, jumping down from the ship and landing lightly in the snow. She gestured to the other Guardians of Kawts. "Like everyone else did."

"'Everyone else' has a fancy uniform," Quill pointed out, trying to shake the snow off his foot. "All I have are tennis shoes."

"Why *don't* you have a suit, Quill?" Madison asked. "You have your own weapon - that stun rifle my dad helped you make."

"It didn't cross my mind until just now," Quill said. "I didn't know I was going to be hiking up a mountain this week."

"We might have an extra pair of boots in the Infini-case," Timothy said. "I'll check with Dr. Maddium."

"Speaking of Dr. Maddium," Jewel said, coming over to the little group. "Everyone else is waiting for us on the other side of the ship."

"Right," Timothy said, fighting off a brief surge of embarrassment. "We should probably get going."

* * *

For the next hour, the Guardians of Kawts struggled over boulders and through snowdrifts, intent on reaching the ruins. Halfway up, they stopped on a narrow ledge, crammed together like sardines as they tried to give their aching muscles a chance to rest. But all too soon, they had to set out again, resuming their painstakingly slow climb.

Nearly two hours after they had landed, Timothy pulled himself up over the final ledge, brushing the snow from his arms. A few moments later, Gearwire appeared beside him. One by one, the rest of the Guardians of Kawts joined them, clustering together on a narrow ledge that ran alongside the edge of the outer dome.

As the last member of Gearwire's crew reached the top of the mountain, Timothy turned to look at the complex behind them. From the ground, the massive, impenetrable dome was an intimidating sight. He gazed up at it in silence, awed by the sheer enormity of the compound.

"I don't think we would have been able to make it up here without Gearwire's ship," Jewel said, taking in the dizzying drop only a few feet away from where they stood.

"That was sort of the point," Suorotiart said. "When they built this place a few hundred years ago, they chose this remote mountain top because it was difficult to access. Anyone who wanted to get in would first have to climb the mountain. And from way up here, the guards could easily spot them and stop them before they ever reached this point."

"All but one," Draagetsew said, a wistful smile crossing his face. "One of the greatest heroes Alpen has ever seen was lost somewhere inside these walls."

"That's not exactly encouraging," Crystal said, arching an eyebrow. "Why can't we just blast a hole in the ceiling over the chamber and retrieve it that way? Between Gearwire's glue gun and Madison's grenades, I think we'd have enough firepower."

"Unfortunately not," Draagetsew replied. "The builders of this facility thought of that angle. They had the ceilings, the dome, and most of the walls laced with invincium - the same stuff that the Golden Knight's armor is made of, if I'm not mistaken."

The Golden Knight nodded, and Draagetsew continued. "Nothing short of a nuclear bomb or the Weather Belt itself could make a dent in this place without having to work on it nonstop for several years."

Crystal shrugged. "It was worth a shot."

Jewel walked up to the dome surrounding the complex, pressing her palm against it. "So if we can't force our way through the dome, how *do* we get in?" she asked, turning to face Draagetsew.

"Excellent question," Draagetsew said, pulling the ancient map out of his pocket. He examined it for several seconds before answering. "The only entrance is a gate a short distance from here." He glanced down at the map again. "That way."

Gearwire nodded solemnly and began to inch along the narrow ledge around the edge of the dome. Timothy followed, trying not to think about the sheer drop in front of him. He shuffled along, keeping his back tightly pressed against the dome.

Enjoy this while you can, he thought grimly. *It's only going to get harder from here.*

Finally, after nearly fifteen minutes of agonizingly slow movements, the ledge suddenly widened out, expanding until it was big enough for all of them to gather once more. Timothy breathed a sigh of relief as he came into the larger space, rolling his tense shoulders. After a few moments, Quill appeared around the bend, and Timothy reached out and pulled him to the ledge.

They stood next to each other, watching as Madison started to round the corner. She had only gotten halfway around when she glanced down. Even from where he stood, Timothy could hear her gasp. She froze, clinging to the surface of the dome.

We forgot about Madison's fear of heights, Timothy thought, the realization striking him like a bolt of lightning. A frown crossed his face as he examined the situation.

She won't be able to stay there indefinitely. If she doesn't finish the climb, sooner or later she's going to fall.

"Don't look down," Quill called out, interrupting Timothy's concerns. "Just focus on getting around the bend." Timothy glanced over at him, surprised. Quill didn't notice, his focus entirely on Madison. "Keep your eyes on me," he said. "And take your time. We aren't in a hurry."

For several moments, Madison didn't move. Finally, she started along the ledge once more, slowly inching her way across. This time, it was Quill who helped her the last few feet.

Quill put his hand on her arm. "Breathe," he counseled gently. Madison nodded and took a deep breath. She exhaled slowly, then gave a weak smile.

"Thanks," she gasped, the tension draining from her shoulders. She moved to the center of the larger ledge and sat down, studiously avoiding looking at the edge. Quill sat down beside her, saying nothing.

One by one, the others trickled over, completing the perilous journey themselves. Before long, they all stood in front of the gate.

The gate seemed to be some kind of old airlock, two great shining sheets of metal that would slide open when the door was unlocked. Framing these was a white, puffy arch, broken into five segments of a strange, sleek metal. On the right-hand side, a control panel was embedded into the frame, a simple computer consisting only of a card reader, a keypad, and two dime-sized lights - one red, and one green.

Draagetsew removed a key card from his shirt pocket and swiped it through the control panel. The door whirred, then emitted a sharp click.

"-nter…. passc-" a robotic voice garbled from the central section of the gate's frame.

Timothy frowned. "What does it want us to-" he started, but Draagetsew cut him off.

"The passcode," he said, examining the map again. He mouthed a series of numbers as his eyes scanned the paper. Then he punched the digits into the keypad, typing each one slowly and deliberately. Timothy counted thirty-seven by the time he was finished.

The whirring noise intensified, then abruptly stopped. Timothy eyed the door warily, suddenly realizing that it was quite possible that the door was equipped with some sort of defenses that they had overlooked. He breathed a sigh of relief as the green light lit up.

The door chuffed softly, then slowly slid open, creaking on its rust-worn hinges. Draagetsew drew himself up to his full height and marched inside. The light began to flash, and the others ran inside after him, the door sliding shut just as the last person entered. Timothy stared up at the first of the concentric walls he had seen from the ship.

We're in, he thought.

Let's just hope we all make it back out.

Chapter 9

Idalbo stared up at the sky, watching Gearwire's ship disappear into the distance. The remaining members of the Guardians of Kawts stood around him, determination growing within them. As the ship vanished from view, Idalbo led the way back into the house, where breakfast was waiting.

"So what's the plan?" Howard asked, shoveling a forkful of scrambled eggs into his mouth.

"Rebellion-building," the Mysterious Man said. "Set up the groundwork for a covert resistance in case they fail."

"And reunite the Kriegerhelden!" Adalbo added.

A smile flickered across Idalbo's face at Adalbo's words.

This mission isn't the only reason you want to see them again, he thought. His smile faded as he recalled what Inn had told him when he had visited Kawts.

I'll have to keep a close eye on them, he realized. *The situation is precarious enough without having to deal with all that.*

"Yes. And reunite the Kriegerhelden," the Mysterious Man said. "But whatever we do, we have to be subtle about it. I don't think the Council's ever really gotten a good look at you two, but if Ethos suspects that we might still be in the area, he's liable to vaporize Alpen and Kawts both."

"I don't think we can count on the Kriegerhelden's assistance," Idalbo said. Adalbo looked up at him sharply, but Idalbo ignored him. "From what Inn told me last time, a lot of them still aren't on speaking terms with each other. It won't be easy getting them to all agree to come, let alone fight together again."

"We have to try," Adalbo said. "We were the ones who got them into this mess in the first place, after all."

No, Idalbo thought. *I got them into this mess.*

But to his brother, he only said, "We'll try. I'm just saying that it isn't going to be as easy as you think."

"I'll stay here," Howard said, breaking the awkward silence that followed. "See if I can figure out a way to counteract that cannon of theirs."

As he finished his breakfast, Idalbo stood and left the room, packing up his gear for their mission. Before the sun had reached its peak, he and Adalbo were already gone, on their way to the heart of Blancstadt.

* * *

Idalbo walked down the cobbled street, his eyes darting around for any sign of Ethos or the Council. Despite his concern, he maintained a normal walking speed, blending in with the crowd of mutants who were visiting the marketplace.

"I think I see Ederba," Adalbo whispered. "In the stall across the street. I'd recognise that painted shell of his anywhere."

Idalbo shook his head. "We need to meet with Inn first. He'll know what the situation is with the rest of the Kriegerhelden."

Adalbo nodded, a smile breaking out across his face. "To Inn's!" he agreed, straightening up a little taller.

Idalbo sighed. "You know she's not going to be too happy to see you, right? She was pretty upset with you when we left. And after what happened with Okceg…"

Adalbo's smile faded. "I know," he sighed. "I just want to see her again."

Idalbo smiled sympathetically. "Let's go," he said, starting off down the winding streets until he reached Inn's café, a small restaurant in the heart of the city. Idalbo pushed the door open, and a tinny bell rang throughout the room. After a few minutes, the café's owner appeared behind the counter, a six-tentacled mutant named Nagninnur - or Inn, as he was more commonly known.

"Just a minute!" he called, his focus on the contents of a drawer below the counter. "I've just got to get this-" He looked up for the first time, and a broad smile broke out across his face. He wiped his hands on the front of his kilt, hurrying out from behind the counter.

"Idalbo! Adalbo!" he boomed. Idalbo winced, and realization flashed across Inn's face. "It's been far too long!" he continued in a much quieter tone, glancing around to make sure no one had overheard.

Idalbo almost laughed. "It has been a while," he agreed. "But you were with us in Kawts just a few months ago."

"Bah!" Inn said. "We've been sorely missing you two over here. Seililyad!" he shouted. "We have visitors!"

"I heard!" the arch reply came from the back of the restaurant. "Now can you tell him to leave?"

Inn slowly turned back to the brothers, one of his tentacles holding the back of his neck. "Yep. She's still mad at you, Adalbo," he said, wincing sympathetically.

Adalbo stared at the ground, and Idalbo couldn't help feeling sorry for his brother.

I never should have asked him to come with me. I should have let him live his life here.

"Well, *I'm* happy to see you two, at any rate," Inn said, breaking the uncomfortable silence that followed. He moved toward the counter and beckoned for them to follow.

Idalbo and Adalbo followed him into the back of the café, where his daughter Seililyad was working. Her tentacles twitched in annoyance when she saw Adalbo, but she said nothing, brushing past him without a word.

Inn made no comment, either not noticing or intentionally ignoring the tension. "I assume you're here to help us take down the Council," he said, rubbing his tentacles together. "What's the plan?"

"It's a bit more complicated than that," Idalbo said. "The Guardians of Kawts already tried to expel the Council. Ethos rigged the entire city to evaporate if we killed him."

The color drained from Inn's face. "We're in big trouble, aren't we?"

"Draagetsew and Suorotiart went with the rest of our team to retrieve the Weather Belt from the compound."

"As I said, we're in big trouble," Inn repeated, shaking his head. "That's a suicide mission!"

"I've seen Gearwire's crew pull off impossible feats on more than one occasion," Adalbo said. "If anyone can complete the task that Penn failed, it's them."

"Alright," Inn said, raising two of his tentacles in surrender. "So why are you two here, then? I doubt it's just for a friendly visit."

"We're trying to get the Kriegerhelden back together," Idalbo said. "Just in case."

"And to be as much of a pain in the Council's side as we can," Adalbo added.

A smile broke out over Inn's face. "Now you're talking!" he said. "It's been far too long since we've had a proper mission!"

"We can't do anything too disruptive," Idalbo said quickly. "Not unless we find a way to disable their cannon first. It's still primed to wipe Blancstadt off the face of the earth."

"Still," Inn said. "I'm looking forward to it." He thought for a moment. "But first things first, I suppose. We need to get the gang back together."

Idalbo nodded gratefully. "Do you know where we could find them?"

Inn scratched his chin idly. "I'm going to be honest with you, I've lost touch with a few of them. I haven't spoken to Legov or Revenant since Okceg's funeral." He thought for a moment longer, then added, "I might have a hunch about where they are. But you'll have to be careful. The Council has spies everywhere - they even managed to dredge up a few old drones from somewhere. They've been keeping a close eye on us."

"Is your café safe?" Adalbo asked. "We'll need somewhere secure to meet when we get everyone back together."

"*If* we can get everyone back together," Idalbo corrected.

A smile broke out across Inn's face. "The Council hasn't quite figured out where my café is," he said. "I've been careful to lose their drones before I get here. I'm not so sure about the others, though. We'll need to arrange some way for them to lose their shadows before they arrive."

"I think Howard Kolt could help with that," Idalbo said. "Do you know where we can find them?"

"Tapfer and Loyola are still working at the castle," Inn replied. "I don't think the Council has figured out that they were Kriegerhelden yet. Revenant's been forced into hiding by the new restrictions on technology, but I think you might find him holed up at his old workshop - you know the place."

"What about Legov, Ederba, and Omor?" Adalbo asked.

Inn scratched his chin thoughtfully. "Ederba went back to being a merchant after the Kriegerhelden broke up. If he's in town, he'll probably be at the marketplace." There was a long pause, then he added, "Legov and Omor were both arrested a week or two ago on trumped-up charges. They arrested Omor's entire troupe and razed his theater. They've scheduled his public execution for later this week. Last I heard, they released Legov a few days ago, though. He might be at his bank."

Idalbo frowned. "We should have come back here sooner. Maybe we could have stopped the Council from taking over."

"No offense, Idalbo, but I don't think your being here would have made a bit of difference. They'd still have this evaporation cannon of theirs, remember?"

"I'd back a good swordsman over their high-tech gadgets any day," Adalbo said. "A weapon like that is only as dangerous as its wielder."

"And unfortunately for us, its wielder is very dangerous indeed," Idalbo said, cutting short his brother's fantasies. "Inn, can we use your café as a meeting place?"

Inn nodded. "Of course. Whatever it takes to bring down the Council."

"Count me in too," Seililyad said, appearing in the doorway. She looked directly past Adalbo, focusing on Idalbo and her father. "The Council cannot be allowed to control Alpen."

The bell over the door rang again, and the group lingered in silence for a long moment. "Well," Inn said, drawing the word out as he turned towards the door. "I should get that. Are you two going to be all right back here?"

"We'll be fine," Idalbo said as Seililyad and Inn left the room. Once they were out of earshot, he sighed.

"What are you thinking?" Adalbo asked.

"We've got our work cut out for us."

* * *

"I can't believe we're actually here," Madison said, looking around the inside of the dome. "Adalbo was always telling us the legends about this place."

"Adalbo?" Timothy said. "When was this?"

"He used to give little concerts around the base sometimes," Madison said. "Sung some Alpenite ballads. I think the last time might have been while you were on that mission with Henry."

"What did the songs say?" Quill asked. "Was there anything that might help us?"

Madison shook her head. "The songs weren't really about the compound itself. They were about the adventures that a famous Alpenite hero had when he tried to find the Weather Belt."

"Penn Echse. The greatest hero who ever lived," Draagetsew said solemnly. "He was lost somewhere in this very complex."

"If this complex killed the greatest hero who ever lived, I think we should maybe reconsider our plan," Crystal said.

"Penn didn't have a map," the Golden Knight said. "Nor access to people who have first-hand experience with the traps inside."

"Well said," Draagetsew said, looking at the Golden Knight with approval. "And Penn was also by himself. For reasons lost to time, his partner-in-crime didn't accompany him on that fateful mission."

"I hate to interrupt, but shouldn't we be focusing on where we're going?" Jewel said. "We don't want to be caught in a trap we weren't expecting."

"We don't have anything to worry about for the time being," Dr. Maddium said. "The first several traps are all physical barriers. Various types of walls. There aren't any surprises until the entrance into the inner circle."

"We should be getting to the first wall pretty soon, though," Draagetsew said, looking around at the trees that lined the path. "If I read the map correctly, it should be right around this corner."

Just as Draagetsew said, the group soon came face-to-face with the first barrier between them and the Weather Belt. Timothy stared up at the massive wall of barbed wire in front of them. The entire wall seemed to be made of the stuff, glinting in the late morning sunlight. Looming over it was an even taller wall that extended nearly all the way to the top of the dome.

"How are we going to get past those?" Quill breathed, his eyes widening.

"One problem at a time," Gearwire said. "For now, all we need to worry about is this wall of razor wire."

"I assume going through it is out of the question?" Crystal asked.

Gearwire nodded, gingerly touching one of the barbs. "It's definitely sharp enough to cause some damage. And my glue gun doesn't get hot enough to melt invincium."

"Could we dig a tunnel under it?" Madison suggested. "Your glue gun could eat through the dirt just fine. And if we needed to, we could use one of my grenades to help."

"The wall extends several meters underground as well," Draagetsew said, consulting the map. "We could dig under it if we absolutely had to, but it would take a while."

"Over it is, then," Timothy said. He thought for a moment, then said, "Madison? Do you think you could use those energy whips of yours to climb up to the top?"

Madison shook her head. "They would probably be strong enough to hold the weight, but that wire would just slice right through them. And then not only would we be back where we started, but I wouldn't have a weapon anymore."

"I think I have an idea," Jewel said slowly. She looked over at Crystal, who groaned.

"I was afraid you were going to suggest that."

"Suggest what?" Quill asked.

"We could use our powers to build a ladder overtop of the barbed wire," Jewel said.

"One layer of filmy crystal at a time," Crystal said. "It'll take ages and be super exhausting."

"How long are we talking?" Dr. Maddium said.

Jewel frowned, squinting at the wall. "With both of us working on it, I'd say about fifteen minutes?"

"Do it," Gearwire said. "It'll be more efficient than a tunnel. And if need be, we can get rid of it once we're all on the other side. Any tunnel we dig would leave an easy solution for the Council."

Jewel nodded, stepping towards the wall. Crystal did the same, facing the wall with her palms extended. A glittering trail of blue light drifted from their hands, solidifying into translucent blue crystal when it touched the wall. They worked in silence for several minutes, deep in concentration.

Timothy watched them as they worked, seeing a blue crystal ladder slowly take shape before his eyes, each thin layer building off of the previous one.

"I wish I could do that," Quill muttered next to him.

Timothy didn't respond, although something about Quill's comment irritated him.

The ladder continued to grow, until finally it reached about two inches thick. The twins both stopped, simultaneously dropping their hands to their sides. They looked a little pale, as if building the ladder had taken a lot out of them.

"Well done," Gearwire said.

"That's all well and good, but how are we going to get back *down*?" Suorotiart said. "Not all of us have wings, you know."

Jewel blinked slowly, swaying a little. "Just give us a moment," she said, sitting down on the grass. Crystal joined her, seeming only slightly less tired than her sister.

"I can't believe this!" Suorotiart said. "You've hardly done anything! You won't last a week in this compound if something as small as that tires you out!"

Timothy felt his anger rising within him. He glanced over at Jewel, but she didn't seem to have heard Suorotiart's comment. He turned back toward the Prime Minister, but before he could reprimand him, Crystal spoke up.

"You try to 3D print something with your hands sometime and tell me it isn't exhausting," she said. "Besides, if you want to get to the other side so badly, you're welcome to fly yourself over there right now. Or maybe you'd prefer to fly the rest of us over?"

"Well, of all the-" Suorotiart started, his wings fluttering in anger.

"Suorotiart," Draagetsew said calmly, putting one of his four hands on the smaller mutant's shoulder. "Don't complain about things you know nothing about."

Suorotiart glowered, but he said nothing. After a moment, he flew over the wall and disappeared on the other side, although Timothy could still hear him muttering to himself under his breath.

"He's just worried about Alpen," Draagetsew said apologetically. "He's not normally like this." He thought for a moment. "Alright. He kind of is. But he's a great advisor. And he really does have Alpen's best interest at heart."

"We're going to have to address this sooner or later," Dr. Maddium said. "We can't afford to be bickering like this once we get deeper in. And Suorotiart has already instigated two arguments in the last hour."

"I'll talk to him," Draagetsew promised.

Over by the wall, Jewel slowly got to her feet. Timothy jogged over to her. "Are you sure you're up for this?" he whispered. "You don't look so good."

"I'm fine," Jewel said. "I'm just a little out of practice yet. And I think this might be the largest layer-by-layer project we've ever done." She turned and looked at Crystal. "Are you ready for part two?"

"I'm right behind you," she said, standing and walking over to the wall.

It took the twins another fifteen minutes to encase the other side of the wall, working slowly from the top down. Moving carefully to avoid stabbing their toes on the razor-sharp wire, the Guardians of Kawts climbed up and over the wall, joining Crystal, Jewel, and Suorotiart on the other side.

Chapter 10

"You know, with everything going on, I never got the chance to thank you," Jewel said as they walked along the forested path to the next trap.

"Thank me for what?" Timothy asked, turning to look at her.

"For coming to visit me in the hospital as much as you did," Jewel said. "I know you must have been busy."

Timothy shrugged, suddenly feeling very self-conscious. "Don't mention it," he said. "It's a shame you didn't have a chance to fully experience the new Kawts before getting dragged into this mess."

Jewel sighed. "Honestly, I feel more at home here with all you guys than I would be back in Kawts. Crystal and I have been double agents for so long - it's hard to make real friends when you're always having to watch your back." A faint smile crossed her face. "When you started asking questions, I was so excited to finally have someone else to talk to other than my sister. Of course, then you got chased out of Kawts…"

She trailed off, a faraway look coming into her eyes.

Timothy felt a pang of sadness at the wistful tone in Jewel's voice.

I wonder what would have happened if I'd stayed in Kawts, he wondered, not for the first time.

"We're here!" Draagetsew bellowed from the front of the column. Timothy abruptly turned towards the front once more, quickly pushing all such thoughts aside.

No. We're in a very dangerous compound. This is no place for reminiscing. His thoughts flickered back to Jewel.

Or daydreaming.

"I think this one's electrified," Draagetsew said, stopping in front of the wall. It looked like an ordinary chain-link fence, stretching several feet over their heads. As if confirming his words, the fence emitted a loud pop, followed by a crackle of electricity.

Timothy stared up at the fence, running through a list of their supplies in his head.

We aren't going to be able to climb over it, he realized. *We don't have anything we can use as a ladder without starting a fire or getting electrocuted.*

"Invincium isn't a conductor, is it?" Gearwire asked, squinting at the fence.

Dr. Maddium shook his head. "No. It is a metalloid compound, but it doesn't conduct electricity."

Gearwire nodded. "That's what I thought." His glue gun leapt into his hand, and he quickly squeezed the trigger, spraying the fence with incredibly hot glue. In the space of just a few seconds, a hole had formed that was large enough to climb through.

Quill stared at Gearwire in shock, and Timothy couldn't help but smile. He had seen Gearwire's lightning-fast reflexes on more than one occasion during his time as a member of Gearwire's crew. But Quill had not, having been under the Council's mind control at the time.

Just wait until you see him in battle, Quill.

"Well," Draagetsew said, visibly impressed. "That looks like a problem solved to me." He nodded in appreciation toward Gearwire, then stepped nimbly through the hole, being careful not to let any part of his body touch the fence itself.

"How did you *do* that?" Quill breathed.

The ghost of a smile crossed Gearwire's face. "A lot of practice."

"You must have trained for months!" Quill said. "When did you find the time to practice that much?"

Gearwire's expression darkened. "It's amazing how quickly you can learn when the fate of the world depends on it." He stepped quickly through the hole in the fence, cutting off any further conversation.

Bewildered, Quill looked toward Timothy for an explanation.

"Kawts isn't Gearwire's first fight," Timothy said. His smile faded as he recalled the handful of battles he had witnessed himself.

Understanding dawned in Quill's eyes. "That's right! Madison was telling me something about that the other day. She said that he came here after fighting in another war with Dr. Maddium and…" He trailed off, searching for the name.

"Henry," Timothy said bluntly. Then he followed Gearwire through the fence, leaving Quill alone on the other side.

You have to cut him a little slack, a voice in his head chided. *He wasn't there. He hasn't seen the things you've seen.*

Exactly. That's the problem. He doesn't understand. I'm not the same person I was two years ago.

He'll understand before long. And when he does, he'll need someone to lean on.

Timothy sighed. He turned back towards Quill, but at that moment, Draagetsew bellowed, "At this rate, we'll be inside the inner ring by tomorrow morning! I can practically see the Weather Belt already!"

Crystal rolled her eyes. "Yay! I can't believe we're almost to the beginning of our journey!" she said, her voice dripping with fake cheerfulness. Jewel elbowed her, and she fell silent.

"She does have a point, I'm afraid," Suorotiart said. "We've only barely begun."

"Bah! We've gotten this far, haven't we? That's farther than just about anyone else has ever gotten before. I'd say that's a reason to celebrate!"

"If we had more time, I might agree with you," Dr. Maddium said gently. "But the Council's only going to be a few days behind us at best. We don't have time to sit around."

"Fine," Draagetsew huffed, unfurling the map with a flourish. He studied it for a moment, then said, "It looks like it's just forest for a while. Peppered with landmines and pitfall traps, of course. The old guard towers are right in the middle of it." He looked up at the Guardians of Kawts. "Back in Penn's time, the guards would live here in the towers and prevent anyone from getting to the Weather Belt. They had to memorize the location of every trap just to get assigned here."

"I take it the guards are no longer in the picture?" Crystal said.

Suorotiart smiled. "After a few hundred years of only having one man get past the first wall, we decided it wasn't worth the upkeep."

"The land mines are still here, though, right?" Madison said. "What's the plan for getting past them?"

"There's a path marked on the map," Draagetsew said. "It's narrow, but it's there."

"Where is this path?" Gearwire said.

Draagetsew studied the trees in front of them. "It should be right about... here." He came to a stop in front of a large boulder, brushing away some of the moss that had grown overtop of it. He grinned. "Right this way, good sirs."

Draagetsew started off through the tangled overgrowth, hacking a path through the dense vegetation with his battleaxe. After a second's hesitation, Timothy followed, his staff ready in his hand. Behind him, Quill, Madison, and the twins were engaged in a lively discussion. For a brief moment, he was tempted to put his staff away and join them, but he resisted.

We're in constant danger now. I can't afford to be distracted. He returned his attention to the path in front of him, tuning out his friends behind him.

I have to be ready. Who knows what we might find in here?

* * *

Idalbo looked up at the sky, checking for any signs of attack drones. Once he was satisfied that he wasn't being followed, he made his way to a run-down old storefront on the outer edge of town. As he slowed to a stop, he glanced behind him, checking one last time for pursuers. Then he slipped inside, walking through the darkness to the back room of the store. When he reached the back wall, he hesitated, searching his memories for the key to the entrance.

After a moment's thought, he picked up the lone can of tomato soup on the shelf and moved it to the other side. The shelf flipped upside-down, dropping the can down a chute hidden in the floor. A shelving unit on the other side of the room slid back, revealing a secret passage. Idalbo walked through it quickly. He heard the system reset behind him, depositing the can back onto the shelf and sealing the passage once more.

Idalbo walked through the darkened halls into a well-lit concrete room. Discarded bits of machinery littered the edges of the room, making the space look a lot smaller than it actually was. In the center of the room, a short mutant with a kangaroo pouch lay on his back underneath what Idalbo took to be a prototype hovercar. Unlike most other mutants, he lacked the irregular, dust-yellow scales that were characteristic of the people of Alpen. The mutant muttered to himself as he worked, grumbling something about having insufficient power.

Idalbo leaned up against the doorframe, watching. "How's business been lately?" he asked, a smile tugging at the corners of his mouth.

The other mutant gave a strangled yelp and sat bolt upright, bashing his head against the contraption that he had been tinkering with. Rubbing his head and muttering, he slid out from underneath the vehicle.

"Sorry about that, Revenant," Idalbo said, trying not to laugh at the other mutant's reaction.

Revenant glared at him, still rubbing his head. "What do you want, Idalbo?" he asked, scowling.

"You know why I'm here. We're trying to stop the Council. We need to rebuild the Kriegerhelden."

"You can rebuild it without me," Revenant snapped. "I'm not working for that bumbling idiot again."

"Inn is not in charge anymore. I am," Idalbo said. "And you know just as well as I do that he is not responsible for Okceg's death."

"Well, that makes one of us," Revenant said, shaking his head. "I warned him that the mission would end in disaster, and he sent Okceg there anyway. You sure picked a great general to replace you when you went off to join Herr Metaltoes!"

"It was a freak accident, Revenant. You know that. He'd already completed the most dangerous part of the mission when he was killed."

"Accident or not, it wouldn't have happened if you had left me in charge. Or, come to think of it, if you had just stayed here and fought your own war with your own people. Tell me, what was so special about this Kawts place that it made you willing to abandon your own country in its deepest struggle?"

Idalbo flinched at the bitterness in Revenant's tone. "Draagetsew specifically recommended me for the mission," he said. "Gearwire needed my help more than Alpen did. The Council is beyond evil, Revenant. I'm disappointed that the Kriegerhelden fell apart once I left, but I don't regret for a minute my time fighting alongside Gearwire's crew. Fighting the very same tyrants who are currently wreaking havoc on Alpen, I might add."

"You can defeat them without me," Revenant said, turning back to his project. "What do I know about strategy, anyway?"

Idalbo grabbed his shoulders and spun him around. "Revenant, listen. The Council has the entire city rigged to evaporate at the touch of a button. You're telling me that you can stomach the idea of anyone having that much power?"

Revenant froze, his eyes hardening. Deliberately, he pulled Idalbo's hands away. "Good luck, Idalbo," he said, turning away again. "You're going to need it."

Idalbo sighed and began walking to the door. He had almost reached the hall when Revenant added, "Idalbo?"

Idalbo turned around. "Yes?"

"Is it true that the Council is after the Weather Belt?"

"That's our suspicion. Yes." Idalbo waited a second longer, but Revenant made no response. Idalbo ran his fingers through his short black hair and turned back toward the hallway, making his way back onto the streets of Blancstadt.

* * *

Idalbo watched the Blancstadt jail, scrutinizing it from the safety of an awning across the street. Glancing around to make sure there were no attack drones in sight, he ambled across the street, making a slow circle around the squat stone building.

It looks like they've upgraded the security a bit since I've been here last, he thought, his eyes narrowing. *It's not going to be easy to break Omor*

88

out.

Still, I need to let him know we're here.

He crouched down by the barred windows of the prison, which were just barely above ground level. He peered inside, scanning the rooms for the tall, gilled mutant. After a minute of searching, he spotted Omor in a cell near the center of the room.

Not ideal, he thought as he unslung his bow. *But I can make it work.* He fingered one of his quills, gauging the distance between the bars of Omor's cell. He took a deep breath, then shot the quill through the bars and into the jail. It sailed through several cells before embedding itself in the wooden leg of Omor's cot. Satisfied that Omor would understand his message, Idalbo slipped away, retreating to Inn's café before anyone could see him.

* * *

"It's simple, I tell you," Draagetsew said, waving his four arms madly. He stood in front of the next obstacle - a second wall of barbed wire, this one considerably thicker than the first. He turned to Crystal and Jewel. "You just need to crystallize it and we can climb over it just like before," he said.

Jewel said nothing, eying the trap warily. "I don't know about that," she said. "Why would the builders have used the same trap twice so close together?"

"Besides," Crystal said, shaking her head. "That first ladder was hard enough, and this wall's even bigger than the last one. I'm not creating another crystal ladder if there's another option."

"Then let's drape a blanket over it," Draagetsew said. "We'll do it the old-fashioned way."

"Sir," Suorotiart began. "If I may - perhaps we should check the map first. This obstacle may be more complex than -"

"Nonsense!" Draagetsew interrupted, throwing his hands down. "It's just barbed wire! Look - I'll prove it!" He removed his bedroll from his pack and unfurled it, tossing it over the fence. The fence sagged slightly, but remained otherwise unchanged. Draagetsew began to climb up the blanket, taking his time as the wall shifted and groaned ominously beneath him.

"See?" he said from a perch halfway up the wall. "Nothing to worry about!"

The wall groaned again, and then suddenly sprung to life, shredding the blanket to pieces. The tightly clustered columns of barbed wire that made up the wall began rotating. Draagetsew let out a cry of pain as the barbs tore into his flesh. Timothy stepped forwards to help, but the Golden Knight pushed him aside. Protected by his invincium armor, he marched unflinchingly into the whirling mass of wire and dragged Draagetsew out. The mutant president had already lost consciousness, resting limply in the Golden Knight's hands. Timothy and Quill exchanged worried glances.

We haven't even reached the building yet, and already Draagetsew's on death's door, Timothy thought. For a moment, images of Henry's death rose to the surface of his mind, but he quickly pushed them aside.

No, he thought, *That's in the past. No amount of dwelling on it can change that.*

Chapter 11

Adalbo stood in the middle of the crowded marketplace, scanning the booths for Ederba, a short mutant with a turtle shell on his back. By the time he had examined three quarters of the street, he began to grow anxious, absently tapping his foot on the cobblestones.

Come on, he thought, mentally checking off one booth after another. *He has to be here. Where -*

A sudden flash of color drew his attention, interrupting his train of thought. A grin broke out across his face.

Ederba's shell, he realized, recognising the painted pattern. *No one else in Alpen has a design quite like it.*

He pushed through the crowd towards the booth when a new realization stopped him cold. He glanced around at the seething mass of people around him, his excitement turning to irritation.

I can't talk with him right now without being seen by several dozen witnesses, he thought. He fell back, recalculating his plan. As an idea began to take shape in his mind, he continued towards Ederba, this time at a more leisurely pace. When he reached the merchant's booth, he wandered alongside it, browsing the merchandise. After a moment, he came to a stop in front of an old clock sitting on the table. Ederba hurried over, sensing a potential sale.

"How much?" Adalbo asked, still staring at the clock.

"That would be twenty five-" Ederba started. He cut off suddenly as he recognized Adalbo. "Twenty five Alpenmark," he continued quickly, his tone unchanged.

"I'll take it," Adalbo said, pulling some money from his pocket and holding it out to Ederba. He paused and withdrew his hand slightly. "Ah!" he exclaimed, looking down at his bare wrist. "I'm late for my meeting!" he turned back toward Ederba. "Would it be possible for you to drop it off tomorrow at the place I'm staying? I'm sure you've heard of it - it's a place called 'Inn's café'. I'll let you in at 6:00 tomorrow morning."

"Will there be other potential customers there?" Ederba asked, raising an eyebrow.

"Perhaps," Adalbo replied with a grin. "We're trying to restructure our company."

Ederba said nothing for a long while, staring off into space. "I'll deliver it tomorrow. And if you're looking for another business partner, I'd be happy to join you."

Adalbo nodded briskly, then disappeared into the crowd once more. After making sure that he wasn't being followed, he made his way to the National Bank of Alpen. When he arrived, he found it closed, the windows boarded up, as if Legov had been gone for years instead of a few weeks. Alarm bells ringing in his head, he peered through the boards and spotted Legov, a short, portly mutant with tusks and an elephant trunk. Adalbo knocked on the door and waved, and the wealthy businessman waddled over.

He opened the door a crack, and Adalbo could see that several deadbolts had been installed. "We're closed," he said angrily, pointing to a sign. "Can't you read?"

He started to close the door again, but Adalbo said, "Wait! Legov, it's me."

Legov squinted at him. "Adalbo?" he whispered, quickly unlocking the door and yanking Adalbo inside. As Adalbo staggered forwards, Legov slammed the door shut behind them and bolted it.

"What-" Adalbo began, but Legov cut him off.

"Spies," he muttered. "They're everywhere." He glanced furtively out of the partially boarded-up window.

Adalbo stared at him warily.

Something's wrong here, he thought. *Legov's never been a particularly trusting person, but this is insane. I've never seen anyone so paranoid.*

"I came here to get your help with… a project," Adalbo said, choosing his words carefully. "But if now isn't a good time, I can always come back later…" He trailed off, noticing Legov's continued muttering. The other mutant didn't reply, continuing to pace the room, pausing every few seconds to peek out of the windows as if in anticipation of an attack.

He's in no state of mind to participate in any sort of mission, Adalbo realized, his heart aching for his friend. *What did the Council do to him?* Anger welled up in him as he watched Legov continue to babble quietly to himself.

The Council's going to pay for this, he vowed, letting himself out the back door and leaving Legov to pace the room alone.

* * *

Slowly, the Golden Knight lowered the unconscious Draagetsew to the ground. Dr. Maddium examined his wounds, his face grave. From what Timothy could see, the wounds seemed to be relatively shallow, but they were numerous, and in some places, there appeared to be severe damage.

"How is he?" Quill asked, paling as he stared at Draagetsew's prone form. "Is he going to be okay?"

"I don't know," Dr. Maddium said.

"Are any of his organs damaged?"

"I don't know, Quill."

"Maybe we should check for broken bones - we'd want to try to fix those first, right?"

"I don't know!" Dr. Maddium snapped, turning his head to look at him. "I'm an engineer, not a paramedic!" He paused, taking a deep breath and then slowly exhaling. "I don't know," he said, shaking his head. "His internal organs are unscathed as far as I can tell, but his skin and muscle tissues are pretty torn up. He's already lost a lot of blood. Probably too much. We can try to stop the bleeding, but after that…" he shrugged. "I don't know what to do."

"We'll have to act fast then," Crystal said, blue light beginning to seep from her palms. "Get the bandages on, and we'll cement them in place."

"Right," Dr. Maddium said, looking around for the bandages. Jewel opened her pack and tossed him several rolls.

"We'll need water, too," he said, his confidence beginning to return.

"I've got it," Timothy said, pulling a gallon container of water from his chest plate as the Golden Knight and Gearwire propped Draagetsew upright. Dr. Maddium took the water from Timothy and rinsed Draagetsew's wounds. The mutant flinched, but did not wake up. Dr. Maddium frowned as he, Timothy, and Madison wrapped the bandages around Draagetsew's arms and torso.

The bandages were soaked with blood before they even finished, and the twins hurried to cover them in a crystal film, slowing the bleeding considerably.

Dr. Maddium sat back on his haunches, running a bloodstained hand through his tangled gray hair. "That's all I can do for him. I've never seen anyone survive losing that much blood."

"With all due respect, he has plenty of extra," Suorotiart said, arching an eyebrow.

Timothy stared at him, feeling his mouth curl into a disapproving frown.

"I'm being serious," Suorotiart said with an irritated glance at Timothy. "He has a lot more blood in his body than a normal human. Combined with our people's accelerated healing abilities, I'd say he's got about a fifty-fifty shot." A smirk crossed his features. "Plus, I'm pretty sure Draagetsew is far too stubborn to die from something as simple as blood loss."

"All the same, I'd feel better if there was something more we could do for him," Gearwire said. "Are you sure that there's nothing else?"

Dr. Maddium shook his head. "I'm not a medical expert. You know that. Anything above basic field medicine is beyond my pay grade. We'd need someone who's been trained as a medic..." He trailed off, an idea striking him.

"The Mysterious Man," he breathed, pulling out his radio beacon. A few moments later, his voice came over the line.

"What happened?" he asked, his tone level.

"It's Draagetsew," Dr. Maddium replied. "He tried to climb what he thought was a barbed wire fence. We tried to warn him, but he wouldn't listen. The fence started rotating, and he got caught in it. I know this is a lot to ask, but I know that a friend of yours was a medic, so I was hoping you might possibly..."

"Know something about medicine?" the Mysterious Man finished, a surprising harshness in his voice. "Having a healing ability is not the same as being a medic. You know that, Maddium."

Timothy listened to the conversation with surprise. *Why is he so upset that Dr. Maddium brought this person up?* he wondered. *What is he hiding? And how does Dr. Madduim know about it?*

"That said," the Mysterious Man continued, concealing his emotions once more. "I might have picked up a few things. Have you stopped the bleeding?"

"Yes," Dr. Maddium replied. "We have him wrapped in bandages and secured them with the twin's powers. That's about all we can do on that front."

There was silence for a moment, and Timothy worried that they had lost contact. Then the Mysterious Man said, "Lay him flat on his back." There was a pause, and then he added, "And try to prop up his feet if you can. About a foot in the air."

Dr. Maddium turned back toward Draagetsew, but the Golden Knight and Gearwire had already carried out the Mysterious Man's instructions.

"Now what?" he asked.

"You'll probably need some sort of IV," the Mysterious Man replied. "Saline, blood, and epinephrine would all help him if you can find them."

Dr. Maddium nodded. "Saline I can do," he said. "Timothy!" he called. "I'm going to need some more water and some salt."

Timothy nodded and took the requested items out of his chest plate. Dr. Maddium pointed to the container of water. "Another gallon?"

Timothy nodded.

"Good," Dr. Maddium said. He was silent for a while, calculating the proper concentration. He measured out a small heap of salt onto his palm and poured it into the water, gently shaking the container to stir it.

As the Mysterious Man rattled off more precise instructions on how to administer the treatment, Dr. Maddium was already rummaging through their supplies. "I could have sworn there was an epinephrine injector somewhere around here," he muttered, tossing things out of the first aid kit and onto the ground. His face grew more and more grave until finally, with a triumphant shout, he removed the injector from the kit, holding it aloft. He shook the injector out of the case and removed the cap, then slammed it into Draagetsew's thigh. Draagetsew flinched, but he did not open his eyes as the medicine flowed into him.

"Make sure you keep him warm," the Mysterious Man added. "Sometimes people who have lost a lot of blood end up going into shock and freezing."

"Right," Dr. Maddium said, pulling a blanket from the Infini-case and laying it over Draagetsew. "Anything else?"

There was silence for a while, then the Mysterious Man replied, "That's all I can remember. Just make sure he stays put for at least a week. Two or three weeks if you can make him sit still for that long. Being a mutant, he might recover faster than most, but we don't want to risk permanent damage by rushing things."

"I'll try my best," Dr. Madduim replied.

"Good luck," the Mysterious Man said. Then he hung up.

* * *

Idalbo and Adalbo had just made it back to Inn's Café when the Mysterious Man radioed them from their base of operations.

"Gearwire would like to speak with you," he said. "Are you in a secure location?"

"As secure as we can be, given the circumstances," Idalbo said, looking at the room around them.

"I'm putting him on the line," Howard said. There was a click, and then Gearwire's voice came through the radio.

"Idalbo? Adalbo? Can you hear me?"

"Loud and clear," Adalbo replied.

"We have nothing but bad news, I'm afraid," Gearwire said. "Draagetsew fell into a rotating barbed wire fence and got torn to ribbons. We think he'll make it, but we're going to be stuck here for at least a week or two. We need you to buy us some time. If the Council reaches us before Draagetsew's back on his feet, we don't stand a chance. And once we're out of the way, the complex itself will be the only thing standing between them and the Weather Belt."

"And then the world is doomed," Idalbo said grimly.

"We'll do what we can," Adalbo said. "But gathering the Kriegerhelden has proven to be more challenging than we thought."

"If you can't get the Kriegerhelden back together, you may have to do it alone," Gearwire said. "If the Council wins this fight, they'll be virtually unstoppable."

"What about the other fail-safe devices?" Idalbo asked suddenly. "We could gather the rest of them and still defeat the Council."

"It is a possibility," Gearwire admitted. "But at this point, it's doubtful if the others even still exist. A race against the Council to collect the most powerful artifacts known to man should be our last resort. But if we fail, it will be up to the Kriegerhelden to do just that."

"We won't let the Council win," Adalbo promised. "Even if it costs us everything."

"Good luck," Idalbo said. "We'll be praying for you."

"Likewise," Gearwire replied, then hung up.

"I don't like this," the Mysterious Man said. "I just can't shake the feeling that they're walking into a trap."

Chapter 12

Timothy was sitting by the mouth of Draagetsew's tent when he awoke several hours later. The burly mutant tried to sit up, but the crystal cast over his body prevented him from doing so. He peered at the casing and frowned, redoubling his efforts to stand. Pain flashed across his face and he immediately stopped struggling.

Timothy ducked back out of the tent. "He's awake!" he called. The others ran over, Dr. Maddium trailing behind with the Infini-case. Timothy stepped back inside as the others began to arrive.

"What happened?" Draagetsew muttered as he looked around the tent. When he saw the looks of concern on the others' faces, however, everything came flooding back.

Dr. Maddium pushed toward the front of the group, a bowl of soup in his hand. He handed it to Draagetsew, who accepted it awkwardly. Dr. Maddium nodded to the twins, and they approached him, raising their hands toward him. Slowly, the crystal dissolved, until Draagetsew could once again move freely.

"I guess you guys were right," Draagetsew said, wincing as he took a sip of the soup. "There was more to the trap than it seemed." A puzzled look flashed across his face. "But how did I get out of there? I passed out pretty much immediately."

"It was the Golden Knight," Dr. Maddium said. "He went in after you and pulled you out."

"Thank you, my friend," Draagetsew said weakly, clasping the Golden Knight's hand.

"It was no act of courage," the Golden Knight said, his face unreadable. "I knew my armor would protect me."

Draagetsew raised an eyebrow, but he said nothing. He tried to sit up, but Dr. Maddium stopped him.

"You have to stay put for at least a week," he said.

"A week? The Council will have caught up with us by then!" Draagetsew protested.

Dr. Maddium shook his head. "It's possible. But the Mysterious Man says that if we try to move on sooner, we run the risk of re-opening your wounds."

"That's a risk I'm willing to take," Draagetsew said, trying to stand again. "If the Council gets ahead of us, the world is doomed."

"The Kriegerhelden are working to delay them," Dr. Maddium said.

Draagetsew seemed to relax. "They're good men," he said. "If anyone can do it, they can." He closed his eyes, and in only a few moments, he was fast asleep.

* * *

That night, Samuel had good news to share.

"Ray told us everything he knows about the Council's plans," he said over the radio. "Volker let Crofton spend an hour or so talking with him before he resumed his questioning. Afterwards, he was more than happy to tell us his story."

"Which was…?" Gearwire prompted gently.

"It's a bit long," Samuel replied. "But I can give you a brief synopsis."

Timothy heard the sound of pages turning, then Samuel's voice came back on the line.

"Like most of the Council members, Ray inherited his position from his father," Samuel said. "He went through the Council's training program and was granted a seat upon his father's retirement. At the time, he was completely unaware of the truth about the Blanks and the Council. Whether this was by accident or by design, he wasn't sure, but for whatever reason, no one ever told him the truth."

Which means that there's still a chance that Aksell is unaware of what the Council's really like, Timothy thought, hope rising within him. But he pushed the feeling aside.

As long as he thinks the Councilmen are the good guys, he'll never fight against them.

"When Ray finally discovered what the Council had been doing, he was appalled. He petitioned the other Council members to put an end to The Race and Blanking. He thought he had made a persuasive case, but the Council was unconvinced. The next morning, his friend Crofton disappeared. Ray said that the message was unmistakable - if he continued to fight against the Council, there would be consequences. Fearing for his family, he gave in and tried to project an image of a loyal Councilman. He seems deeply sorry about everything he helped the Council to do."

"If that's true, then why did he refuse to talk earlier?" Gearwire said, one eyebrow raised.

"According to Crofton, he was concerned that we were planning to kill him once he'd told us what he knew. Which is an understandable assumption, considering that the Council would likely have done exactly that."

"Do you believe him?"

"I do," Samuel replied after a moment's thought. "He always struck me as the most miserable person in Kawts. If this is all just an act, it's an act he's been cultivating for decades."

Gearwire nodded slowly. "What did he say the Council was planning?"

"As it turns out, the answer is not much. At least, not that they shared with him. It seems that Ethos didn't trust him very much, which Ray thinks is why he was assigned to guard the route to Alpen. But he was able to confirm that the Council intends to go after the Weather Belt as soon as they get themselves established in Alpen."

Gearwire's face grew more grave. "That shouldn't take them much longer," he said. "Unless the Kriegerhelden can do something to stop it."

"There is one other thing," Samuel said. "Ethos seemed to have been playing his cards pretty close to his chest, but Ray is pretty sure that he's struck a deal with the Orgwar."

"The Orgwar?" Gearwire repeated, a slight tremor in his voice. "What kind of deal?"

"It seems to be roughly the same plan they had when they started turning Kawts into a giant munitions factory - the Council will work with the aliens in their conquest of Earth and provide them with resources and slaves; and in return, they will be rewarded with a governorship of a cluster of planets. It seems Ethos is no longer satisfied with just ruling Kawts."

Samuel's words hung ominously in the air. A shiver ran down Timothy's spine as he imagined some unknown aliens coming to the Council's aid.

"He plans to use the Weather Belt to take over the world," Gearwire breathed, the color draining from his face.

"Ray believes so, yes," Samuel replied. "And he knows that as of the last time Ethos contacted the Orgwar, they offered him governorship of an entire star system in exchange."

"Then it's all the more vital that Idalbo and Adalbo are successful,"

Gearwire said.

"Why? What are they doing?" Samuel asked.

"Draagetsew got caught in one of the traps earlier today," Dr. Maddium said. "We think he's going to be fine, but he's going to need to remain here for a couple of weeks. We've let Idalbo and Adalbo know that they need to find some way to delay the Council's arrival."

"I'll be praying for them. And you guys," Samuel said after a long pause.

Gearwire smiled grimly. "Thanks. We're going to need it." He reached out his hand to turn off the radio, but Samuel had one more question.

"What about Ray?" he asked. "What do you want us to do with him?"

Gearwire sighed, contemplating the options. "You really believe he's telling the truth?"

Samuel hesitated for a moment. "Yes. I think he's telling the truth. His story's consistent with what I've observed about him."

Gearwire nodded slowly. After a long pause, he said, "Keep him in custody for now. See if there's anything more you can get from him about the Council's plans. We'll reevaluate the situation once we've had a chance to test some of his intel."

"Will do," Samuel replied, then hung up.

* * *

Idalbo sat in the back room of Inn's café, waiting in tense silence as the clock ticked slowly closer to six o'clock. He glanced up at the clock, then across the room to his brother. He sighed heavily.

"The moment of truth," he said, forcing himself to smile.

"The moment of truth," Adalbo repeated, staring restlessly at the open door.

Idalbo stared at the clock again. 5:55. *Tapfer and Loyola will be here,* he reassured himself. *But will Revenant?*

A bell rang in the café, and Idalbo's head snapped towards the entrance. He could hear the murmurs of Inn's voice as he pointed the guest in their direction. A few moments later, Ederba appeared in the doorway, holding a clock.

"Special delivery," he said with a grin, passing the clock to Adalbo. Idalbo gave his brother a quizzical look, but Adalbo only smiled in response. Ederba took a seat, joining them in their waiting. At 6:01, Loyola arrived, followed by Tapfer at 6:05, his kangaroo-like tail swinging back and forth impatiently.

As the time neared 6:15, Idalbo had just about given up hope of anyone else arriving. The bell rang one more time and Revenant entered the room, looking around at the group as if daring somebody to comment. He took a seat on the opposite side of the room and stared off into the distance, avoiding making eye contact.

Seililyad slipped into the room without a word, sitting down in the seat furthest away from Adalbo. Inn entered last, closing the door behind them and choosing a seat that was not too close to any one mutant.

We have our work cut out for us, Idalbo reflected with a sigh as he watched his friends all try to avoid interacting with each other. He exchanged a glance with Adalbo, then slowly stood.

"It's great to see you all again," Idalbo started weakly. Behind him, Revenant snorted. "It's been far too long since we've had all the Kriegerhelden in one place," he continued, undeterred.

"Maybe there's a reason for that," Revenant muttered under his breath.

Idalbo sighed. "Look. I know that some of you are upset about my decision to go to Kawts. Seililyad, I know that you and Adalbo didn't end things well when we left. And I know that all of us are keenly aware of the fact that Okceg is no longer with us. Things have been said that shouldn't have been said. It may be that those friendships we once had have been permanently severed. But we have a common enemy here. The Council came here seeking the Weather Belt. If we can't stop them now, there will be no future for Alpen. Can we all agree to put aside our differences long enough to defeat them once and for all?"

There was silence for a long time. Then Revenant said, "Count me in. I'll work with you all one last time, for Alpen's sake. But don't expect me to be happy about it."

"I'm in too," Seililyad said with a brief glance at Adalbo.

"Me too," Inn said, standing.

One by one, the rest of the Kriegerhelden followed his example, pledging themselves to the mission of expelling the Council from Alpen.

So far, so good, Idalbo thought, the ghost of a smile touching his face.

* * *

Timothy stared into the fire, his mind far away. Draagetsew's injuries had brought back memories he would rather have forgotten. Images of Henry's death flashed before him, intermingled with memories of Jewel's near-fatal injuries during the Battle of Kawts. Timothy pushed the thoughts aside, trying to stave off his grief and fear.

Jewel sat down beside him, concern written across her face. "How are you doing, Timothy?" she asked. "You've seemed a little... off these last few days."

"I'm fine," Timothy said. "I'm just... worried about Draagetsew."

Jewel frowned. "Are you sure that's it? You got really serious out of the blue yesterday before Draagetsew even got injured. Is there something else that's going on?"

"We're getting further into a very dangerous place," Timothy replied. "We can't afford to be goofing around."

Jewel looked at him incredulously. "Just because we're somewhere dangerous doesn't mean we have to be serious all the time. I mean, look at the Golden Knight! He has more fun when he's in dangerous situations than when he's doing ordinary things."

So did Henry. But it didn't do him any good.

"Gearwire's always serious," Timothy said. "And he's the most level-headed one here. He never lets his emotions get in the way."

"Just because Gearwire does something doesn't mean it's a good idea for you to do it," Jewel said gently. "Or, for that matter, that it's a good idea for Gearwire to be doing it. Gearwire may be a great captain, but he's not perfect."

Timothy sighed. "It's just... we've already lost too many people. Henry's dead. Maurice is probably dead. You almost died during the Battle of Kawts. I can't lose anyone else."

"Henry died knowing exactly where he was going," Jewel said. "And from what I remember about your brother, so did Maurice. And I'm still here."

"I don't know what I would do if I lost you," Timothy said. "Or Quill. Or Gearwire - or any of the others. We haven't even gotten to the dangerous part of the compound yet, and already, Draagetsew might not make it through the night. It would take a miracle for us to get through this whole thing unscathed."

"What makes you so sure we won't get a miracle?" Jewel said, a slight smile on her face.

Timothy opened his mouth to respond, but no words came out. Before he could find his tongue, a commotion broke out from the direction of Draagetsew's tent, and he jogged over, grateful for the interruption.

"What are you doing?" Dr. Maddium demanded, staring Draagetsew down.

Draagetsew, who had already partially disassembled his tent, ignored the question. "We need to keep moving," he answered gruffly. "We can't let the Council catch up with us."

"That may be true," Dr. Maddium replied. "but we also can't go anywhere until you're completely healed."

"I feel fine," Draagetsew grunted.

Dr. Maddium gave him an icy stare. "You got torn to ribbons by a rotating barbed wire fence only yesterday. Mutants may heal faster than most, but you and I both know that you haven't fully recovered. I'm surprised you were even able to get yourself this far."

"I'm fine," Draagetsew repeated, heaving the central tent pole up over his head. He gasped as the violent movement re-opened his wounds. Red streaked across the bandages that covered his body. Timothy watched with horror as he collapsed.

"Help me with him," Dr. Maddium said, half-managing to catch the burly mutant before he hit the ground.

Timothy and Quill ran over to him, helping him reset Draagetsew's tent while Crystal and Jewel applied another layer to the crystal compress that now coated Alpen's president.

Timothy frowned as he helped Dr. Maddium and Quill lay Draagetsew back down in his tent.

He's going to kill himself if he keeps trying stuff like this, he realized. *Mutant or not, we have to convince him to rest somehow.*

Chapter 13

"I feel fine!" Draagetsew exclaimed, pacing angrily in front of the fire. Timothy watched him closely, the mutant's pacing making him vaguely uncomfortable. It had been six days since his injury, and he had finally recovered enough to be up and walking around.

"You're not fully healed yet," Dr. Maddium said. "You need to wait a few days longer. It could be up to a week before you're well enough to travel. Especially when that travel is through a maze of deadly traps." Draagetsew opened his mouth to protest, but Dr. Maddium continued. "And furthermore, if you decide to ignore our advice and continue on anyway, I will have the twins cover you in crystal again until you're completely immobilized."

Hurt flashed in Draagetsew's eyes. "Gearwire," he pleaded. "You can't seriously be okay with this! You know me. I'm perfectly fine!"

Gearwire shook his head. "Sorry, Draagetsew. But Thomas is right. It's too risky. We need you to make it through the ruins alive. And so do the people of Alpen. If we have to do that by force, so be it."

Draagetsew's protests died away, replaced by a muted grumbling. Finally, he sat down beside the fire, a resigned look in his eyes. "Alright," he said at last, shaking his head. "I'll wait. But don't expect me to like it."

* * *

After they had been in the compound for a full ten days, Dr. Maddium deemed Draagetsew ready for travel. Idalbo had informed them the day before that the Council was rapidly finishing their preparations for the trip to the Weather Belt compound. If the Kriegerhelden failed to delay them, the Council would be ready to set out within the next four days. It would take them another two days to reach the compound, time which Gearwire planned to use to build up as much of a lead as they could. The threat of the Council catching them looming over their heads, they quickly packed up their camp and prepared to cross the rotating fence.

Timothy pushed his fear aside as he watched Suorotiart fly back and forth over the deadly barrier, bringing each person's packs and gear over to the other side. As he finished, the Golden Knight walked resolutely into the whirling thicket of razor wire. Sparks flew as the invincium fence clashed against the equally strong metal of his armor. After a few seconds, the Golden Knight disappeared from view completely, an earsplitting shrieking sound the only sign that he was still inside.

About thirty seconds later, the sound abruptly stopped, and Timothy allowed the tension to drain out of his muscles. The silence seemed to stretch for ages before Suorotiart confirmed what they had all hoped.

"He made it through," he announced, flying the Golden Knight's armor back to the outer side of the fence. He handed the armor to Timothy, who quickly put it on. As Timothy turned to face the wall, he once again shoved aside a feeling of nervousness.

Here goes nothing, he thought. He exhaled heavily, then marched into the fence. The horrible shrieking sound returned with a vengeance, amplified several times over from the interior of the armor. Combined with the sight of razor-sharp bits of metal flying past his face, it was enough to set his nerves on edge.

What if the armor breaks? he worried. *Or what if it falls off? Maybe I put it on wrong! What if-*

He shook his head angrily, pushing the thoughts away. He pressed onwards, spurred on by the knowledge that he was already halfway there. After what seemed like an eternity, he stumbled out of the trap. He breathed a sigh of relief as he removed the Golden Knight's helmet and handed it to Suorotiart.

Suorotiart disappeared again over the top of the wall, and soon the sound began again as another member of the Guardians of Kawts crossed the barrier. For the next half-hour, this process repeated itself, until every member of their party had made it across. Dr. Maddium handed the Golden Knight his armor, and he quickly put it back on. Most of the gold paint had been scratched off, but otherwise, it seemed to be completely intact.

"Three walls down, one to go," Draagetsew said, the hint of a smile tugging at the corners of his mouth. "Isn't this fun?"

* * *

"Can someone please pass me that screwdriver?" Revenant barked, elbow-deep in a mess of wires.

Idalbo passed the tool to him, and Revenant took it with a grunt. The rest of the Kriegerhelden stood in a semicircle around him, watching. Idalbo shifted uncomfortably on the concrete floor of Revenant's hidden workshop. No one dared to speak, and the resulting silence was broken only by Revenant's mutterings and the clatter of tools.

As the silence stretched on, Idalbo began absently fiddling with one of his quills. The quiet was suddenly shattered by Revenant's triumphant shout. He yanked something out of the device and lifted it over his head, grinning like a madman.

"What is that?" Tapfer asked, one eyebrow raised.

"This," Revenant said, his grin spreading wider than Idalbo would have thought possible. "Is the thing that's going to get Omor out of the Council's clutches."

"Yes, but what *is* it?" Inn snapped, his tentacles twitching in frustration.

Revenant glared at him. "We need to get Omor and his troupe away from the Council alive, right? But if the Council knows we've broken him out, they may start attacking the people of Blancstadt until we surrender. Hence, we need a way to rescue them without the Council knowing about it. Hence," he held up the device again. "This thing." He stuffed the device in his pouch and walked over to a nearby workbench. "I'm going to make more of these and work them into a set of suits. Whoever is involved in the attack on the execution will need to wear one. And Omor and his troupe will wear the rest."

"How are we going to get them to put on the suits?" Ederba asked. "It's not like we can just ask them politely to delay the execution so we can give the prisoners a change of clothes."

"I don't know!" Revenant snapped. "Apparently, tactics aren't my responsibility. Why don't you ask our fearless leader?"

Idalbo frowned, sensing that the Kriegerhelden were about to break into a heated argument. But before he could speak, a voice called out from the dimly lit hallway behind Revenant.

"I think I might have a solution to that problem," the voice said as it stepped into the light. Idalbo stiffened, recognising Legov at once. He looked haggard, and had huge bags under his eyes, but it was unmistakably him. Legov smiled weakly. "Hello, everyone. I take it Adalbo told you about our little... ah, discussion. It's... been a rough couple of weeks. But I'm ready to rejoin the Kriegerhelden. And I think I have a plan."

***

As the sun began to set, Gearwire called for the group to come to a stop. He walked up to Draagetsew. "Is there a place where we can safely set up camp for the night?" he asked.

Draagetsew studied the map. "Just up ahead," he answered, looking off down the path. "where one of the guard towers used to be. We can stop there."

Timothy breathed a sigh of relief as they emerged from the brush, grateful for the chance to rest his aching muscles. He removed his armor and sat down on the grass, staring up at the ruins of the guard towers. Both were in a state of disrepair, and one of them had partially collapsed, leaving a scattered pile of rubble around its base.

Draagetsew pounded on the doorframe of the more intact tower, sending sound waves reverberating across the structure. He poked his head inside and shouted something towards the ceiling. As the echo returned, he nodded approvingly.

"I think this one's still sturdy enough to camp out inside," he said, giving the doorframe another punch. Timothy heard a loud creak and eyed the tower warily.

"You are not getting me to set up camp inside there," Madison said. "It looks like it could collapse at any moment. We'll be crushed by falling rocks in our sleep!"

"It's sturdier than it looks," Draagetsew countered. "But anyway, there's something I need to show you on the top floor." He stepped inside the tower. "Follow me!"

Timothy exchanged glances with Madison and Jewel.

Jewel sighed. "Alright. Let's go."

Timothy stepped inside the tower, followed closely by Jewel and Quill. Crystal and Madison brought up the rear, each of them prepared to react in case the tower fell. Timothy stared up the center of the tower, marveling at how the dying sunlight reflected off of the dust as it drifted to the ground. From this angle, he could see clearly the gaping hole in the tower's upper floors.

Draagetsew stood halfway up the spiral staircase that wound around the outside of the tower, tapping his foot impatiently. "Are you coming or not? We don't have all day."

Timothy took a cautious step onto the staircase, flinching at the creaking sound it made. Gingerly, he lowered his foot onto the next step, then slowly eased his weight onto it. The stair held firm, and Timothy breathed a sigh of relief. He flitted up the rest of the stairs lightly as a mountain goat, skipping any steps that seemed too weak to support his weight.

Draagetsew led them up the winding staircase, finally coming to a stop in front of an ancient wooden door. He jiggled the knob and frowned. Then he charged the door with his shoulder, splintering it into hundreds of tiny pieces. He stumbled into the center of the room, narrowly avoiding falling through the hole in the floor. The room appeared to have been a bunk room at one time, the remnants of empty beds still lining the walls. Draagetsew's eyes shone with excitement as he righted himself, rubbing his massive hands together as he looked around the room.

Timothy watched him warily. "Is there something we should know about this room, Draagetsew?" he asked, a feeling of dread creeping over him.

"Just a minute," Draagetsew said, waving a hand dismissively in his direction.

"What is he doing?" Jewel whispered, looking on with concern.

"Nothing foolish, I hope," Crystal said, joining them.

"Aha! There it is!" Draagetsew exclaimed suddenly, reaching underneath one of the beds and pulling out a large seaman's chest. He looked up at the others. "Come on!" he urged, beckoning them forward. "There's something in here that might benefit you guys."

Timothy raised an eyebrow. "What kind of-" he began, but Quill had already joined Draagetsew in kneeling beside the chest. Timothy sighed as he followed his friend. The twins and Madison reluctantly followed suit. Draagetsew grinned and then threw open the lid of the chest, revealing five armbands, each looking like it had been carved from a different colored gemstone.

For a moment, Draagetsew was silent, staring at the rings in amazement. Then he reached into the chest and pulled out the black ring. He handed it to Timothy. "Put it on," he said eagerly.

Timothy didn't move, looking at Draagetsew like he had lost his mind. "Go on," he urged. "Trust me!"

Timothy raised an eyebrow, but he complied, slipping the ring onto his arm. No sooner had he done so than Draagetsew threw a punch at his face. Timothy ducked under the attack and took a step closer to Draagetsew, sweeping the mutant president's legs out from under him before he had a chance to react.

Draagetsew hit the ground hard, and Timothy realized too late that he had just attacked the leader of a large country. He looked down at Draagetsew in horror, but Draagetsew jumped back to his feet, beaming. "Yes!" he shouted. "That was amazing!"

Now I know *he's gone crazy,* Timothy thought. *Gearwire's not going to be happy about this.*

"How did you do that?" Quill asked, his mouth hanging open.

"Do what?" Timothy asked, frowning.

"What you just did! You were almost as fast as Gearwire!"

"What? How...." Timothy looked around in confusion before settling on Draagetsew. "What did you do?"

"Nothing," Draagetsew said, smiling. "It's all in the ring."

"How could a ring let him do that?" Madison asked.

"The ancient legends say that these rings were created by Marathon shortly before his death during the War of Heroes. He transferred his powers into them in case anything should happen to him."

"He made a magic ring," Timothy said skeptically.

Draagetsew shook his head. "No. He had superpowers of his own - a lot like the twins. He simply transferred them into these rings. One ability in each one."

"That sounds... kind of unrealistic," Quill said. "No offense."

"It is possible," Jewel said. "Gearwire has a device that can siphon our powers into other people. It doesn't seem like too much of a stretch to assume that someone could invent some sort of superpower-battery."

"Exactly!" Draagetsew said. "That's exactly what this is! These rings were used by the guards who lived in this tower - they had a lot of free time to experiment with them. They aren't as strong as they used to be, but they're still more than enough to give you a leg up in battle."

He turned towards Timothy. "The black one is the agility ring. I figured it might come in handy if you have to sneak past any Council spies."

His words hit Timothy like a ton of bricks. "Wait - you want *me* to use this? A powerful ancient artifact?"

Draagetsew nodded. "I've discussed it with Gearwire and Dr. Maddium. There's five of you, and five rings." He reached into the chest again and pulled out a blue ring, handing it to Quill.

Quill accepted it eagerly, slipping it onto his arm. "What power do I get?" he asked.

"Endurance and durability," Draagetsew replied, a mischievous gleam appearing in his eye as he kicked Quill squarely in the chest.

Quill slid across the floor, slamming into the wall. Panic welled up in Timothy as he heard the sickening thud.

Not Quill too, he thought. *Not again.* He ran over to his friend, but Quill jumped back to his feet, beaming.

"I barely even felt that!"

"That ring will drastically reduce any injuries you sustain," Draagetsew said. He turned to the twins and Madison, but Crystal held up a hand to stop him.

"I'm not taking one of those if it means you're going to punch me."

"Well, luckily for you, the other three can't really be tested that way." He reached into the box and tossed the remaining three rings to them, the red going to Madison, the yellow going to Jewel, and the green going to Crystal. "Madison, you have the strength ring. It boosts your strength to unusually high levels. According to the stories, that particular ring has lost more of its power than the others over the years, but you should still be able to easily lift the weight of a small refrigerator while using it."

"Cool," Madison said, slipping it on.

"Crystal! Or Jewel?" Draagetsew shook his head. "Whichever one of you has the yellow ring will have enhanced speed. And the green ring grants flexibility."

Before anyone could say anything further, the tower groaned and creaked, shifting ominously. Timothy froze, sensing something was amiss. The tower creaked again, and a brick fell to the floor.

Draagetsew smiled sheepishly. "Maybe the tower wasn't quite as sturdy as I thought it was," he admitted. Another brick fell to the floor. "And maybe I shouldn't have whacked it quite as hard as I did."

"Run!" Timothy shouted as the floor of the tower began to give way beneath him. Everyone dashed for the stairs, running down them as fast as they could. Jewel reached the bottom first, nearly a minute ahead of the others. A large chunk of stone landed in the middle of the staircase, and Draagetsew and Madison quickly pushed it over the side. They were almost to the bottom when the stairs themselves collapsed, dropping them the last several feet to the ground. Timothy hit the ground hard but immediately rolled back into his feet, diminishing the shock of the impact. Out of the corner of his eye, he saw Quill sprawled out on the floor, the ring on his arm glowing. Seconds later, he too was back on his feet and making a beeline for the exit.

Timothy had almost reached the door when a large piece of the tower fell from the ceiling. He dropped to the ground, sliding under it just in time. A feeling of dread came over him as he got to his feet. He scanned the rest of the group, realizing that Crystal was still inside the tower. He turned back towards it just in time to see her squeeze through the tiny gap between the ground and the fallen part of the tower moments before the entryway collapsed completely.

Timothy breathed a sigh of relief as he dusted himself off. The tower gave a final groan, then collapsed in a cloud of dust. Timothy coughed as the centuries-old particles of stone and mortar entered his lungs. When the dust finally settled, all that remained of the tower was a pile of rubble.

"On second thought, I think we'll be sleeping out here tonight," Draagetsew said.

Chapter 14

It only took them a few minutes to set up their camp, arranging their tents in a circle around a fire Gearwire had built between the two dilapidated guard towers. Timothy slipped off into the trees to look for firewood, having been assured by Draagetsew that there were no traps this close to the towers.

As soon as he was out of sight of the camp, Timothy breathed a heavy sigh and sat down on a nearby log. The tension of the last couple days was beginning to catch up with him, and for a long while, he didn't move, resting his eyes. After what seemed like just a few minutes, he realized he had been on the brink of nodding off. Reluctantly, he got to his feet, running his finger over the ring Draagetsew had given him.

He should have given this to someone else, he thought. *I mean, imagine if Gearwire had this. He'd practically be unkillable.* For a long moment, he stared at the ring, deep in thought. Finally, he walked deeper into the forest, picking up sticks and smaller pieces of logs.

As he returned to the camp with an armful of logs, he saw Draagetsew sitting by the fire, waving his arms about wildly. The rest of the Guardians of Kawts sat spellbound in front of him. Timothy slipped over to the fire and deposited the sticks onto the ground.

"And Penn fought the bandits off with only a single arrow! Sent them running right back to Prime Minister Mahgnitton!"

"That's not quite the way it happened," the Golden Knight said.

"There were only five bandits, not twelve. And Penn rarely used arrows. He preferred to use his sword."

"How do you know that?" Quill challenged, eying him skeptically.

Draagetsew's eyes grew wide. "You're *that* Golden Knight," he breathed. "I always wondered, but I never really *thought* that you might actually be…"

The Golden Knight nodded. "I was Penn's partner. At least, until Prime Minister Mahgnitton tricked him into going after the Weather Belt. It was a few weeks after he left that Dr. Maddium recruited me to be part of Gearwire's crew."

"Amazing," Draagetsew whispered, looking like a little kid in a candy store. "Is it true that Penn used to rob the Prime Minister's caravans? And did he really once defend an entire village from a massive flood?"

"If we make it out of here alive, I promise I will answer all of your questions, Draagetsew," the Golden Knight said. "But not now. We have more important concerns now than sorting out the truth from a bunch of old legends."

Draagetsew opened his mouth to protest, but at that moment, Gearwire's radio squawked to life.

"….ere's been….o sign….f the Counci-," Samuel said. "I thin…. they're….ot com….ng." Gearwire frowned and glanced over at Dr. Maddium.

"I was afraid this might happen," he said. "Invincium has been known to block certain kinds of signals. I'd be surprised if we could hear anything out of this radio by tomorrow night."

"Did you hear that?" Gearwire asked Samuel. "We'll probably lose contact with you by tomorrow night."

"Oka-" Samuel answered. "….at should I ….o about ….ay?" he asked.

Gearwire frowned. "I can't hear you, Samuel. Can you repeat that?"

"Ray…. should I…. about ….ay?"

"Let him go free for now," Gearwire said. "But keep an eye on him.

Don't allow him to have any weapons, and don't let him leave Kawts."

"-ill do," Samuel replied. Then the radio went dead.

* * *

Idalbo ran his finger along the edge of his bowstring as he waited beside the window - the same window where he had been stationed during Gearwire's unsuccessful attack on the castle weeks earlier.

Here's hoping history doesn't repeat itself, he thought grimly, lowering his bow. In the square below, Revenant and Inn waited, both disguised as emissaries of the tree people.

The ghost of a smile touched his face as he watched his friends. It hadn't been lost on him that the two had seemingly begun to put aside their differences when they had begun preparation for this mission, even if only to have a better chance of succeeding.

And yet, Idalbo noted, *Neither of them complained about being put on the same team. Maybe they're doing better than I thought.*

He plucked a quill from his back and notched it into place on his bowstring, He exhaled deeply, then drew it back, hesitating for only a moment before releasing it.

The quill sailed through the air before embedding itself in the arm of the guard at the gate. The guard shouted in pain, and Idalbo knew instantly that he had hit Deyeneek.

Serves him right, Idalbo thought, remembering the guard's strong Council sympathies.

"The way is clear," Idalbo said into his radio. "For now, anyway."

"Thanks. We've got it from here," Inn replied, his excitement plain in his voice.

"Good luck," Idalbo said. He clipped the radio to his belt, slinging his bow over his shoulder as he slipped out of the building.

* * *

"We're good to go," Inn reported, grinning wildly. He unholstered his axe from his belt.

"Let's get moving, then," Revenant said, readying his own weapon. For a moment, neither of them moved. Finally, Revenant said, "Look. About what happened with Okceg - I know it wasn't your fault. You did the best you could in a bad situation. And you did a much better job of leading than I ever would have."

Inn's face softened for a moment. "Thanks. And we couldn't have done any of this without your inventions." He heaved a great sigh and twirled his axe in a circle, his eyes shining. "Now let's go take the Council down a peg or two, shall we?"

Revenant grinned back at him, and then the pair charged into the castle, shoving past the injured guard into a courtyard filled to the brim with attack drones. For a brief moment, Inn hesitated. Then he let out a mighty battle cry and charged the drones, hacking them to pieces even as he danced out of the way of their bullets. Revenant stood behind him, picking off the drones one by one with a powerful compact laser pistol, reducing them to black lumps of slag.

Unprepared for the ferocity of the attack, the drones retreated a short distance away. It was all the opening Inn needed, and he kicked open the door to the castle. He heard the sharp pop of gunfire from outside, but he continued onwards, trusting Revenant to protect himself. He was not disappointed, and before he even reached the storeroom, Revenant had joined him, stashing his pistol in his pouch.

"Ready?" Revenant asked.

Inn nodded. "Of course." He rammed his shoulder into the door, smashing it off its hinges. The pair darted into the room, Inn already scanning the shelves and casks for the supplies the Council had bought for their journey. Opening a hidden pocket in his disguise, he draped the supplies in old rags, liberally soaked with oil. Revenant appeared beside him, a lit match in his hand.

"Here goes nothing," the shorter mutant said, tossing the match onto the pile of food and tools. The fire flickered out for a second, then flared to life, spreading with startling ferocity across the crates of supplies. Inn nodded approvingly and ran out of the building, Revenant close behind him. In the courtyard, they were once more forced to fight off attack drones, but fortunately for them, none of the Councilmen were present.

Fighting their way through the drones, they emerged at last onto the streets of Blancstadt, quickly losing the drones in the familiar maze of back streets. Removing their disguises, they ran onwards to the center of town, spreading rumors of a fire at the castle as they went. By the time they reached the site of the execution, the crowd had already begun to murmur, as if sensing that something was not right.

As Inn and Revenant's report reached them, the crowd's reaction shifted from a vague anxiety to fear. The murmuring rose to a clamor, and within moments, fighting broke out in the center of the crowd, instigated by Adalbo and Legov. Several of the members of Alpen's castle guard broke away from the prisoners to deal with the riot. At the Council's instruction, several more were dispatched to investigate the disturbance at the castle. Inn grinned at Revenant as he turned back toward the café. Their task was complete.

* * *

Idalbo stood in the center of the crowd, his heart pounding. He slipped his bow out from under his cloak, notching a quill onto the string. He exhaled heavily, then donned a wooden mask, shrugging his hood over his head.

I'm only going to get one shot before they get to me, he thought. *Let's make it count.* He charged up toward the dais where Omor and his theater troupe were awaiting their execution, shouting at the top of his lungs.

Before he was even halfway to the platform, the Council had begun to respond, drawing their weapons in the blink of an eye. Idalbo quickly drew back his bow and aimed it at Ethos. But before he could fire, something thudded into his side. A red warning flashed across the screen inside his mask. Idalbo crumpled to the ground, his bow slipping from his fingers. The quill he had intended for the head Councilman went wide, sailing harmlessly over his head.

So much for that idea, Idalbo thought with a sigh. He watched as Ethos sent two of the Councilmen over to his prone form to make sure he was truly dead. As they drew closer, Idalbo couldn't help but smile. Out of the corner of his eye, he saw Tapfer and Loyola help the prisoners into the suits that Revenant had made. Suits that were identical to the one Idalbo now wore.

Before the Councilmen could reach Idalbo, Omor suddenly broke free from the ropes that held him and charged the Council, brandishing one of Idalbo's own quills as a sword. The rest of the troupe followed after him, slipping from the grasp of the guards. The guards tried to pursue them, but Tapfer and Loyola blocked their path, tripping over each other and ending up sprawled out across the platform.

Ethos stared at the former prisoners as they drew nearer and nearer. There was no hint of emotion in his eyes as he raised his pistol and began to fire. Mere seconds later, the entire group was lying motionless on the dais.

Idalbo felt rough hands heave him into a semi-upright position and begin hauling him across the plaza. He flinched, but the skin-tight bodysuit he wore prevented the movement, flashing another warning before his eyes.

"Dump the bodies outside of town," Ethos said with a wave of his hand. "You are all dismissed for now," he told the crowd, then hurried off toward the castle to investigate the fire for himself.

For the next several minutes, Idalbo was dragged through Blancstadt, completely unable to move.

How much longer is this going to take? He wondered, a bead of sweat trickling down the back of his neck. *I'm starting to get a little claustrophobic.*

To his great relief, the Councilmen soon reached the edge of town. They slowed to a stop, searching for a suitable place to dispose of Idalbo and the others. Suddenly, Idalbo found himself flying through the air. He hit the ground hard, rolling into the bottom of a ditch. One by one, the others joined him, all in a similar state of paralysis. As the Councilmen's voices faded away, Idalbo was left in a profound silence, praying that the rest of the Kriegerhelden would find them soon.

In the end, nearly half an hour passed before Ederba and Revenant appeared at the top of the ditch. Revenant slid down to the bottom and removed Idalbo's facemask, his fingers flying over the keyboard inside. The mask dinged softly, and Idalbo's suit suddenly lost its rigidity. He breathed a sigh of relief and gently extricated himself from the pile. He quickly peeled the suit off of him while Revenant repeated the process on the keypads hidden on the other suits.

"I should have known you were the wizard behind this, Revenant!" Omor shouted as soon as he was released. "What was that?"

Revenant smiled. "That was a compilation of all the data I could find about human anatomy and bullet wounds," he said. He grinned wider. "There's a chip in each of those suits that's programmed to know exactly what happens when a person is shot in a certain way, and then instructs the suit to mimic the effects, all while keeping the wearer completely safe."

Omor nodded, his eyes wide. "Impressive."

"I've been working on it off and on ever since… well, since you-know-what. I figured it might come in handy to be able to appear, for all practical purposes, dead. Still haven't come up with a good way to de-activate it from the inside, though," he added with a shake of his head.

"Still," Omor insisted, "It's the most realistic way to fake your own death I've ever seen. You could even make altered versions for actors. Can you imagine how realistic we could get with something like that?"

"There'll be plenty of time to think about that later," Idalbo said with a slight smile. "For now, we just need to get you and your troupe back to our temporary base of operations. We've still got a lot of work to do."

* * *

"Everybody up! It's time to get moving!"

Timothy groaned and opened his eyes, awakened by Draagetsew's bellowing. For a moment, he considered going back to sleep, but he quickly thought the better of it. Sighing, he sat up and crawled out of his tent, yawning.

"You are aware that it's only five o'clock, right?" Dr. Maddium said, hiding a yawn of his own. "There's no rush."

"We still have a lot of traps to get through, remember?" Draagetsew said, far too cheerfully for the hour. "The sooner we start, the more traps we can get through in a day. And the more traps we get through in a day, the sooner we get the Weather Belt and free Alpen!"

"I appreciate your zeal, Draagetsew, but these traps will be considerably harder to get through if we're all half asleep," Gearwire said. There was a long pause, then he added, "I'll get the coffee."

Fifteen minutes later, everyone was huddled together in a rough circle, nursing cups of coffee. Timothy took a sip of the brown beverage and resisted the urge to immediately spit it back out. He forced himself to swallow and take another sip.

I don't get how anyone likes this stuff, he thought, making a face at his mug. Still, he drank every drop, relishing the warmth. By the time they finished packing up their camp, he was wide awake.

"So what's first on the agenda today?" Quill asked.

Draagetsew looked upwards, craning his neck to see over the trees. "That," he said, pointing to the massive wall looming overhead. "We should be only a few hours away if we hurry."

"We'd best get moving, then," Gearwire said. "As long as we're up, we might as well make use of the time."

Draagetsew unfurled the map from his pocket, leading the group deeper into the trees. As predicted, it took them several hours to reach the next obstacle, stumbling out of the trees directly in front of the massive wall.

Timothy slowly lifted his head, taking in the sheer enormity of the structure. The top of the wall was at least forty feet above the ground by his estimation, nearly touching the bottom of the dome. Now that he could see it up close, he noticed the tiny bits of metal and glass that jutted out of it at odd angles, making any attempt to climb it guaranteed to end in severe lacerations.

Of course. They had to make this complicated.

"Do you think you could create a ladder for this wall, too?" Quill asked, turning to the twins.

Jewel shook her head. "We can't risk it. The wall's too high. With how slippery that last ladder was, someone would fall off."

"Not to mention the fact that I'm not sure I'd be able to climb the ladder if we did make it," Crystal said. "I'd be lucky to still be *conscious* after a project that big."

"We have a rope in our supplies," the Golden Knight said. "We can climb over the old-fashioned way."

Gearwire shook his head. "That might work for you and me. But everyone else will get their feet sliced to ribbons."

"Are we sure we *have* to go over it?" Madison asked, her face paling slightly as she eyed the top of the wall.

Madison was barely able to force herself to climb up to the library roof last year, Timothy recalled. *There's no way she's going to climb over this wall.*

"The Council will have wiped Alpen off the face of the map before we ever get into the inner circle at this rate!" Suorotiart said, looking rather irritated.

"Quiet!" Draagetsew said, looking up from the map once more. "It looks like there is a way to go through the wall instead," he said, looking around at the group. There's a secret door somewhere around here."

"I'll fly over to the other side of the wall and have a look around," Suorotiart said. "If I can find the exit, it'll help us locate the entrance." Before anyone could object, he shot up into the sky, his batlike wings flapping rhythmically.

"I guess the rest of us had better get looking on this side, then," Crystal said. "Unless some of us want to try to find the door from the *top* of the wall instead." The tone of her voice made it clear what she thought about Suorotiart's suggestion, but no one commented on it. Instead, they approached the wall, getting as close to it as they dared while they scanned the structure for any signs of an entrance.

They had been searching for several minutes when a movement caught Timothy's eye. He turned to look at it, frowning slightly. Nothing happened, and he turned back to the section of wall in front of him, only for the movement to catch his eye once more.

I must be seeing things, he thought, squinting at the spot where the movement had seemed to come from. He was just about to turn away again, when suddenly, the wall flickered. Timothy swallowed hard and slowly reached out his hand toward the spot. Instead of touching sharp bits of shrapnel, his hand found nothing but empty space.

"I think I found it!" he called out, waving the others over to him. He repeated his discovery again, this time allowing his hand to go all the way through, disappearing into what seemed to be a solid surface.

"Good job, Timothy," Gearwire said, nodding approvingly. "If you don't mind stepping aside, I'm just going to test something." He drew his sword from its sheath and stuck it into the spot, flicking it from side to side until he hit something. Slowly, he traced the outline of a rectangle in the air, his sword grating against the concrete wall.

He's feeling out the exact dimensions of the doorway, Timothy realized. *That's genius.*

Having gone all the way around the border, Gearwire brought his sword to the center of the space, waving it wildly. Finally, he returned his sword to its sheath. "Doorway seems clear," he said. "If there are any traps waiting for us on the other side, they aren't motion activated. And I didn't feel any tripwires or anything like that."

"Then what are we waiting for?" Draagetsew said. "Let's go catch up with Suorotiart!" He plunged through the gap in the wall, vanishing from sight. Timothy took a deep breath and followed him in, emerging into an almost pitch-black room. The only source of light was a dimly glowing green crystal mounted on the wall, a bit like a cut diamond, but about the size of Timothy's fist. He stared up at it, puzzled.

Suddenly, Timothy froze, overcome by the feeling that someone was watching him. A shiver ran down his spine, and his heart began to beat a little faster. The sensation quickly faded, but something still didn't feel quite right. He became aware of a gentle pressure inside his head, as if something was trying to get inside his brain. He pushed back against the feeling, but the pressure only increased, until it was almost painful. Timothy grunted and brought his hand up to his forehead, massaging his temples. The pressure redoubled, and he stopped fighting it, allowing whatever it was to do what it was trying to do. Images from his past flashed before him, unprompted, and Timothy began to breathe faster.

What is going on? What is this thing doing to me? What if I lose control of my-

Diagnostic complete, a voice said directly into his mind. *Preparing the subject now.*

A short hissing sound came into the chamber, as if someone had released air from a balloon. Timothy's eyelids grew heavy, and he staggered up against someone in the darkness.

This was a trap, he realized. *It's putting us to sleep. I have to-*

He took a couple of steps toward what he thought was the exit, only to collapse to the ground as the gas began to take effect. As his limbs grew heavier, he stared up at the glowing jewels in the corner of the room, silently blaming them for what was happening. Then his eyes closed and everything went dark.

Chapter 15

Idalbo lay on his back outside the ramshackle house, staring up at the sunset.

We still have a long way to go, he thought. *But it's nice to be able to rest for a while.*

A frown crossed his face as he remembered how quickly the Council had rebuilt their stash of supplies - mostly by threatening the local merchants with execution if they didn't 'donate' to the expedition.

Still, now that most of the Council is in the ruins, it leaves us with a lot more freedom to move around.

A black speck appeared on the horizon, catching Idalbo's eye. He sat up and squinted at it, trying to determine what it was. As the speck drew closer, he realized with a sudden jolt of fear that it was Gearwire's ship.

"Mysterious Man! Howard!" he shouted, dashing inside to grab the radio beacon. "There's something out here you need to see!" Idalbo ran back outside, followed closely by Howard. The Mysterious Man took one look at the speck and disappeared inside, emerging seconds later with a portable telescope. As he set up the tripod, Idalbo opened the channel to his brother's radio.

"Adalbo!" he said, glancing around anxiously as he waited for his brother to respond. In the heat of the moment, the brief delay before Adalbo's voice came on the line felt like hours.

"What is it?"

"Gearwire's ship is flying back towards Alpen."

There was silence for a while. "What? He should be inside the central building of the complex by now."

"That's exactly the problem," Idalbo said. "We're keeping an eye on it from the base, but we'll need you to investigate as soon as it touches down. Something's not right."

"It's turning towards the city," the Mysterious Man confirmed, peering through the telescope. "It seems to be heading to the castle."

"I'm on my way," Adalbo said. Idalbo could hear the rustling in the background as he donned his disguise and ran out into the streets of Blancstadt. A tense silence followed, neither Adalbo nor the Mysterious Man having anything more to report.

"I'm standing a block away from the castle now," Adalbo said at last.

"The ship still seems to be on track," the Mysterious Man confirmed. "Wait - now it's turning a bit to the south."

"Why would they be going to the south side of Blancstadt?" Howard mused aloud.

"It's been largely abandoned since the end of the war," Omor said, coming up behind them. If you wanted to land a ship in the city without anyone noticing, that would be the place to do it."

Howard frowned. "It can't be Gearwire, then. He would have come back here."

"We don't know that for sure," Idalbo said, hoping that the scientist was wrong. "He might have some other reason for not landing the ship here." Howard didn't reply, and Idalbo knew how painfully unrealistic his suggestion had been.

"Okay. I'm in position," Adalbo said. "I see the ship."

"Good. Keep us posted," the Mysterious Man said.

"And be careful," Idalbo said. "Make sure they can't see you. Just in case."

"Will do."

"The ship's coming in for a landing," the Mysterious Man reported after a long pause. He looked up at Idalbo, his face pressed into a grim frown. "Whoever's in that thing doesn't seem like they're used to flying. Gearwire's not the pilot."

Idalbo felt his anxiety rising as the silence returned. After what seemed like hours, he heard Adalbo gasp.

"It's the Council," he confirmed. "All of them."

The statement hit Idalbo like a ton of bricks. His head spun as he realized what this meant.

If the entire Council is back in Blancstadt, that means they never intended to go inside the complex in the first place. But they still went through the act of preparing for an expedition to get the Weather Belt. Why would they go through so much effort to make us think they were hunting the Weather Belt? Unless...

"There's a mole in Gearwire's crew," the Mysterious Man said, coming to the same conclusion as Idalbo.

Idalbo picked up the radio beacon, punching in the numbers as quickly as his fingers could type them. But instead of Gearwire's voice, all he heard was static. His shoulders slumped as he realized they were too far into the ruins for the signal to reach them.

"This is not good," the Mysterious Man muttered. "We have to call Samuel. With Gearwire gone, he's our best shot for figuring this out."

It took Samuel a while to answer, only heightening Idalbo's discomfort.

"Hello?" he asked, sounding puzzled. "Who is this?"

"We have a problem," the Mysterious Man said. "We believe that the crew in the Weather Belt complex have a traitor in their midst. Someone who plans to hand the Weather Belt over to the Council."

"Have you tried radioing Gearwire?" Samuel asked.

"They're too far into the compound. We can't reach them."

There was silence on the other end of the line. "We'll be there as soon as we can," Samuel said at last. "In the meantime, try to see if you can figure out any clues about the traitor's identity. Or what exactly they're planning to do. Perhaps there's still a way for us to get a message through."

"I can try to build a signal booster," Howard said. "With Revenant's help, I might be able to have something up and running in a few weeks."

"Good," Samuel said. "With luck, we'll be there before you finish."

"One more thing," Volker interrupted before Samuel could hang up. "Make sure you keep a very close eye on the Council. This may just be a ploy to trick us into leaving Kawts undefended."

Idalbo nodded. "We'll let you know if they show any signs of leaving," he replied.

"You should mention it to Ray," the Mysterious Man suggested. "See how he reacts."

"Good idea," Samuel said. "We have a lot to do if we have any chance of getting there in time. Keep us updated with anything new you find. We'll see you later." Then he hung up.

Idalbo and the Mysterious Man exchanged a worried glance.

The Mysterious Man was right, Idalbo realized. *They're walking right into a trap.*

* * *

Timothy groaned and opened his eyes, blinking in the bright sunlight that shone on his face. The events of the previous hours came flooding back to him, and he froze, scanning the place he now found himself in.

He sat propped up against the tall wall, facing a large stretch of grass, beyond which the forest resumed once more. Over the tops of the trees, he could just barely make out the outline of the central building of the complex, which housed the Weather Belt itself.

Seeing no imminent danger, Timothy slowly got to his feet.

What happened in there? he wondered. *How long have I been out?* His eyes widened as he realized for the first time another very important detail. *And where is everyone else?*

Timothy paced along the wall, trying to quell the panic that threatened to rise up within him. Then he stopped, shaking his head. "We're going to be fine," he told himself. "I survived by myself in the forest for months back in Kawts." A flicker of fear returned, however, when he thought of his friends.

But what about Jewel and Quill and Madison and Crystal? he thought. *They haven't had the same experience. Gearwire and the Golden Knight will be fine, but will they?*

He shook his head, clearing his mind. "Worrying about that isn't going to do us any good," he said. "There's nothing I can do to help them until I find them." With this thought in mind, he set off toward the trees.

He hadn't gone far before he heard someone calling his name. He turned around to see Jewel running towards him, waving her hand over her head. Timothy ran over to her, his fears beginning to dissipate.

"Jewel! Thank goodness you're okay! Have you seen the others?"

Jewel shook her head. "I was about to ask you the same thing," she said. Then she smiled. "I'm so glad I found you."

"Me too," Timothy said. "I was worried that I might not see you guys again."

A brief silence followed. Then Jewel said, "So what now? Whatever that thing in the wall was doing, it seems to have split us up."

Timothy nodded, frowning. "It felt like it was looking for something in my head," he said. "Did you feel that too?"

"Yeah." Jewel shuddered. "For a moment, I was worried that it was going to turn us into Blanks."

"Why would the Weather Belt complex need to mess with our heads?" Timothy said. "This place is deadly enough without that."

"I don't know," Jewel said. "But if we want to get out of here alive, we're going to have to keep moving. The sooner we find out what's happened to the others, the better."

"Agreed. I just hope they're all still alive."

"I'm sure they're fine," Jewel said, but Timothy could hear the uncertainty in her voice.

I hope you're right, he thought, trying not to think of the alternative. He forced himself to focus on Jewel, ignoring the anxiety that threatened to overwhelm him. *I can't lose another friend.*

Chapter 16

Timothy yawned and crawled out of his tent, squinting in the morning sunlight. He and Jewel had traveled together for the rest of the day, finally setting up camp when the sun began to set. But despite the distance they'd covered, they had yet to find any signs of the others.

Timothy stifled another yawn, glancing over at Jewel's tent.

We shouldn't have stayed up so late talking last night, he thought, debating with himself whether he should wake up his traveling companion. He frowned, noticing that the flaps on Jewel's tent were open. His blood ran cold when he realized the tent was empty.

What if there was another trap here? he thought, his panic chasing any thought of sleep from his mind. *What if she got taken somewhere else? Or what if she's-*

"Timothy!" Jewel called cheerfully from behind him. "Good morning!"

Timothy felt the tension draining out of his body as he realized she was safe. As Jewel approached the tents, he said, "Where were you? I thought something had happened-"

Jewel smiled sympathetically. "Sorry about that. I was praying under that tree over there," she said, pointing. "I needed to be alone with God for a bit."

"Why? What good is that going to do?" Timothy asked.

"In case you forgot, we're in a bit of a situation right now," Jewel said with a smile. "God's the only person I know who could help us find the others. Assuming they're still alive."

Timothy shook his head. "And assuming he's real," he said. "And if that's true, why didn't he save Henry? Or allow the Council to rule Kawts for as long as they did?"

"Believe me, those are pretty high on my list of things to ask him someday, too," Jewel said. "But I've seen enough to trust that he knows what he's doing."

"What do you mean?" Timothy asked, something in Jewel's tone giving him pause.

"It's a bit of a long story," Jewel said. "I can tell you everything once we get underway, if you want. But first, let's have breakfast. I'm starving."

* * *

Timothy and Jewel walked through the forest for several hours, keeping to the narrow path that snaked between the trees. As the sun rose higher in the sky, Timothy spotted a massive gate in the distance. The pair drew closer to it, their conversation dying out. When they were only a stone's throw away from it, they stopped, wary of what might lay ahead.

Timothy stared up at the gate, which stood nearly ten feet tall and appeared to be made of some sort of white stone, slightly yellowed with age. The archway was attached to a high wall made of the same material, heading off into the trees as far as the eye could see.

"What is it?" Jewel asked, craning her neck to try to see around the corner and into the walled-off area itself.

Timothy opened his mouth to reply when suddenly, a shout rang out across the forest.

"Jewel!"

Timothy turned to see Crystal emerge from the trees, the look of relief plain on her face. She ran over to her sister, hugging her fiercely. In spite of his relief at seeing another one of the Guardians of Kawts alive, Timothy couldn't help but feel a slight twinge of irritation at Crystal's presence.

"Crystal!" Jewel said. "Thank goodness you're okay! Where have you been?"

"I woke up by that wall a few days ago," Crystal said. "I'd rather not talk about what happened between then and now."

"Wait," Timothy said. "Did you say a few days ago? We've only been on this side of the wall since yesterday."

"Well, this is day three for me," Crystal said. "I thought you guys were all dead."

"Why's that?" Timothy asked, dreading the answer.

"I said I didn't want to talk about it," Crystal said. "But I found some... bodies. Evidently, they were fakes, since you two are still clearly alive."

"We've got to get out of here," Jewel said, shaking her head. "The sooner we find the others and get the Weather Belt, the better."

"You won't hear me objecting to that," Crystal said. "Let's keep moving."

"I'll do a sweep for traps up ahead," Timothy said, unsheathing his staff. "Follow me."

With that, he took a cautious step through the archway, feeling out the ground in front of him with his staff. When he had tested the entire section of floor with no signs of a trap, he took another step forwards, repeating the process. After a few moments, he reached the end of the dividing wall that hid the rest of the trap from view. As he rounded the corner, his heart sank.

"It's a maze," he said, taking in the winding network of corridors laid out before him. A large red warning sign spray-painted on the wall caught his eye, and he added, "And by the looks of things, there are plenty of surprises waiting for us."

* * *

The trio slowly made their way through the maze, Timothy using his staff to sweep for any unexpected dangers. Behind him, Jewel caught Crystal up on everything that had happened to them over the last day and a half, Timothy speaking up only when Jewel left something out. They had just finished their account when the maze suddenly opened up onto a large round room.

One side of the room was piled high with gold and jewels, the mounds of treasure glittering in the sun. The other side of the room appeared to be some kind of workshop, the tables lined with a plethora of strange devices.

"What is this place?" Timothy breathed, looking around the room with wary awe.

"It almost looks like a treasury of some sort - or an armory," Jewel said. She took a tentative step deeper into the room.

"The bigger question is, *why* is this place?" Crystal said, walking over to the workbench. She examined the devices on the table. "If these are what I think they are, this is some next-level tech."

"It must be some sort of backstage area," Timothy said, putting away the shuriken he had pulled out when they entered the room.

"Or it's a storehouse to prepare us for what's coming next," Crystal said. "I'm telling you, these devices make that mind-reading wall look like a party trick." She picked up one rather large raygun. "I mean, a device that can eliminate friction? That could come in handy."

"I wish Draagetsew were here," Jewel said. "He'd be able to tell us what this place is."

Timothy fell silent, a strange, distant sound catching his ear. He frowned, trying to place it. Then it hit him.

Footsteps.

Motioning for Crystal and Jewel to stop talking, he leaned toward the source of the sound.

There's too many of them for it to be Gearwire and the others, he realized, detaching a shuriken from the leg of his suit.

Before Timothy could warn his companions, a cluster of long-legged robots burst out in front of them, weapons raised. For a moment, Timothy and the robots stared each other down. Then the robots opened fire, giving Timothy only barely enough time to dive out of the way. He rolled to his feet, swinging his staff at the legs of one of the robots, dropping it to the ground. Before it could recover, Timothy threw a shuriken at its head, shearing through it. Behind him, he heard a shout, and he turned to see a pair of robots bearing down on Jewel, who stood with her arms outstretched toward the oncoming robots.

Why isn't she using her powers? He wondered, noticing how none of the robots had been encased in crystal. His eyes met Jewel's, and he knew instantly that something was very wrong.

Timothy pivoted, sending two shurikens whizzing through the air toward the approaching robots. The shurikens took the robots in their chests, dropping them instantly. As soon as the robots fell, their remaining companions turned and fled, disappearing into the maze.

Timothy ran over to Jewel, who was staring at her hand in disbelief. "Are you okay? What happened?"

"They- they took Crystal," Jewel stammered, looking up at him. "And I couldn't do anything about it."

Timothy frowned, alarm bells ringing in his head. "What do you mean?"

"I couldn't stop them," Jewel repeated, more to herself than to Timothy.

"We'll just have to go after them," Timothy said, unclipping another shuriken from his suit. "They can't have gotten far yet." He turned to follow the retreating robots, but Jewel grabbed his arm, her eyes wide.

"Timothy, you don't understand." She looked him directly in the eyes as she continued. "My powers aren't working."

Timothy blinked. "What?"

Jewel thrust out her hand toward a nearby wall. Instead of being coated by familiar blue crystal, the wall remained blank. A note of panic crept into her voice as she continued. "Something in this place is preventing me from using my powers. I'm defenseless."

"You're not defenseless," Timothy said, stalling for time while his mind raced to come up with a solution.

"My powers are the only weapon I've ever trained to use," Jewel said. "I can't fight without them!"

Timothy took a step back, running his hand through his hair. "Let's just stay calm," he said. "I'm sure we can figure this out."

"Stay calm? Those robots took Crystal! And without my powers, there's nothing I can do about it."

As she had been talking, Jewel's breathing had quickened, until now, she was on the verge of hyperventilating.

She's going to pass out if she doesn't calm down, Timothy realized suddenly. *I have to do something.*

"You don't need powers to fight the robots," Timothy said. "I mean, look at Gearwire. He doesn't have any powers."

"Even Gearwire wouldn't be able to do much without his glue gun or his robot legs," Jewel said. "My powers *are* my weapon, Timothy."

"You don't have to have a weapon to fight. Think of Maurice and

Samuel and Quill. They all helped fight the Council, and they didn't have a single weapon between them."

"And all of them also had Crystal and I to bail them out if things went wrong," Jewel said, although her panic seemed to be beginning to subside.

Timothy took her hand, looking her directly in the eyes. "We're going to figure out what's happened to your powers," he said. "But first, we need to focus on figuring out where they're bringing Crystal."

Jewel nodded, taking a deep breath and exhaling heavily. "You're right," she said. "One crisis at a time."

Timothy turned his attention to the maze itself, staring off in the direction that the robots had gone. The robots were nowhere to be seen, having vanished utterly into the trap.

I hope I can still track them, Timothy thought, glancing back at Jewel. *Otherwise, we're in trouble.* He exhaled slowly, starting off in the direction where the robots had disappeared. It wasn't long until he reached a crossroads, paths going off in four different directions.

Timothy came to a stop, frowning as he inspected the paths.

I don't see any tracks, he thought, bending closer to get a better look. The walls and floor of the maze were made of stone, not leaving any signs behind. He straightened up, prepared to tell Jewel the bad news. To his surprise, she seemed more optimistic than she had just moments before. It didn't take long for him to find out why - in her hand was a small silver sphere.

"Is that one of Crystal's smoke bombs?"

Jewel nodded. "It was lying in the entrance to this path," she said, pointing to the second one.

"It looks like Crystal is leaving us a trail," Timothy said. "Let's go. We've got to catch up with her before she runs out of trail markers."

The pair ran off down the path, retracing the robots' route through the maze. Along the way, they collected several of Crystal's smoke bombs, stashing them in Timothy's chest plate.

"We'd better be almost there," Jewel said as they approached another crossroads.

Something in her tone struck Timothy as off. He turned to look at her, but she just pointed off down one of the passageways. Lying in the middle of the floor was a green armband, seemingly carved out of a gemstone.

"Crystal's ring," Timothy said. "Which means she's probably running out of things to leave behind."

"What do we do now?"

"Follow this path until we reach another crossroads. Then we'll have to figure something else out."

He started down the path, Jewel right behind him. They hadn't gone far, however, before they heard angry shouting from somewhere ahead of them. Timothy and Jewel locked eyes, both of them thinking the same thing. They burst out into a run, making their way toward the sound. Not having any trail markers, they made a few wrong turns, but even so, they soon emerged from the maze, standing atop a low hill.

Timothy stopped cold as he saw what was at the bottom of the hill. A sleepy little village was laid out before him, lifted straight from the medieval ages. His heart skipped a beat. On the streets of the town were people.

Chapter 17

For a long time, neither Timothy nor Jewel spoke.

Finally, Timothy stammered, "How?"

"I - I don't know," Jewel said, the loss of her powers momentarily forgotten. "Maybe they're the descendants of the guards who used to work here."

"Draagetsew said there were no more guards. Why are they still here?"

"I suspect there's quite a lot about this place that Draagetsew doesn't know," Jewel said.

Then, as the urgency of their situation came back to her, she asked, "Where's Crystal?"

Timothy grimaced, scanning the hillside below them. There was no sign of Crystal or the robots who had taken her.

Okay. Now it might be time to panic, he thought.

"I... I don't know," he said at last. He shook his head. "Maybe the people in that town saw something."

Jewel gave him a weak smile. "Let's go."

Staff in hand, Timothy started down the hill, keeping an eye out for any signs of their quarry. Yet even to his trained eye, he was unable to spot any signs of recent passage.

I don't like this, he thought, pausing halfway down the slope. *It feels like we're walking into a trap.*

Jewel appeared beside him. "We need to keep our eyes open. Something about this is wrong."

"Agreed."

Taking one last look at the village before him, Timothy made his way down the rest of the hill, walking along the dusty dirt road into the little settlement. The few people who were out on the streets paid no attention to him, going blissfully about their business.

"Why aren't more of them mutants?" Jewel muttered beside him.

Timothy's eyes widened, realizing for the first time that only a handful of the people he could see had the mutant's characteristic dust-yellow scales.

"Nothing about this place makes sense," he said, scanning the row of buildings for somewhere they could find information. Most of the buildings seemed to be closed for the day, the sole exception being the inn and restaurant at the end of the street.

That's as good a place to find information as any.

Keeping his weapons at the ready, Timothy jogged off down the dusty street, bursting into the inn. The innkeeper looked up calmly as he entered.

"Can I help you?"

"We're looking for someone," Jewel said. "She was taken by a group of robots from the maze on the top of the hill."

The innkeeper screwed up his face. "Let's see…" He shook his head. "I don't know anything about any robots. Or a maze, for that matter. But I can get you a room or two if you're planning on sticking around."

"What do you mean, you don't know anything about a maze?" Timothy interrupted. "It's right outside of town."

The innkeeper thought for a moment. "Doesn't ring a bell."

"We were just there," Jewel insisted. "There was a huge room in the middle filled with treasure and gadgets."

The innkeeper gave her a look. "I've heard a lot of tall tales over the years from travelers coming through here. Tales of treasure and magic artifacts are more trouble than they're worth."

"This isn't a story," Jewel said. "I'm telling you, we-"

"Jewel."

Jewel stopped, looking up at Timothy. Timothy pointed out the window in the direction of the maze. Both maze and hill had disappeared, replaced by an endless grassy plain. The pair fell silent, struggling to come to terms with what they were seeing.

"This is a dream," Timothy muttered. "It has to be a dream. There's no other way this makes sense."

"We've still got a couple of rooms available," the innkeeper said after a while. "Whatever you're looking for, you won't find it in the dark. Might as well stay here for the night."

Timothy exchanged glances with Jewel. "If it is a dream, we don't have anything to lose," she whispered. "Maybe things will make more sense in the morning."

Timothy nodded slowly. He turned to the innkeeper. "We'll take the two rooms," he said.

The innkeeper reached beneath the desk and pulled out a pair of keys. "Come with me," he said. "I'm sure you'll find your stay here enchanting."

* * *

"Thanks for helping me out back there," Jewel said. She and Timothy were sitting in one of the rooms the innkeeper had shown them, the sun having already set. "I just... when I realized I couldn't use my powers..." She trailed off. "It's always been one of my biggest fears. That somehow, I would lose my abilities, and then I wouldn't be able to help the people I care about. It was like waking up one day and realizing I couldn't move."

Timothy nodded, stopping himself from saying, 'I know what you mean' just in time.

"That must've been terrible," he said instead.

"Thanks." Jewel sighed. "I haven't been without my powers since the day Gearwire recruited me," she said, allowing the blue light to flow from her palms, creating a thin coating of crystal on the surface of the wall. "I guess I'm not used to being an ordinary person."

"Even without your powers, you still wouldn't be ordinary," Timothy said. "Not many people would be willing to do the kinds of things you've done for Kawts, powers or not."

Jewel smiled at him. "Thanks."

The silence between them lingered for a moment, then Timothy spoke. "There's been something I've been meaning to talk to you about." He hesitated a moment, then said, "How did you handle being a part of Gearwire's crew for all those years? Even just since the Battle of Kawts, it's been one thing after another. I feel like I don't have time to be an actual person."

Jewel smiled sympathetically. "Is that why you've been so reluctant about going on missions lately?" she asked. She fell silent for a while, staring off into the distance.

"When I first joined Gearwire's crew, he sent us on missions almost nonstop," she said at last. "Crystal and I hardly even had time to do our homework for school. I was about ready to quit. The only thing that kept me working with him was a sense of responsibility - I felt like I couldn't just stand by and do nothing when I had the power to do something about it."

Timothy nodded. "Yeah. I kind of thought you would say something like that."

"I'm not finished," Jewel said. "It got to the point where I just couldn't do it anymore. I was stressed out constantly, and I couldn't sleep. It took Crystal and Pastor Shepherd to help me realize something - I couldn't do everything myself. If I didn't take the time to take care of myself, I wasn't going to be able to do anything to stop the Council at all. So I contacted Gearwire and told him I couldn't do so many missions. I told him to only give me missions that it was important for me specifically to do."

She shrugged. "Gearwire listened. He stopped giving me so many missions, and my work for the rebellion improved drastically." She turned to Timothy. "You just need to tell him how you're feeling. You can be part of Gearwire's crew and still have a life."

Timothy nodded. "Thanks. I'll have to talk to Gearwire once we find him." He stopped. "Assuming we all get out of this alive."

Chapter 18

"This is such a charming little town," Timothy said, sitting down beside Jewel in their usual booth. He took a deep breath, relishing the cool morning breeze. The very air seemed to add to the allure of the little settlement.

Jewel smiled, and Timothy was suddenly struck by the joy it brought him.

I wish every day could be like this, he thought, returning Jewel's smile.

"It's the kind of place you wish you never had to leave," Jewel agreed. A shadow flickered across her face. "But Timothy… didn't we come here for a reason?"

Timothy waved the comment away. "Who cares why we came? Whatever reason we had for coming here, I'd say it was an excellent decision."

"I'm not complaining," Jewel said. "It's been nice to be able to just relax. Not to have to worry about anything. I just wish Crystal were here with us."

At the mention of Crystal, Timothy frowned, his eyes narrowing. "Now that you mention it, didn't the reason we came here have something to do with Crystal?"

Jewel nodded slowly. "It was such a long time ago," she said. "But I think you might be right."

Exactly how long has it been? Timothy wondered, trying to pinpoint when they had come into town. *The days have all kind of blurred together,* he realized. His forehead furrowed as he tried to think back to what they had been doing before they arrived in town. A memory bubbled to the surface of his mind, and he felt the blood drain from his face. He turned to look at Jewel, but she had apparently already come to the same realization.

"Crystal!" she shouted, looking like she'd just seen a ghost. She locked eyes with Timothy. "We came here to rescue Crystal! How many days have we been in this town?"

Timothy felt a cold stab of fear run through him as he waved the innkeeper over to their table.

"Innkeeper," he said. "How long have we been here?"

"A few minutes," he said, looking puzzled.

"Not the table," Timothy said. "How long have we been in town?"

"You've always been here," the innkeeper said. "As long as I can remember, anyway. And I've lived here all my life."

Timothy swallowed hard. "Thank you," he managed. The innkeeper nodded and hurried away.

"This place is a trap," Jewel said, confirming what he had already been thinking. "We must be drugged or something."

Timothy nodded. "And there's no telling how long it's been since we arrived." As the memories of their mission flooded back to him, his eyes widened. "For all we know, the Council's already gotten their hands on the Weather Belt."

"We need to find my sister and get out of here," Jewel said. "Before we get sucked in again."

"Agreed," Timothy said, forcing himself to ignore the small part of him that wished they could stay in the little town forever. He pulled himself to his feet. "But where would we even start?"

"I knew we'd catch up with you somewhere," a voice said from the doorway of the inn.

Timothy turned around to see Ethos and Aksell behind him. He reached for a shuriken before realizing that his armor was back up in his room.

Guess I'll have to improvise, he thought, rising to his feet.

"That's close enough," Timothy said, holding his hand slightly behind his back, as if hiding a weapon. "If you take one more step toward us, you're going to wish you hadn't."

"For once, I couldn't care less," Ethos said, deliberately moving closer to them. "Fact is, we need your help."

"Why should we believe you?" Jewel asked, her hands raised.

"Because we've gotten ourselves in over our heads," Aksell said. "The Orgwar are coming. And they have no interest in working *with* any humans. The Weather Belt is our only chance at stopping them."

Timothy and Jewel exchanged glances.

"What happened to the rest of the Council?" Timothy asked.

"They're being held in the catacombs beneath this town," Ethos said. "That's why we need your help. The two of us don't stand a chance at breaking them out alone. Besides," he added with a disdainful smirk. "I figured you people have more experience with jailbreaks."

"We only came into this town in the first place to find Crystal," Jewel said. "Our team is more than strong enough to get the Weather Belt without your help."

Ethos gave an exasperated sigh. "They're being held in the same network of tunnels, you fool!" he spat. "As a matter of fact, the room where your sister is being held is under this very inn!"

Timothy froze. "What did you say?"

"Let me put it in simpler terms: you help Aksell and I free our team, and we'll help you free yours."

"Fine," Jewel said. "But we're rescuing Crystal before we do anything else."

"I am not in a bargaining mood," Ethos said darkly.

"That sounds fair," Aksell said, stepping between his father and his friends. "Dad, they don't trust you. You need to give them something."

"I don't particularly trust them either," Ethos said, but some of the venom had gone out of his voice.

"But I do," Aksell said. He turned to Timothy and Jewel. "I don't know how you two got yourselves wrapped up in all this, but I do know you won't back out of a promise."

"If you show us where Crystal is being kept, we'll help you free the rest of the Council," Jewel said. "You have my word."

"Timothy?"

Timothy nodded. "Me too."

Ethos frowned. "Fine. Follow me."

Without another word, he turned and started off to the back room of the inn. As Jewel followed after him, Timothy dashed up the stairs, retrieving his gear from his room. By the time he returned, Ethos had already subdued the innkeeper, and with Aksell and Jewel's help, had pried open a hidden doorway.

Ethos noticed Timothy's wardrobe change, but he made no comment, disappearing down the dark, sloping tunnel.

* * *

"I need you to be completely honest with me, Aksell," Timothy whispered as they made their way down the winding passageway. "Is Ethos telling the truth?"

Aksell looked betrayed. "Of course he is. I know you don't trust him, but he really is a good man."

"Aksell," Timothy said. "This is important. If there's any chance that Ethos wants the Weather Belt for any purpose other than fighting off the Orgwar..."

"I've seen the messages, Tim," Aksell said. "He's telling the truth."

Timothy nodded. "Okay. I believe you." He hesitated a moment, then added, "You still think that we're the bad guys, huh?"

"You are the ones trying to overthrow the government."

"And the Council are the ones invading other countries in retaliation," Timothy said.

"It's more complicated than that," Aksell said. "You haven't had the training I have."

Timothy shook his head sadly. "No, Aksell. I haven't. I was trained by Samuel, not a member of the Council. And I trust him a lot more than I trust your dad."

Before Aksell could reply, Ethos interrupted.

"This is the place," he said, coming to a stop. "Right around the corner."

As Timothy and Jewel approached the bend in the passageway, Timothy glanced over at Ethos.

So far, he's shown no signs of betraying us, he thought. *Then again, Ethos is an excellent actor.*

Stifling his reluctance to turn his back on the head Councilman, Timothy peered around the corner.

On the other side was a medium-sized room with a series of several cages suspended from the ceiling. One of these was currently occupied by Crystal, and another, much to Timothy's surprise, was occupied by Madison and Quill.

Standing in the middle were a band of robots, scanning the room at regular intervals. Timothy ducked back into the passageway, trying to formulate a plan.

"What's the situation?" Jewel whispered.

"Looks like about fifteen robot guards," Timothy said. "Center of the room."

"Are they the same kind as the ones that you fought earlier?"

"As far as I can tell."

"Do you remember what you told me about that mission you and Henry went on?"

Timothy hesitated, glancing over at Ethos and Aksell, who stood a few feet away. "You mean the one with the drones?"

Jewel nodded. "How would you feel about doing something like that again?"

"You mean distract the drones while you free the others? It's worth a shot, I guess."

Jewel shook her head. "No. I distract the drones and give you a chance to get in behind them."

"Absolutely not. Jewel, I almost died last time. I'm not letting you get killed by these robots," Timothy said, his mind flashing back to when Jewel had been impaled during the Battle of Kawts.

Jewel smiled softly. "It's not up to you," she said, turning and running into the room. "Just make sure you destroy those robots!" she called back over her shoulder.

Timothy hesitated for a second, then ran out after her. The robots seemed not to have noticed him, their attention focused on Jewel. He skidded to a stop, assessing the situation.

Jewel isn't going to have long before those robots get her, he thought. *And I'm only going to have one shot at surprising them.*

Moving quickly, Timothy detached all the shurikens from his suit, launching them at the robots in quick succession. Seven of the robots fell to the ground, Timothy's shurikens finding their mark. The eighth one went wide, coming dangerously close to hitting Jewel. Timothy recalled the shurikens to his hand, even as the surviving robots turned to face him. He managed to drop two more of them before they turned and fled, escaping into the maze.

Timothy ran over to Jewel, helping her to her feet where she had fallen. There was a slight burn on her arm where a bullet had grazed her, but she seemed otherwise unharmed.

"Don't *do* that!" Timothy said. "You didn't even give me time to prepare! You could have been killed!"

"I knew you wouldn't let that happen," Jewel said, grinning as she tried to catch her breath.

"I hate to interrupt, but we really need to get out of here before those robots come back," Crystal said. "If you two would quit staring into each others' eyes and let us out of these cages, we'd appreciate it."

"Right," Timothy said, flushing slightly. "Hang on." He hurried over to the cages, sawing through the bars with one of his shurikens. With Jewel's help, they managed to get the others out in just a few minutes.

"You have no idea how good it is to see you, Tim," Quill said as he climbed out of his cage, retrieving his rifle and his pack from against the wall. "We haven't seen anyone else all day!"

"What do you mean, all day?" Timothy asked. "Have you seen the others? What happened to them?"

Quill's forehead furrowed, a puzzled frown crossing his face. "You guys are the first people Madison and I have seen since we woke up by that wall this morning. We tried to come through this maze and got stuck in here a few hours ago." He glanced around at the others. "Am I missing something?"

"Only a couple of days," Crystal said. "I woke up by that wall three or four days ago already."

"And Timothy and I have been stuck in this town for who knows how long," Jewel said.

"So we don't even know if the others are awake yet," Madison observed.

"Not to mention the fact that we could easily pass right by them in a place this big," Timothy said.

"We'll find them sooner or later," Jewel said, touching Timothy's arm.

"I hope so. In the meantime, we'd better keep moving."

"Aren't you forgetting something?" Ethos asked, entering the room with Aksell by his side.

Their newly rescued teammates reached for the weapons, but Timothy held up a hand to stop them.

"They're with us," he said. "For now, anyway. It sounds like the Council got themselves into a similar trap as you three did. We made a deal that they would show us where you were being held in exchange for us helping free the rest of the Council."

"With all due respect, that's a terrible deal," Crystal said.

"What's done is done," Jewel said. "I wasn't about to leave you down here."

"Touching," Ethos said. "The rest of my men are trapped in a room at the end of this hallway," he said, pointing to a doorway on the far side of the room. "I'll be waiting for you there if you ever decide to uphold your end of the bargain." With that, he turned and disappeared, muttering to himself in the darkness.

* * *

Idalbo paced restlessly across the tiny living room of their temporary base.

We need to figure out who the traitor is. Before it's too late. He began to walk even faster, glancing at the clock on the wall before remembering that it was broken. He shook his head.

Adalbo's bound to have explained the situation to the Kriegerhelden by now. We'll have to infiltrate the castle again. And this time I won't be able to help them. The Council's border guard has been on high alert since we

156

broke Omor out of jail.

Howard Kolt looked up from the amplifier he was tinkering with as Idalbo passed by him yet again. "If you keep this up, you'll wear out the floor," he observed, his eyebrows raised in amusement.

Idalbo ignored Howard's attempt at a joke and continued pacing, wracking his brains for a solution. *There's got to be someone who's been behaving strangely recently. There has to be! But who?*

Chapter 19

"Are you sure about this, Tim?" Quill whispered as the group walked down the hallway in the direction Ethos had disappeared. He glanced at Aksell, then added in a lower tone, "I mean, it's Ethos. You know he's not going to let us just walk away."

"He's kept up his end of the bargain so far," Timothy said. "We never would have found you three if he hadn't shown us where to look." He fingered one of his shurikens. "That said, it never hurts to be a little skeptical."

Quill nodded, sidling over to Aksell and striking up a conversation, though Timothy noticed his eyes didn't leave Ethos.

"This is the place," Ethos said, coming to a stop in front of a gaping doorway.

Madison pulled a lantern from her pack. The lantern flickered to life, revealing a floor that sloped downwards to a central point. Stepping carefully to avoid any unforeseen obstacles, she approached the room. Suddenly, Ethos darted forwards, shoving her out onto the sloping floor.

Madison slid toward the pit in the center of the room, the lantern falling from her fingers. She grabbed one of her whips, flicking it at Ethos. The weapon wrapped itself around his ankle, jerking him backwards into the room. Then the two of them disappeared into the pit, a distant tinkle of breaking glass the only sound that could be heard.

Quill didn't move, staring helplessly at the spot where Madison had been standing only moments before. All the color had drained from his face.

Timothy reached the door in an instant, only a little behind Jewel. He peered into the inky blackness, but he saw no signs of Madison.

"Madison?" Crystal called out, fear replacing cynicism in her voice.

There was no answer from the pit, and Timothy fought to keep his mind clear.

We can't lose anyone else, he thought, hoping against hope that Madison was still alive. *We have to get down there somehow.*

He started to step into the room, only to almost trip on a thin wire stretched across the doorway. He staggered backwards, not wanting to fall into the same trap as Madison had.

"Madison!" Quill shouted. "Are you okay?"

There was still no answer, and Timothy forced himself to put aside his concern, focusing solely on the solution to the problem. Even so, he couldn't escape the nagging dread that gnawed at the edges of his mind.

"First order of business is to get a better look at what we're dealing with," Timothy said, trying to keep the tremor out of his voice. He reached into the compartment of his chest plate, pulling out another lantern. He lit the wick, holding it overhead as he peered into the room. Despite the strength of the light, it barely illuminated half of the room, leaving the far side shrouded in darkness.

This isn't going to work. I need a better vantage point.

He glanced up at the ceiling of the room, which was only a few feet over their heads. An idea slowly began to form in his mind, and he turned to the twins.

"Jewel? If I threw this lantern up near the ceiling, could you trap it up there?"

Jewel thought for a moment, then slowly nodded. "I- I think so. Maybe."

"Good. Get ready." Timothy turned back toward the doorway, hurling the lantern towards the center of the room. A trail of blue light flashed past him, and the lantern stopped its arc, suddenly encased in a chunk of blue crystal that fixed it to the ceiling. From its new location, the lantern lit up the entire room, although the light was dim and bluish by the time it left its crystal sheath.

As the steeply sloped floor came into view, Timothy's eye was drawn to a horizontal beam running along the outside of the room.

That almost looks like a railing, he thought, frowning. He glanced down at the tripwire in front of him, then back up at the horizontal beam. He exhaled heavily, fixing his eyes on what was in front of him. Then he gingerly stepped over the tripwire and leapt across the corner of the floor, grabbing the edge of the railing with his hand. As he pulled himself towards it, he realized that there was a walkway behind it which was completely flat.

Timothy pulled himself underneath the railing, rolling onto the walkway. For a moment, he didn't move, breathing heavily. Then he slowly got to his feet, testing the ground to make sure it wasn't slippery.

"There's a walkway over here," he said, turning back to the others. "I think it'll give us our best angle for getting Madison out of there."

Jewel was by his side in an instant, Crystal following closely behind. Timothy removed a coil of rope from his chest plate, tying one end around the railing. The other end slid across the floor, vanishing into the hole.

"Someone's going to have to climb down there after her," Jewel said.

"I'll do it," Quill said, joining them on the platform. Before any of them could object, he tossed his stun rifle to the floor and slid underneath the railing, using the rope to control his fall. As Quill vanished into the pit, Timothy had a brief surge of worry that the railing wouldn't be strong enough to hold the weight of two people.

There's nothing I can do about that now, he realized, shaking off the thought. *Hopefully, the railing was one of the things they laced with invincium.*

The rope went taut, and several minutes later, Quill's head appeared above the edge of the pit, dragging Madison's limp form up with him. He had slipped Madison's ring onto his arm, and it glowed faintly as he pulled the two of them hand-over-hand up the rope. When he reached the railing, Crystal and Jewel pulled Madison onto the platform, while Timothy helped Quill up.

"How is she?" Timothy asked, dreading the answer.

"She's still breathing," Jewel said.

"I think she's just unconscious," Quill said, his gaze fixated on Madison. "I found her leaning up against a huge spike at the bottom of the pit. It looked like she slid down the side."

"It doesn't look like she's bleeding anywhere," Crystal said, helping Jewel to slowly lower Madison to the walkway.

"Did you find Ethos down there?" Timothy asked. "He might be able to tell us what happened."

Quill hesitated, taking his eyes off of Madison for the first time since he had emerged from the pit.

"About that… Ethos was actually impaled on the spike. But… he wasn't bleeding or anything." He glanced over at Timothy. "Tim, he was a robot."

"Where's Aksell?" Crystal said suddenly.

Timothy looked around, realizing for the first time that Aksell was no longer present. "There's something weird going on here," he said.

"We can worry about that later," Jewel said. "For now, we just need to focus on Madison."

Timothy swallowed hard as he watched everyone crowd around Madison.

I might lose another friend today, he realized, struggling to ignore the feeling of dread that stirred in his stomach. *The sooner we get out of here, the better.*

Chapter 20

"So what now?" Crystal asked. The little band had returned to the surface once more, and were sitting around a table at the inn. Aksell was nowhere to be found, having slipped away in the confusion.

"Ethos implied that there were other holding facilities under this town," Timothy said. "We might be able to find the rest of our team down there."

"Ethos almost just killed Madison!" Quill shot back. "AND he was secretly a robot! That doesn't exactly make him the most trustworthy source."

"I hate to agree with Quill, but he's got a point," Crystal said. "Ethos isn't trustworthy at the best of times. And if we've learned anything from this adventure so far, it's that nothing is as simple as it seems here."

"I'm with Timothy," Jewel said. "It might be a trap, but are we really willing to risk leaving one of our crewmates behind because the source was questionable?"

"Looks like it comes down to me," Madison said, looking from one side of the table to the other. She thought for a moment, then sighed. "We have to at least try to look for them," she said at last. "But I'm not spending the night in this town. I think we've seen enough to know that won't end well."

"Where would we even start?" Quill asked.

"I think the best place to start would be to check the back rooms of some of these other buildings," Jewel said. "Unless anyone has a better idea."

"Works for me," Crystal said, shrugging. She stood. "Now let's get moving before we all get hypnotized."

The group made their way outside, inspecting the row of buildings that lined the main road of the little town. After a brief debate, they decided to begin with the clock tower, working their way around from there.

After inspecting the outside of the building, they managed to find a door on the right-hand wall, which swung open easily when they pushed on it. Timothy took a cautious step into the brightly lit room, his staff and shuriken at the ready. To his surprise, the room seemed to be empty, except for three of their team members standing in the center.

Dr. Maddium looked up sharply as the door opened. His hair was more wild than usual, and his eyes were wide, making him look disheveled and slightly crazed. "Don't close that door!" he shouted, sprinting towards them.

Crystal reached out and grabbed the doorknob, stopping it just seconds before it closed. Dr. Maddium caught up to them, pushing the door open as far as it would go. Suorotiart and the Golden Knight followed him over, seeming to be in various degrees of madness themselves. Dr. Maddium held the door open while the others ran through it. Timothy followed them out, not quite sure what to think.

"What's going on here?" Quill asked, watching the trio's behavior with concern.

Dr. Maddium took a deep, shuddering breath, then slowly exhaled. "It's a simulated time loop," he said, looking up and down the street like he was seeing it for the first time. "We kept reliving the same moments over and over."

"How long were you in there?" Madison said, concern written across her face.

Dr. Maddium shook his head. "I have no idea. A few days at least, I think. It's all kind of blurred together." He put one hand against the wall to steady himself, breathing heavily.

"Have you guys gone through any other traps?" Crystal asked.

"And do you know what happened to Draagetsew and Gearwire?" Timothy said.

"Maddium and I met up shortly after we woke up on this side of the wall," the Golden Knight said. He seemed slightly rattled by the previous trap, but he seemed less affected by it than Dr. Maddium. "When we came into town, a strange man begged us for help - he called himself Ethos I. When we agreed, he tricked us into going into that room."

Timothy exchanged glances with Jewel, noticing how closely the Golden Knight's story paralleled what had happened with them and Ethos I's descendants - Ethos the Ninth and Aksell.

"I stumbled across them a little while after that," Suorotiart said. "Unfortunately, I didn't get the message to leave the door open until it was too late."

"Something weird is going on here," Timothy said, shaking his head. With the help of the others, he recounted what had happened to them since they arrived in the village.

"I think I can explain a good bit of that," Dr. Maddium said from his place by the wall. He seemed to have recovered somewhat from his ordeal, his familiar composure returning.

"The air here is laced with a chemical compound called L.O.T.U.S. It suppresses long-term memory and critical thinking. That's why you two were lulled into forgetting about the mission," he said to Timothy and Jewel.

"But how did they get a robotic version of Ethos?" Crystal asked. "Surely he wasn't around when this place was built."

"That's because of the trap inside the wall," Dr. Maddium said. "Those green crystals inside the wall - they were part of a mind reading technology pioneered by my old teacher. Working with some of Alpen's scientists, I developed a program that would enable the crystals to seek out and record the greatest fears, desires, and enemies of each person who entered the wall. It would then send that information to a processor hidden somewhere in this complex, where another program would arrange the available paths to fit them."

"What do you mean, 'fit them?'" Timothy asked.

"To test the character and intentions of each person who sought the Weather Belt, the program attempts to guide them to traps where they must prove that, should the good of the world require it, they can work with their greatest enemy, face their greatest fear, and surrender their greatest desire."

Timothy's mind flew back to the various challenges they had faced since they had reached the interior wall.

Almost everything that's happened over the last few days has made me face the possibility of losing another teammate, Timothy thought. *And Ethos is probably all of our greatest enemy. Did the program think living in this town with Jewel was my greatest desire?*

"So when we thought we were working with Ethos and Aksell…" Quill started.

"You were really working with robotic duplicates based on memories that the wall was able to pull from your heads. The fact that the five of you had extensive interactions with the two of them would have given it a lot more to work with - made it harder to realize you were talking to a fake. And since you knew that the Council had probably already reached the compound, you didn't think twice about it."

"How could they have pulled off such detailed physical replicas?"

Crystal said. "There's no way they already had an Ethos robot primed and ready to go."

"That's another part I had a hand in," Dr. Maddium said. "It's a hologram-based cloaking technology I got from my old lab partner. Gearwire has the same technology installed in his robotic legs, as a matter of fact."

Timothy nodded, remembering when Gearwire had transformed himself into Henry to scare off the Council during the Battle of Duncan's Ridge.

"So if we haven't run into a trap for all three of those things yet…" Madison said.

"Either there wasn't a trap in the complex that could be used to address it, or it's still yet to come," Dr. Maddium said, smiling sympathetically. "Or maybe you've already faced it and didn't realize it. It bases its judgements on what you actually believe to be your greatest fear, desire, and enemy; not what you consciously tell yourself to be the case."

"So which one of your greatest enemies is Ethos I?" Crystal asked, arching an eyebrow at Dr. Maddium and the Golden Knight.

"I admit, that one's a bit of a puzzle," Dr. Maddium said. "While I was involved in the fight against Ethos I, I never actually saw the man myself."

"And I can't recall ever having met him," the Golden Knight said. "Though he gave me a surprisingly strong sense of déjà vu."

"If you're done comparing notes, we have a lot of lost time to make up," Suorotiart said. "Need I remind you that the real Council is on their way here as we speak? If they haven't arrived already."

Timothy nodded. "Right. You three didn't happen to figure out what happened to Gearwire or Draagetsew while you were in there, did you?"

"No…" Dr. Maddium said, looking up and down the street once

more. "But now that I'm getting a good look at this place, I have my suspicions. Come with me."

Motioning for the others to follow, Dr. Maddium set off down the dusty dirt road, following the path out of the village.

"Do you know where we're going?" Quill whispered to Timothy as they walked.

"No idea," Timothy whispered back. He hesitated for a moment, then added, "But I think Dr. Maddium has seen this place before. Look at how confidently he's moving."

After a few more minutes of walking, Dr. Maddium came to a stop in front of a solitary farmhouse. He knocked on the door, and Gearwire opened it.

"We've been waiting for you to show up!" he said, a broad smile on his face. He beckoned them forward. "Come in!"

Timothy glanced over at Dr. Maddium, who nodded. Turning back toward Gearwire, Timothy stepped into the farmhouse, surreptitiously removing one of his shurikens as he did so.

The strange stuffiness of the room took him by surprise, causing him to cough several times. For a moment, he forgot why he had come. Then the sight of the others following him inside cleared his mind once more.

It's that LOTUS thing that Dr. Maddium was telling us about, he realized. *The air here is thick with it.*

On his guard once more, Timothy looked around the room. To his shock, several others had already gathered around the kitchen table, Henry among them.

"Quill! Timothy! I was hoping you would be joining us someday!" Gearwire was saying, motioning to the chairs behind them. "Please. Take a seat!"

Timothy's forehead furrowed. *How is Henry here? I watched him die. And what on earth is Gearwire talking about?*

"I almost forgot to introduce you," Gearwire continued, apparently oblivious to Timothy's concern. He gestured to the people accompanying him. "This is my original crew. Gwen Aria, Duncan Trevor - and you already know Henry. MacGregor had to run an errand, but he should be back in a few minutes. Officer Riss -"

"Gearwire," Dr. Maddium said gently, interrupting his introductions. "Gearwire, all these people are long dead. They aren't really here. They're robotic replicas stripped from your own memories."

"You still haven't figured it out yet, have you, Thomas?" Gearwire said, shaking his head. A bemused smile crossed his face as he added, "You and I are dead too. All of us here are."

Something in Gearwire's tone made Timothy pause. "Gearwire, where exactly do you think we are?" he asked.

A shadow flickered across Gearwire's face, but only for a moment. "We're in Heaven, of course."

Timothy shook his head. "We're all still in the Weather Belt complex. And none of us are dead."

"I know it'll take some time to get used to," Gearwire said. "It's a big transition."

Timothy glanced back at Jewel. For once, he was at a complete and total loss of what to do.

How do you convince someone he's not actually dead? And what if we can't convince him? We don't stand a chance of getting through this complex without Gearwire's help.

"Excuse me," Crystal said, pushing past Timothy. She walked up to Gearwire, then, before anyone could ask what she was doing, she punched him in the face.

Gearwire staggered backwards, his hand flying to the place where he had been hit.

"If you were dead, that wouldn't have hurt," Crystal said matter-of-factly.

"I… No. You can't trick me. I'm not leaving."

"Gearwire, you know this isn't real," Dr. Maddium said, coming to the front of the group. "I can see it in your eyes. This is just another trap in the Weather Belt complex - these robotic duplicates will coax you into staying here, until eventually, the gasses in this room will make you fall asleep. Permanently."

Gearwire shook his head slightly, his eyes wide.

He almost looks afraid, Timothy realized.

"Even if it is a trap, I'd rather stay here."

"I've tried to reason with you, Milkop," Dr. Maddium said, a warning tone in his voice. "I wanted you to make the right decision without any help. But as your friend and oldest remaining crewmember, I can't let you do this. We need your leadership to get through this compound alive. We need your experience in knowing how to stop the Council once we obtain the Weather Belt - the very monsters you and I both bear some responsibility for creating. The world needs you, Milkop."

For a long moment, Gearwire was silent, looking back and forth between his current and original crews.

"You should have let me die here in peace," he said finally. Without lifting his gaze from the floor, he unholstered his glue gun, firing it at the nearest of the robotic duplicates.

The robot sparked and fell to the ground, a gaping hole through its middle. Gearwire turned and looked at the fallen robot, seeing the metal and wires underneath the facade. He seemed to sag forwards as he spoke again.

"Let's go."

* * *

They made good time through the forest, emerging a few hours before sundown. The building in the center of the ruins loomed overhead, the top vanishing into the clouds.

Gearwire slowed to a stop just outside the door, the others gathering in a loose group around him.

"We'll set up camp here for the night," he said. Timothy glanced over at him. They were the first words he had spoken since they had left the village, the group having moved through the remaining traps in subdued silence. He seemed older somehow, and more tired than Timothy had ever seen him.

By the time their camp was set up, Gearwire had already disappeared into his tent, closing himself inside.

"Are we going to talk about what happened today?" Crystal said, breaking the silence that followed in Gearwire's wake.

"Yeah," Quill said. "That's the second time someone has called Gearwire 'Milkop' in the last few weeks. Is that the same Milkop who led a rebellion against the Council a hundred years ago?"

"That's not quite what I'm concerned about," Crystal said. "I'm more worried about whether Gearwire's going to be able to lead us through the rest of the complex."

"You should have listened to me earlier," Suorotiart said. "I said that it was dangerous to follow a man whose background you don't know into a place like this."

"As much as I hate to agree with Suorotiart, I think he has a point this time," the Golden Knight said, looking at Dr. Maddium. "Clearly, Gearwire's past is affecting the mission."

"Gearwire will be fine," Dr. Maddium said. "He's just had a pretty big shock, that's all. He'll be back on his feet in a day or so." He glanced over at Gearwire's tent, then continued in a lower tone, "Gearwire doesn't want me telling you guys any of this, so I won't say much. But at this point, it is affecting all of us. You deserve an explanation of today, at least."

"A lot of you have heard that Kawts isn't Gearwire's first fight. That's true. Me and Henry were part of Gearwire's crew during the Robot War. Our crew went on the missions too dangerous for anyone else to go on. We were the best squadron in the entire human army. The Security Council was so impressed by our skills that Gearwire was eventually promoted to overseeing the entire defense. We won the war. But most of our crew didn't live to see it. The deaths shook all of us, but they were especially hard on Gearwire. He felt responsible because he was the one in charge."

That trap was Gearwire's greatest desire, Timothy realized. *He wanted to be with his crew again. No wonder he was convinced he was in Heaven.*

"But why did you call him 'Milkop?'" Quill pressed.

"That part's not exactly relevant to what happened today," Dr. Maddium said. "Suffice it to say, that's the name he went by during the war. Whether he's the same Milkop you're thinking of, I will leave to your imaginations to decide."

"All I know is, he'd better recover quickly," Suorotiart said. "If he can't keep his head in the present, we might have to have the doctor take over."

"Just give him some time," Dr. Maddium repeated. "And remember, you didn't hear any of this from me."

With that, he turned away, disappearing into his own tent. One by one, the others also turned in for the night, no one breaking the silence that followed. As Timothy crawled into his tent, he couldn't help but think about what he had seen that day.

Gearwire seemed so sure he was in Heaven when we found him. I suppose I might have thought the same thing if I had woken up one day and Maurice and Henry were standing next to me.

He stared up at the fabric overhead. *Both of them seemed so sure there was a real place like that waiting for them.* He sighed, shaking his head.

I wish I could believe it myself.

Chapter 21

Timothy sat up, hearing the low murmur of voices outside his tent. As he crawled outside, he spotted Gearwire and Dr. Maddium standing near the entrance of the room, deep in conversation. Slipping on his armor, he made his way over to where they stood.

"I don't know. No one's seen him in a while," Dr. Maddium said as Timothy approached.

Gearwire sighed. "I don't like it. This place is dangerous. And he has our only map."

"We've gotten this far without one," Dr. Maddium said. "It wouldn't be ideal, but we could pull it off in a pinch."

"How are you feeling this morning, Gearwire?" Timothy asked. Gearwire and Dr. Maddium started violently, noticing his presence for the first time.

"Don't *do* that, Timothy!" Gearwire gasped, the barest hint of a Scottish accent creeping into his voice.

"Sorry," Timothy said, giving him a sympathetic smile. "Force of habit, I guess. But how are you doing?"

"I've had better days," Gearwire said with a haggard smile. "But I think I have everything straight again." He looked over at Timothy. "You didn't happen to see Draagetsew at all the last couple of days, have you?"

Timothy shook his head. "Not since we went through the wall."

Gearwire nodded slowly. "That's what I thought. We're going to have to go in blind."

"Speaking of which," Dr. Maddium said, turning to Timothy. "Would you mind waking the others? I've got just enough fuel stashed away in the Infini-case to get one more fire going. We might as well have one last hot meal now that we're mostly back together again."

Timothy nodded and slipped back to the camp. It took him only a few moments to rouse the others, and before long, they had all gathered around Dr. Maddium's fire.

Between Gearwire and Dr. Maddium, it took over an hour before the food was ready, although several large pots of coffee were made in the meantime. Timothy's stomach growled as the smell of pancakes filled the air.

They must have been saving this for today, he realized. *Things are only going to get more difficult from here.*

One of us might die today.

Around him, the others appeared to be having similar thoughts, the gaps in their friendly chatter filled by melancholy silence. It was nearly three hours after they had woken up that they finally began to pack up their camp, each of them reluctant to begin the next leg of their journey.

"So what's the plan?" Quill asked as Dr. Maddium packed the last of the cooking gear back into the Infini-case.

"There isn't one," Gearwire said, standing. "Without Draagetsew's map, we have no idea what we're walking into. We're just going to keep going through traps until we find Draagetsew or reach the Weather Belt."

"Or die in the process," Suorotiart said.

"Yes," Gearwire said. "Or die in the process."

Timothy glanced over at Quill and Jewel, trying to ignore the butterflies in his stomach.

Dying is not an option, he thought. *We've gotten this far. We can't lose anyone now.*

* * *

"Are you sure this is a trap?" Quill asked, staring down the seemingly endless, brightly lit hallway.

"Not completely," Dr. Maddium admitted. "But I think after everything that's happened so far, that would be a safe bet."

"It looks like we're just going to have to test it and find out," Madison said, reaching into her utility belt and pulling out a small, ravioli-shaped grenade. She tossed it out into the hallway, and it skittered across the floor. For a second, nothing happened, and Timothy began to wonder if it really was just an ordinary hallway.

Then the walls began to move, marching relentlessly towards the center. Dr. Maddium watched the process carefully, timing how long it would take for the walls to meet. After about thirty seconds, the walls crashed together, crushing the grenade and staying there for several more seconds before returning to their original positions.

Timothy stared at the mangled remains of the device, his heart sinking. *There's no way any of us are going to get through this before the walls close,* he realized with horror. *You can't even see the other side from here.*

"I don't think it's quite as dangerous as it appears," the Golden Knight said. He stared down the hallway, his eyes narrowed. "There's a notch carved out of the wall there," he continued, pointing. "It looks like it might be just big enough to fit a person."

Gearwire took out a pair of binoculars and studied the wall. For a long moment, he was silent, and Timothy felt his anxiety increasing as the silence lengthened.

"That's not the only one," Gearwire said. "They're spaced at fairly regular intervals along this hallway. It just might be possible to cross between them before the walls collide. But it seems that each alcove is only big enough for one person to fit at a time."

"How long did you say this death hall was?" Suorotiart asked.

"I'd estimate it at about a mile," the Golden Knight said, squinting off into the distance. "Is everyone going to be ready for that?"

"We have a little too much practice running mile-long races," Quill said, a smile tugging at the corner of his mouth.

Timothy frowned, his mind flying back to the annual races that had been a part of their lives in Kawts.

Last time you joked about The Race, you got turned into a Blank, he thought, but he said nothing.

For a moment, no one spoke. Then Quill gave a shout and charged into the hallway, sliding into the first of the alcoves just before the walls slid shut. Timothy held his breath as he waited for the walls to recede.

Come on, Quill. Come on!

As the walls retreated once more, Quill reappeared and dashed to the next hollow. A cheer went up from the rest of the Guardians of Kawts, and Timothy breathed a sigh of relief. As the walls slid shut, Madison stepped up to the doorway, preparing to run for the first opening the instant the walls retracted. Suorotiart then took her spot, followed by Crystal and Jewel.

"Quill's made it across," Gearwire announced as the number of people who had not yet entered the trap dwindled. He lowered his binoculars, stashing them back in the Infini-case. Then the walls opened, and he too ran out. Before long, only Timothy remained on the far side of the hallway. The next time the walls opened, he was already moving, barely managing to make it to the first depression before the walls collided around him, plunging him into complete darkness.

Despite what he had witnessed so far, he still felt a brief stab of fear as he waited for the walls to slide open.

What if they stay closed this time? No one will be able to get to me. I'll starve to death - or would I asphyxiate first?

He took a deep breath to calm himself. Then the walls opened again, and he sprinted to the next hollow.

This process repeated itself dozens of times over the next several minutes before the other side of the hallway finally came into view. As the walls clamped shut around him once more, Timothy realized with relief that this was the last hollow before he reached the other side. He tried to slow his breathing, which had degenerated into ragged gasps. He had only partially succeeded by the time the path opened again, and he sprinted for the end, mustering up all his remaining energy.

He was halfway there when he suddenly tripped, sprawling out across the floor as the walls continued their relentless march towards him. He quickly scrambled to his feet again and started to run, but the damage had already been done.

I'm not going to make it before the wall closes, he realized, a chill running up his spine. Then he pushed the thought aside.

No. I can still make it. I just need to run faster. He strained forward, but his body refused. He was already at his maximum speed.

Panic and despair washed over him as he watched the walls get closer and closer. But before they could crush him, Jewel dashed back out into the hallway, slightly blurred as the yellow band on her arm glowed faintly. She spun around to face the rest of the Guardians of Kawts and lifted her palms towards the door frame, encasing it in a sheath of crystal. The walls continued to grind onwards until they met the crystal barricade. They slowed to a halt, but it was clear from the fractures rapidly spreading throughout the crystal that it would not last much longer.

Timothy was only a few yards away from them now, pushing himself to sprint as hard as he could as he eyed the cracks snaking across the crystal boundary. Then, without warning, the crystal shattered, showering Timothy in fragments. With almost superhuman speed, Jewel reached out her hand and yanked Timothy inside just as the walls slammed shut behind him. He took two steps, then collapsed on the floor, gasping for air.

Timothy leaned up against the wall with his eyes closed, trying to catch his breath. Dimly, he was aware of Dr. Maddium and Suorotiart arguing about something, but he tuned them out. Quill and Jewel stood over him, concern written across their faces.

"Are you okay, Tim?" Quill asked. Timothy held up a hand to stop him. "Right. You need to catch your breath first. Sorry."

Timothy breathed in slowly, then exhaled in a rush. Quill extended a hand to him, and Timothy took it, pulling himself to his feet. Jewel hugged him fiercely, and after a moment of startled hesitation, Timothy hugged her back.

"You just saved my life," he said as Jewel released him. "Thank you."

Jewel took a step back, her face turning pink. "Someone had to do something. I couldn't just let you die." For a long moment, the two stared at each other, neither quite sure what to say next.

"Well, I for one, am glad you did what you did," Quill said, breaking the awkward silence. He glanced over at the rest of the Guardians of Kawts. "I think Dr. Maddium is probably ready to move on if you've recovered…"

"Right," Timothy said, nodding. "Uh… I think I'm fine now."

"We should probably get over there." Jewel said.

"We should," Timothy agreed, yet he didn't move. Jewel turned and walked back over to the rest of the group, leaving Timothy and Quill alone.

"I think she likes you," Quill whispered as soon as Jewel was out of earshot.

Timothy looked at him incredulously. "What?"

"And," Quill said with an impish smile. "I think you like her, too."

"Come on, Quill! That's absurd!" Timothy protested, silencing the voice in the back of his mind that had just been wondering that very thing.

"Is it?" Quill asked, raising an eyebrow. Then, before Timothy could say anything further, he turned and jogged back to the others.

* * *

Timothy lay awake in his tent, staring up at the fabric over his head. After making it through the hallway, they had gone through a few more minor traps before setting up camp for the night, stopping in a large maintenance room. As he lay there, trying to fall asleep, his mind kept coming back to what Quill had said.

Is it possible that I might have feelings for Jewel? he thought. *I guess we have been spending a lot of time together lately - ever since her injury.* His mind drifted back to their days trapped in the village.

I almost thought there was something there when we were at the inn. Then again, we were both drugged at the time. He shook his head.

Even if Quill's right, the middle of the Weather Belt complex is no place for stuff like that. I can't afford to be distracted worrying about it.

Pushing his thoughts aside, he rolled over and tried to fall asleep. He was on the verge of dozing off when a low mumbling sound caught his attention. He lay motionless, trying to determine what the source of the sound was. As the mumbling grew louder, he realized that the

Golden Knight was talking in his sleep, although Timothy couldn't quite make out what he was saying.

His curiosity satisfied, he allowed himself to relax, the Golden Knight's indecipherable mumbling lulling him to sleep. Just as he drifted off, he thought he understood a single word.

Ethos.

* * *

"What's this all about, Adalbo?" Revenant asked. "I thought we'd already completed our mission."

"Unfortunately not," Adalbo said, looking at the faces of his former comrades. "The Council returned to Blancstadt earlier this week. In Gearwire's ship."

"They weren't planning on going after the Weather Belt after all," Tapfer said, rubbing his chin.

"But why?" Loyola asked. "It's the only thing powerful enough to bring them down! Why would they just disregard it?"

Seililyad studied Adalbo's face. "You think they have a mole in the ruins."

Adalbo nodded. "It's the only explanation that makes sense. The only reason a bunch of people as shrewd as the Councilmen would ignore something that big is if they had another way to get their hands on it. The only thing that fits is that they have a traitor planted among Gearwire's crew."

"Just to be clear," Revenant said, raising his hand, "you're asking us to help you find out who, right? You're not accusing one of us?"

Adalbo shook his head. "I trust you guys. And even if the Council could corrupt one of you, the odds that you would end up in possession of the Weather Belt are slim. No, it has to be someone in Gearwire's crew. They're too confident for it to be anything else."

"So what's the plan, then?" Seililyad asked. "We can't exactly spy on Gearwire's crew right now."

"It is a long shot," Adalbo admitted. "Our only option is to spy on the Council. See if we can find some correspondences between them and the mole. Howard Kolt is working on a signal amplifier in hopes that we can get a message through to the rest of the crew. But it would be best if we could give them some indication of who's behind this when we do."

"We'll keep our eyes open," Tapfer promised. Beside him, Loyola nodded in agreement.

"If we see anything suspicious, we'll let you know immediately."

"Espionage is all well and good, but sooner or later, we're going to have to launch another invasion of the castle to get our hands on the evidence," Inn said. "Unless you two think you can steal the proof we're looking for out from under the Council's nose without them suspecting you."

"That's a question for another day," Adalbo said quickly. "For now, we just need to figure out where they might be keeping such documents - assuming they exist. And if you happen to hear or see anything out of the ordinary, let us know."

Loyola nodded, his long tail twitching. "You can count on us."

* * *

"Is everybody ready?" Gearwire asked, standing in front of the thick metal door.

"We're as ready as we can be," Madison said. "Let's do this."

Gearwire nodded, slowly easing the door open.

As Timothy led the way into the dimly lit room beyond, Suorotiart knelt down a few feet away and began preparing one of the lanterns they had brought. He had barely gotten it lit before he was suddenly jerked out of sight, and the lantern was sent skittering away into the darkness.

Timothy's eyes widened as the light of the lantern revealed what was lurking in the room. Standing in a semi-circle around them were robotic animals of all shapes and sizes. A robotic tiger stood on top of Suorotiart, staring down at him. For a moment, no one moved. Then the robots charged.

Chapter 22

As the robots drew nearer, Suorotiart's muffled shouting drew Timothy's attention, and he turned to look at him. The robotic tiger on top of him raised its clawed paw to deal a finishing blow to Alpen's prime minister. Timothy's eyes darted between the tiger and the approaching robots, assessing the situation.

Suorotiart doesn't have a chance, he realized. *Not when he's pinned to the ground like that.*

As the first of the robots reached them, Timothy came to a decision, throwing one of his drone-shearing shurikens at the tiger as he ran towards it. The shuriken reached the robot and bounced off, skittering away across the floor.

They're made of invincium, he realized, the sinking feeling in his gut growing. He unslung his staff from the sheath on his back and threw himself at the tiger, striking it with the staff moments before they collided. There was a sickening crunch, and Timothy gasped and clutched his shoulder, waves of pain radiating through it. He rolled to his feet, watching warily as the tiger did the same. Timothy switched his staff to his other hand, keeping his injured arm close to his body.

The tiger leapt at him, and Timothy only barely avoided its claws. The band on his arm glowed brightly as he rolled under it, wincing as he landed on his injured arm. He jumped back to his feet behind the tiger, granting him a brief reprieve while the robot tried to figure out where he had gone. As it moved its head from side to side, Timothy was suddenly struck by an idea.

He leapt onto the tiger's back, letting his staff clatter to the ground. He collided with the robot with a jarring crash and began to slide off, but he quickly snagged his fingers in the gap between the robot's neck and its head. The tiger started thrashing violently, and Timothy's grip began to loosen. He popped a shuriken off into his hand and pulled himself up the robot's back, grimacing as the movement sent a fresh wave of pain through his shoulder. He gritted his teeth and made one more attempt to lunge forward, thrusting the shuriken into the gap in the tiger's armor.

Sparks emanated from the robot's neck as its legs buckled. Then, with a haunting creak, it collapsed, giving Timothy only just enough time to jump clear before it hit the ground. Breathing heavily, he slowly walked over to his staff and picked it up. He stood there for a moment longer, desperately trying to catch his breath. Then he charged back into the battle.

* * *

Timothy scanned the battlefield as the robotic hippopotamus he had been fighting crashed to the ground. Of what had originally been several dozen robots, only five remained. Out of the corner of his eye, Timothy caught a glimpse of Draagetsew entering the room and tackling a robotic grizzly bear in what seemed to be a relatively even fight.

To his right, Quill had just dropped a robotic shark with his stun rifle, firing his quarrel into the narrow slits that made up its gills. Dr. Maddium was facing off against a crocodile, pummeling it with blasts of crackling electricity from the gauntlets of his battle suit. Madison was fighting a robotic gorilla, and as Timothy watched, she flipped over its head, one of her electrified whips wrapped around its throat. Gearwire was engaged in a duel with a robotic ostrich, severing its leg and finishing it off with an upward thrust of his sword.

A movement to his left caught his eye, and he pivoted to see a massive robotic snake slithering quickly towards the place where Crystal and Jewel were lying, trying desperately to recover from their fight with a robotic wooly mammoth. He felt a stab of fear as he readied a shuriken, hoping that he wouldn't be too late.

As Timothy drew nearer, the twins struggled to their feet. The way they had been forced to use their powers against the mammoth had clearly taken its toll on them, and they swayed unsteadily, struggling to stay awake. A defiant light shone in their eyes as they turned to face the snake. But Timothy could tell by the look on their faces that they knew they had no hope of defeating this new threat.

Timothy threw the shuriken at the snake, readying his staff as he ran. The shuriken bounced off of the snake's invincium plating, and it turned, its glassy eyes searching for its attacker. Timothy threw himself at the robot, battering it with his staff in a dizzying blur. The snake swung its tail at him, but he ducked under it, severing the last segment of the snake's body with a well-timed cut with a shuriken. The snake flicked its tail at him again, and again, Timothy dodged it, kicking the tail back towards the robot.

As he advanced towards it, the robot seemed to retreat.

Good, Timothy thought, readying another shuriken. *Nothing is going to happen to Jewel on my watch.* For a moment, he faltered, surprised by his own thoughts.

The twins - he corrected himself. *I won't let anything happen to either of them if I can help it.*

He turned his attention back to the snake, but it was too late. The snake lashed out with its tail once more, and this time, Timothy was not fast enough to avoid it. The tail hit him in the chest with a painful crack, knocking him backwards onto the floor. Timothy gasped for air, his ribs screaming in protest. Before he could even realize what was happening, the snake had coiled itself around his body, slowly beginning to contract.

Timothy's armor began to buckle as the snake tightened around him, increasing the pressure on Timothy's injured ribs and making the fresh bruises on his shoulder flare up anew. Timothy jerked his hands upwards in a last, desperate attempt to regain control, but it was too late. His arms were already securely pinned at his sides.

As the snake tightened its grip further, Timothy fought to retain consciousness, struggling against the waves of pain and the awful pressure on his ribcage. Timothy closed his eyes, preparing himself for the end.

I guess I'll finally find out if Henry was right about an afterlife.

The pressure continued its relentless increase, and it became harder and harder to breathe. Then, to Timothy's surprise, it stopped. Puzzled, Timothy opened his eyes to see a thin layer of crystal coating the inside of the snake's coil. He looked up to see Jewel standing a few feet away, swaying with exhaustion. She gave him a weary smile before collapsing to the ground.

All thoughts of giving up were pushed from his mind.

There's got to be a way out of this, he thought, watching warily as cracks began spiderwebbing across the crystal. He imagined with horror what would happen if the crystal broke before he could come up with a plan. The snake would slowly squeeze him to death, shoving shards of crystal into his torso as it did.

No! Stay focused! Jewel gave you another chance to escape! You can't waste it! You have to find a way to....

He trailed off, an idea striking him. He touched the side of his leg, popping a shuriken off into his palm. He brought the shuriken as close to the snake as he could, watching with bated breath as more cracks snaked through the crystal.

I'm going to have to time this perfectly.

Mentally, he rehearsed his next move. The crystal shattered, and Timothy stabbed the shuriken upwards into a gap in the snake's armor, grimacing as the crystal shards sliced into his skin through the gaps in his armor.

The snake continued to try to contract, pressing the shuriken closer and closer to Timothy until it was in danger of puncturing his own armor and stabbing him instead. Timothy pushed back with all the leverage he could muster, and the snake shuddered, then fell into two halves.

The bottom half immediately went limp, but the top half continued trying to strangle Timothy, seemingly unaware that it was now considerably shorter than it had been only a few moments before. Timothy quickly got to his feet, kicking aside the snake's lifeless form before driving the shuriken home into the uppermost gap in the snake's armor. The snake's head continued to try to slither toward Timothy, but the rest of its body was no longer responding. It lay there, unmoving, as Timothy wearily surveyed the battlefield.

Dr. Maddium and Madison had teamed up against a robotic sabertooth tiger, Madison holding it in place with her whips while Dr. Maddium bombarded it with blasts of electricity from his gloves. Draagetsew was fighting a robotic buffalo, having somehow dispatched the robotic grizzly bear he had been wrestling.

Only Draagetsew would be crazy enough to challenge a nearly indestructible robot in hand-to-hand combat. Timothy thought with a weary smile. *And win.*

A flash of movement caught his eye, and he turned to see Quill leaping into the air, grabbing onto the talons of a robotic hawk. The hawk flew upwards several dozen feet before it realized that it had acquired a passenger. Timothy's heart sank as it let out a shriek and dived suddenly toward the floor. Just before it hit the ground, it veered sharply upwards.

Quill twisted away from the ground, only barely avoiding a fatal collision. The hawk soared up near the top of the room, and Quill swung himself onto the bird's back. He shoved the muzzle of his stun rifle into a gap in the robot's armor and fired, letting out a triumphant shout. His exuberance quickly turned to terror, however, as he fell, plummeting toward the ground nearly thirty feet below.

Timothy ran toward him, but he could tell already that he would never make it in time.

And even if I did, there's nothing I can do to prevent him from hitting the ground.

A yellow blur flew past him and grabbed onto Quill, desperately trying to counter his downward plunge. Timothy realized with surprise that it was Suorotiart, his wings straining as he tried unsuccessfully to keep Quill from hitting the invincium-laced floor.

The two crashed to the ground in a heap, Quill's armband glowing fiercely. Timothy reached them just as Suorotiart disentangled himself from the pile, assessing himself for injuries. Timothy ran past him, kneeling beside Quill's prone form.

No. No, not again, he thought, desperately searching for any sign of life. He breathed a sigh of relief as he saw Quill's chest slowly begin to rise and fall. Draagetsew arrived by Timothy's side a few moments later, having just dispatched the last of the robots. One by one, Gearwire, Dr. Maddium, and Madison followed.

They were a sorry sight. Gearwire was bleeding from dozens of shallow cuts inflicted by a swarm of robotic bees. Dr. Maddium had a long gash on his lower leg. One of Suorotiart's wings was twisted at an odd angle, and Madison had a series of scratches on her arm.

"Is everyone alright?" Dr. Maddium asked, breathing heavily.

"Quill-" Timothy said, fighting back tears. "He fell from the top of the room. I think he hit his head."

Dr. Maddium's face immediately grew grave. "I'll see what I can do," he said. He looked around at the small group surrounding them, and his frown deepened. "The rest of you, see if you can figure out what happened to the others while I try to help Quill. If anyone has serious injuries, let me know."

Timothy wandered away from the group to search for the others, but his mind kept coming back to Quill. The rest of the Guardians of Kawts were weighed down by similar concerns.

None of them noticed the security camera hidden in the shadows in the top corner of the room. A small red light blinked on and off as it recorded the battle and its aftermath. Deep in the ruins, an ancient thing awoke and watched the footage, analyzing it for each person's strengths, weaknesses, and fighting strategies. Then its highly sophisticated mind began to devise a few strategies of its own.

Chapter 23

"We might as well set up camp here for the night," Draagetsew said as he returned to the makeshift hospital Dr. Maddium had set up around Quill. "I doubt we'll be in any shape to move on anytime soon." He set the twins down on the ground beside him, both still unconscious.

"Good idea," Gearwire said. "Why don't you, Madison, and Suorotiart start setting up camp. Timothy and I will help you as soon as we find the Golden Knight."

Timothy nodded and started after the rebel leader, wincing as the movement sent waves of pain through his bruised arm. Gearwire was silent as he scanned the room, his face a stony mask. Timothy tried to imitate him, but his concern for Quill showed plainly on his face.

Gearwire walked over to a robotic turkey and gave it a slight kick, nudging it aside. Finally, he turned to Timothy.

"I know this isn't something you want to hear right now," he said. "You've been through a lot fighting the Council. A lot more than someone your age should be put though," he added with a sad smile. "But I need you to be prepared. A fall from the ceiling of this room is almost guaranteed to be fatal. The ring that Draagetsew gave him will reduce some of the damage, but not all. Based solely on that, I'd give Quill only about a fifty-fifty chance of survival. That number could change based on what Dr. Maddium figures out about his condition, but his odds are still not good."

Timothy fought back tears as Gearwire finished speaking. "I don't think I can handle losing Quill again. Not after what happened to Henry."

Gearwire's face darkened. "I'm sorry, Timothy. I never should have sent you two to the gate. No one is to blame for Henry's death but me. I was the commander. I should have anticipated the Council's mobilization."

Images of Henry flashed before Timothy's eyes, his shirt bloody as he struggled to breathe. His final words had been to remind Timothy of his mission.

"Henry didn't blame you," Timothy found himself saying, much to his surprise. "He said that he wouldn't have missed fighting alongside you for anything."

Gearwire smiled faintly. "That sounds like Henry." He turned back towards Timothy. "But we were talking about Quill. If the worst does come to pass, you know that Dr. Maddium and I will be there-"

"I think I see something," Timothy interrupted, pointing to a gold-colored object lying on the floor beside a robotic ankylosaurus.

Gearwire turned to look, and Timothy breathed a silent sigh of relief.

I can't handle talking about Quill dying. Not yet.

"Good eye, Timothy," Gearwire said, picking the object up. It was the Golden Knight's shield. He glanced around the area, searching for any sign of his crewmember. Finally, his eyes came to rest on the broken robot itself.

Timothy followed his gaze, guessing what Gearwire was thinking. "You think he's under that dinosaur?" he asked.

Gearwire nodded. "Regardless of whether he's dead or alive, his shield ought to be nearby. And underneath the dinosaur is the only place I can see that might be able to conceal him from view."

"I'll go get Draagetsew," Timothy said, jogging off towards their camp.

Dr. Maddium limped out to meet him, his leg wrapped in a hastily applied bandage. "Did you find him?"

"We think he may be under one of the robots. We're going to need Draagetsew's help." Timothy turned to go back to Gearwire, but he paused. "How are they? The twins and Quill?"

Dr. Maddium sighed. "The twins will be fine. It looks like nothing more serious than exhaustion from over-exerting their powers. But Quill… I don't know. He's stable for the moment, but he probably has a concussion. And I think he might be in a coma."

"You said you found the Golden Knight?" Draagetsew asked, coming up to the pair.

Timothy nodded. "We think he's trapped under a robot. We need your help to move it."

"Let's go then," Draagetsew said, rolling his shoulders and stretching his arms. "Show me where."

Timothy led Draagetsew back to where Gearwire waited. Together, the three of them rolled the massive robot away, although even with Draagetsew's incredible strength, the robot was almost too heavy.

With the robot out of the way, the Golden Knight's body was clearly visible, his arm bent at an unnatural angle. Gearwire strode over to him, inspecting him for signs of life. "He's still breathing," he reported, standing. "Shallowly, but still breathing." He looked at the Golden Knight's arm. "I suspect he's gone into shock."

"I'll take him," Draagetsew said grimly, scooping the Golden Knight up in his arms and carrying him back to their camp.

Dr. Maddium gave him a thorough examination. "I think I agree with Gearwire," he said. "His armor seems to have spared him the worst of the pressure. But his arm is definitely broken. As long as we can keep him from going into shock, he should be fine."

The most serious injuries treated as best he could, Dr. Maddium turned his attention to the others, doing his best to patch them up. Quill and the Golden Knight were moved into a larger tent in the center of the camp, where Dr. Maddium could keep a close eye on their conditions. Time seemed to crawl by, and it seemed like weeks had passed before night finally arrived.

* * *

Timothy and Madison were sitting by Quill's side when Gearwire entered the hospital tent around midnight.

"How are they doing?" Gearwire asked.

Dr. Maddium sighed wearily and turned to face him. "They haven't changed since we found them. No better, no worse." His voice broke. "I just - I don't know what to do. I should have paid more attention to medical matters."

"You've done all you can," Gearwire said. "Why don't you turn in for the night. I can keep an eye on them for a few hours."

Dr. Maddium started to protest, but Gearwire put his hand on his shoulder. "You're exhausted, Thomas. You need to sleep. Go to bed."

"You're right," Dr. Maddium said after a long pause. He slowly got to his feet and ducked out of the tent. "Thank you."

"You two should try to get some sleep, too," Gearwire said, turning to Timothy and Madison.

Timothy shook his head. "I need to be here with Quill. In case something happens."

Gearwire nodded. "I suspected you might say that." He reached outside the tent and pulled out two rolls of blankets. He tossed one to Timothy and one to Madison. "I brought your bedrolls. I'll wake you up if anything changes."

After a moment's hesitation, Timothy accepted the blankets, unrolling them onto the ground. The last thing he saw before he fell asleep was Gearwire praying between his injured crewmembers, tears streaming down his face.

** * **

Adalbo leaned back in his chair with a sigh, rubbing his eyes. Papers were strewn about the table in front of him, detailing everything they could remember about each of Gearwire's crew members. All the Kriegerhelden, save Tapfer and Loyola, were gathered around the table, scanning the files for any hints about the traitor's identity.

Adalbo glanced at the file in his hand, then tossed it onto the table.

None of this makes any sense, he thought, shaking his head. *They've all proven themselves to be loyal to Gearwire time and time again. I've fought alongside each of them for far too long not to have noticed if one of them was a Council sympathizer.*

"I notice that there are a few profiles missing from this pile," Revenant observed, interrupting Adalbo's thoughts.

Adalbo turned to look at him. "Go on."

"We don't know for sure that the traitor is even in the ruins at all. He could be...."

"You suspect the Mysterious Man," Adalbo said, picking up on Revenant's hints.

Revenant nodded. "Aside from the Golden Knight, he's the one we know the least about. I mean, 'mysterious' is literally in his moniker. And he's one of the only two crewmembers who operate under an assumed name."

"Three, actually," Adalbo corrected. He considered Revenant's statement for a moment. "It's certainly possible," he agreed. "Technically, I can't even guarantee that it isn't Idalbo. And he has no sure way to clear me either. Everyone's a suspect until we can obtain a copy of the Council's communications with the traitor." He thought for a moment longer, then added, "But I think it's unlikely to be someone out here. They're too confident to trust their plan to someone who won't be there when the Weather Belt is retrieved."

"Unless they're bluffing." Seililyad said.

Adalbo nodded. "Unless they're bluffing," he agreed. "Which is all the more reason we need to find those documents as soon as possible." He turned to Inn. "Did Tapfer and Loyola say that they've figured out where they might be yet?"

Inn shook his head. "Not yet. They have it narrowed down to just a few places, though."

"Tell them to keep searching. We need more than just speculation."

* * *

Timothy sat up and opened his eyes. As he looked around the little tent where he had spent the last two nights, he was met once again by the same intense despair that had accompanied him ever since Quill had been injured.

Both of the patients had improved a little over the past day. The Golden Knight had regained consciousness and even gotten up and walked around, his arm in an improvised sling. Quill, however, remained unconscious, and Timothy knew that Gearwire and Dr. Maddium had already begun to tentatively discuss what they should do if Quill never woke up.

196

"How are you holding up?" Jewel asked, ducking into the tent.

"He's not getting any better," Timothy said. "Dr. Maddium thinks he's in a coma."

"I wasn't asking about Quill," she said, sitting down beside him.

Timothy tore his gaze from Quill's prone form to face her. "Quill is dying. And even if he isn't, he will be soon. It's only a matter of time before Gearwire decides we have to leave him behind. How do you think I'm doing?"

Hurt flashed across Jewel's face, and Timothy immediately regretted his outburst.

"He's my friend, too, Timothy," Jewel said. "And you know Gearwire isn't just going to leave him behind."

"Not even if the fate of the world rested on it?" Timothy shook his head. "He would sacrifice Quill in a heartbeat."

Jewel took his hand, clasping it between hers. For a long moment, neither spoke. "We'd stay back with him. If Gearwire decided to move on. You, me, Madison, and Crystal. And Quill."

Timothy turned back towards Quill, trying to conceal the tears that ran down his face. "It's just like what happened with Henry," he choked out at last. "I couldn't get to him in time, and now I'm going to have to watch him die."

"What happened to Henry wasn't your fault," Jewel said with a surprising fierceness. "And neither is what happened to Quill. And besides, Henry's in a better place now."

"But what about Quill?" Timothy said bitterly. "Even if Henry was right, what would happen to Quill if he died right now?"

Jewel was silent, and Timothy looked over to see tears pooling in her eyes. Neither of them spoke again until Gearwire called everyone out for breakfast.

The day dragged on, and still, Quill seemed no closer to recovery. Everyone took turns visiting Quill and monitoring his condition.

Timothy, Madison, and Dr. Maddium remained in the tent for the entire day, Dr. Maddium only leaving when Gearwire again ordered him to rest late that night.

Timothy was awakened in the middle of the night by a desperate shout from Madison. Even before he opened his eyes, he knew that something had happened to Quill. Part of him was tempted to just go back to sleep and pretend for a few more blissful hours that this nightmare was only a dream. But even as he had the thought, a wave of guilt washed over him.

Quill might be dying right now, and you'd rather pretend he's fine than be present for what might be his final moments.

Timothy sat up, blinking as his eyes adjusted to the darkness. Quill's silhouette was dark against the lantern that Gearwire had hurriedly lit. Timothy felt a stab of fear as he realized that Quill wasn't breathing. Gearwire thrust the lantern into his hands, his face graver than Timothy had ever seen him.

"Hold this," he ordered, kneeling beside Quill. It took him only a few seconds to confirm that he had truly stopped breathing before he started to push down on Quill's chest. Timothy watched with a lump in his throat, hoping against hope that he wasn't too far gone for CPR.

Draagetsew burst into the tent, wild-eyed. He took one look at Gearwire and stopped cold. After standing there in stunned silence for a few moments, he knelt down beside Gearwire. Without saying a word, he took over the chest compressions, leaving Gearwire free to manage the others, who were beginning to gather outside the tent.

For nearly thirty minutes, Draagetsew continued to perform CPR, the rest of the Guardians of Kawts looking on with a sense of horrified helplessness. Several times, Gearwire and Dr. Maddium offered to spell him, but Draagetsew refused, grunting something about his heightened endurance. After what seemed like hours, Quill started to cough, and Draagetsew took a step back, ready to jump back in if necessary. But Quill continued to breathe on his own, although his breathing was shallow and erratic.

By the time the day was over, Quill had stopped breathing altogether a total of three times. Each time, he had been revived by Draagetsew, but it was plain to see that he was unlikely to survive much longer.

"The only thing left to do is pray," Dr. Maddium said when the Golden Knight asked about how Quill was doing. "Even if I had the best training and equipment in the world, I don't think there's anything I could do for him at this point."

* * *

When Gearwire entered the tent that night, Dr. Maddium was busy praying for Quill, his mouth moving soundlessly. Gearwire stood off to one side, not wanting to interrupt.

Dr. Maddium finished his prayer and looked up at Gearwire. "There's nothing I can do for him. Nothing at all," he said, tears beginning to form in his eyes.

Gearwire said nothing for a long moment. Finally, he said, "It's out of your hands, now, Thomas. You tried your best. All we can do now is wait. And hope."

"I know. I just wish there was more I could do."

Timothy, who had been unsuccessfully trying to fall asleep on the other side of the tent, felt his heart sink. Dr. Maddium's words had confirmed what he had already suspected - there was no hope for Quill's recovery. Ever since his announcement earlier in the day, a grim silence had settled over the camp, although Timothy knew that the others still clung to the hope that a miracle might occur.

Even if there is a being who could heal him, he clearly doesn't care enough to do anything about it, Timothy thought, remembering Henry and everyone else who had died at the Council's hand.

But what if you're wrong? A small voice in the back of his head nagged. *What if there is a being that could heal Quill? Isn't it worth a try?*

He sighed, rolling onto his back. *If there's anyone out there listening, please heal Quill.*

He waited a moment, listening to Quill's erratic breathing. There was no change.

Chapter 24

It was just before dawn when Timothy was awakened by another shout. He sat bolt upright, fearing the worst. To his surprise, he saw Madison, grinning ear to ear. Timothy's brow furrowed as his exhausted brain tried to figure out what was happening. A movement to the left of Madison caught his eye, and he turned to face it.

Quill was sitting up in his blankets, a dazed look on his face. He blinked in confusion, looking around at the inside of the tent. For a moment, Timothy was sure that he was dreaming.

"He's awake!" Madison shouted again, and Timothy put his doubts from his mind.

If this is a dream, it's a lot better than real life. And if this is real-

A smile spread across his face, and he hurried over to his friend, just in time to hear him mutter something about a dream. "Quill. How are you - how are you feeling?"

Quill stared at Timothy for a long moment, seeming to struggle to remember. Recognition flashed suddenly in his eyes. "Timothy! I'm fine, I think." He squinted. "There was some kind of robotic bird, right? I think I hit my head on something when I fell." He glanced around at his friends' faces, his eyes narrowing. "How long have I been out?"

"Nearly three and a half days, Quill," Dr. Maddium said, ducking into the tent. "You've been in a coma for three and a half days. We didn't think you were going to make it through the night."

"Well, I… uh - I feel fine now," Quill said. He tried to stand up, but Dr. Maddium stopped him.

"You need to take it easy. At least until I've had the chance to make sure you don't have any further injuries."

"And meanwhile, I suspect everyone else will want to hear the good news," Gearwire said, nodding to Timothy and Madison. "Why don't we go tell them while Dr. Maddium checks on Quill?"

Timothy flew out of the tent, his relief making him feel light as a feather. Madison and Gearwire were right behind him.

"Quill's awake!" he exclaimed when Jewel emerged from her tent, bleary-eyed. Jewel stared at him, Timothy's words taking a few moments to sink in. Her eyes widened as she realized what he had said.

"That's great!" she said, struggling to speak. "Is he - how is…"

"Dr. Maddium is with him right now," Timothy said. "But he seems completely fine."

Soon, the clamor in the camp rose to a deafening level as the Guardians of Kawts heard the news. After a few minutes, Dr. Maddium emerged from the hospital tent. He held a finger to his lips, trying to calm the noise.

"He's sleeping," he said. "He's weak, and he needs rest. But he's going to be okay." He smiled wearily. "Wake me up if anything changes," he said, then disappeared into his own tent.

As Gearwire addressed the rest of the Guardians of Kawts, Timothy realized for the first time how exhausted he was. The ecstasy of realizing that Quill was awake had already begun to wear off, leaving him with the emotional exhaustion of the last few days. Without bothering to hear what Gearwire was saying, he crawled into his own tent, falling asleep within seconds.

* * *

By the next morning, Quill had recovered sufficiently to move around freely. In fact, Dr. Maddium had been completely unable to find anything wrong with him. And so, after conferring with Gearwire and Quill, it was decided that they would set out again that very day.

There was a general air of cheerfulness among the Guardians of Kawts as they packed up their camp. Timothy allowed himself to relax a little, forgetting for one moment all they still had to get through. The camp was packed up in record time, and before long, they were ready to begin.

"What's next?" Quill asked brightly.

Draagetsew squinted down at the map. "It's hard to say," he said. "There's nothing printed here. It looks like someone jotted the label onto the finalized blueprint in pencil."

"Can you make it out?" Gearwire asked. "This place is too dangerous to walk into blindly."

"I'm not sure," Draagetsew replied. "Something about D.R. Lois Caving?"

"Let me see that," Suorotiart said, snatching the map from Draagetsew's hands. He examined it for a moment, tapping his foot impatiently. "That says 'Dr. Lars' Ravine,'" he said at last, giving Draagetsew a dirty look. "Lois Caving, indeed," he added under his breath, handing the map back.

Draagetsew shrugged. "Okay. Dr. Lars' Ravine it is. That still doesn't tell us much."

"Don't you know *any* of our history that isn't about your idol, Draagetsew?" Suorotiart shot back. "Dr. Lars was the scientist behind the technology that created mutantkind!"

"Be that as it may, I'm still not sure that helps us figure out the next trap," Draagetsew said. "What kind of trap would a rogue geneticist make?"

Dr. Maddium and Gearwire exchanged glances. "Hopefully, we won't have to find out," Gearwire said. "Let's try to get through this trap as quickly as possible."

"If you insist," Draagetsew said with a shrug, flinging the door open to reveal a massive ravine. Timothy swallowed hard as he stared at the dizzying drop in front of him.

"That looks dangerous," Quill observed, taking an unconscious step back from the doorway.

"Please tell me we aren't going to be climbing down there," Madison added, turning white as a sheet.

Gearwire frowned, then looked up at the ceiling. Timothy followed his gaze, noticing how the ceiling tiles rubbed back and forth over each other. "I'm afraid we don't have much of a choice," he said. "There's no way we'll be able to attach anything to those. At least not without a very serious risk of the rope coming loose or being cut off. It looks like our only option is down."

"I'll get the rope," Dr. Maddium said, turning back towards the entryway to rifle through the Infini-case. Gearwire nodded absently, staring down into the ravine. He seemed lost in his thoughts, fiddling with the hilt of his glue gun.

As he watched Gearwire's reaction, Timothy began to feel a glimmer of fear. *Something about this ravine has him worried,* he realized. He turned away from Gearwire and began double-checking his own weapons. *Anything that can make Gearwire that concerned has to be dangerous.*

Dr. Maddium returned with the rope, handing it to Gearwire. He accepted it with a nod, coming back to the present. "Suorotiart, we're going to need you to fly down the side of this cliff and see if there's anywhere we could stop before the bottom. I don't think this rope is long enough to reach all the way down," he added, examining it.

"I know, I know," the winged mutant said, already lighting one of their lanterns. As the flame flared to life, he grabbed it and flew down into the canyon, listing heavily to one side because of his injured wing.

"We're going to have to climb down," Gearwire announced once Suorotiart had gone. "Then we'll have to cross the ravine from the bottom and climb back up the other side." He looked at Madison. "Do you think you'll be able to make it?"

"I'll be fine," Madison replied, trying to keep her voice level as she met Gearwire's gaze.

"I hope you're right," Gearwire said as he turned toward Dr. Maddium. He whispered something that Timothy couldn't quite make out, and Dr. Maddium's eyes widened. A worried frown crossed his face.

"You think so?"

Gearwire nodded. "That, or something worse. Just be on the lookout."

"What's going on?" Timothy asked, taking a couple steps towards the pair. Gearwire opened his mouth to reply when Suorotiart returned, landing awkwardly on the edge of the cliff.

"There's a small ledge about thirty feet down," he reported. "And there's a larger one about ten feet below that."

"How many people do you think could fit?" Gearwire asked, abruptly switching his focus.

Suorotiart didn't answer for a moment, calculating. "No more than two or three on the first one," he said. "But I'd say almost all of us could fit on the second."

"Fly back down and wait for us on the first ledge," Gearwire instructed. "We can reassess the situation once we get down there."

"Sure thing, boss," Suorotiart muttered under his breath. Then he threw himself into the air once more, spiraling down towards the outcropping below.

Gearwire ignored the mutant's sarcasm and took the rope from Dr. Maddium, tying one end to the door they had just emerged from.

"What do you think is going to happen when we get down there?" Timothy repeated.

"It's probably nothing," Gearwire replied, his fingers moving with practiced efficiency. "Just keep your weapons handy."

"If it's something that could be that dangerous, we should know what we're walking into," Timothy insisted.

Gearwire tugged on the rope, slamming the door shut behind them. "Draagetsew? Could you give this a yank for me, please?" Draagetsew nodded and picked up the end of the rope, jerking it toward him. The rope pulled taut, but it - and Gearwire's knot - held firm. Satisfied that the rope would hold, Gearwire turned back towards Timothy. "I can't tell you what's down there because I don't know. But I did know Dr. Lars. He will have put something very dangerous in that ravine. I just can't say what."

Before Timothy could say anything, Gearwire turned back toward Dr. Maddium. "Thomas, I'll need you to hold down the fort up here while I take a look at the situation down there. Draagetsew, you're with me."

In an instant, he had the rope in his hand and was leaning out over the yawning cavern behind him. Then he was gone, rappelling down the cliff face with professional ease. After a few moments, his voice rang up from the ledge. "All clear! Draagetsew, you're next!"

Draagetsew approached the edge of the cliff and picked up the rope, beginning his own descent. He was quick with his four arms, but even so, he couldn't quite match Gearwire's speed.

Timothy craned his neck to watch as Draagetsew disappeared from view. He shuffled a little closer to the edge of the cliff, just managing to catch a glimpse of the four-armed mutant as he arrived on the platform below. Gearwire greeted him with a nod, then the trio began to examine the platform below them, huddled together as they planned their path.

Timothy stepped back again from the edge, fighting off a sudden attack of vertigo.

The less time I spend near the edge of the cliff, the better, he thought, wandering over to where Quill, Jewel, and Crystal were giving Madison a pep talk.

The minutes stretched on with no instructions from Gearwire, and he began to get worried.

What could be taking them so long? he thought, leaving his friends behind to risk another look over the edge of the cliff.

When he was only a few yards away from the edge, Draagetsew's voice called up from below. "All clear! Send someone else down!"

Timothy glanced behind him. The others were still deep in their conversation, trying to coach Madison through her fear of heights. Timothy turned back toward the cliff, shrugged, and walked to the edge, wrapping one end of the rope around his hand. He took a deep breath and leaned out over the yawning abyss. Slowly, he began his descent, grimacing as the movement put pressure on his still-healing injuries from the animal pit.

Draagetsew greeted him at the bottom, unwrapping the rope from around him. Timothy couldn't help but breathe a sigh of relief as Draagetsew called out for the next person to come down.

"Once they get here, you'll want to climb down to the next platform," he said to Timothy as the next crewmember began their descent. "Gearwire's already waiting for you down there."

Timothy nodded, leaning over the edge to try to spot Gearwire from above. His head swam, and he almost toppled forward into the void. He took a step back to steady himself, then looked over the edge again, more cautiously this time. A slight tremor shook the platform, and

Timothy jerked back just in time to see Draagetsew help the Golden Knight to his feet.

One by one, each of the Guardians of Kawts climbed down the side of the cliff, gathering together on the larger of the two ledges. As the last of them arrived, Suorotiart flew back up to retrieve the rope, starting the entire process all over again.

They made their camp that night on a larger-than-normal ledge a short distance from the bottom, Gearwire deeming it unwise to spend the night on the canyon floor.

* * *

Timothy's eyes flew open, suddenly alert. He lay awake in his tent, listening intently.

"You'll never win."

Timothy's eyes widened. "Ethos," the voice muttered. The sound died away into muted mumblings, then added, "too powerful."

It's just the Golden Knight, Timothy realized with a sigh of relief. *He's sleep-talking again. That seems to be happening a lot more since his injury.*

The mutterings continued, and Timothy listened idly as he tried to fall back asleep.

I think he's having a conversation with someone in his dream, he decided at last, noticing the lengthy pauses between some of the Golden Knight's words. *Or maybe it's a memory,* he thought. *He seems to say roughly the same thing every night. At least the parts I can decipher, anyway.*

As the Golden Knight's nightly ramblings died away into silence once more, Timothy realized that the warrior wasn't what had woken him up. He listened carefully, but silence had returned to the camp.

He was on the verge of giving up and going back to sleep when he heard the sound again. A low rumbling sound echoed through the canyon, only barely audible. It was followed by several rapid, scratching sounds that sent a shiver down Timothy's spine.

Picking up his staff from beside his head, he crawled out of his tent, peering over the edge of the outcropping in search of the source of the sound. The bottom of the canyon was shrouded in darkness, but Timothy thought he saw a shadow moving among the rocks. He shivered, but the noise did not come again. He sat on the edge of the ledge for another fifteen minutes, watching and listening, but to no avail. Finally, he sighed and crawled back into his tent, shaking his head.

Must have been my imagination, he thought. *Or maybe it was the Golden Knight after all.* He climbed back under his blankets and quickly fell back asleep.

But even as he drifted off, something began to move on the canyon floor below. It stared up at the distant light from the top of the canyon and let out a blood-chilling howl.

Chapter 25

Timothy sat in front of his tent, nursing a cup of warm water as he stared off into space. His thoughts were once again on the strange noises from last night. The more he thought about it, the more certain he was that there had been something very real - and potentially very dangerous - behind the sounds. So when Gearwire left the circle of the main camp, Timothy followed him.

"Gearwire - can I talk to you for a second?"

Gearwire turned around, noting the concern on Timothy's face. "What is it?"

"It might be nothing," Timothy said. "But I heard some strange noises last night. I didn't see anything down there, but…" He hesitated, then continued, "I can tell you're concerned about something in this canyon. I thought you might like to know."

Gearwire nodded. "I would be very surprised if we were the only living creatures in this canyon right now," he said. "Thanks for telling me." He turned to leave, heading back towards his tent. Then he stopped and turned partially back around. "Timothy? Just keep an eye out. And keep your weapons close."

"Tell me the truth. What do you think is down there?"

"I honestly don't know. And that's what worries me."

Then he disappeared into his tent, leaving Timothy to wonder about the former rebel's words.

It took them half an hour to pack up their camp. Then the process of the previous day repeated itself, Draagetsew and Gearwire leading the way down ledge by ledge. It was still a few hours before noon when they reached the bottom of the ravine. The second Timothy's feet touched the ground, he unslung his staff from his back, ready to face whatever it was that he had heard the night before.

Gearwire noticed the action and pointed to a cluster of the thirty-foot-tall mushrooms that dotted the canyon floor. A trail of slime snaked through the fungi, reaching nearly halfway up their stalks.

Something definitely lives down here, Timothy thought with a shiver, scanning the forest as the others arrived one at a time behind him.

At Gearwire's insistence, they had lunch early, at the base of the cliff. He seemed reluctant for them to bring exposed food deeper into the forest, an observation which did nothing to calm Timothy's nerves. Before long, they were trekking across the canyon floor, Timothy mimicking Gearwire and Dr. Maddium in their wary watchfulness. An hour into their march, however, they had yet to see any further evidence of life, and Timothy began to relax.

Maybe whatever was making all that noise last night has moved on. He inched his way to the front of the column to ask Gearwire about it when suddenly, Gearwire's radio crackled to life.

"......ear me?" a voice garbled over the radio.

"We hear you, Howard," Gearwire replied, his face grave.

"......gnal ....lis-en ......won't ......rep-" the radio crackled. "The...... mole...... ruins." There was static for several seconds, and Gearwire's frown deepened. Then the static cleared enough for them to hear one final word. "Beware."

The Guardians of Kawts stood in stunned silence, trying to make sense of Howard's cryptic message.

"How did he manage to get a signal through?" Gearwire asked Dr. Maddium, breaking the silence at last.

Dr. Maddium took his time before replying. "I'm not sure," he admitted. "My guess is that we're far enough underneath the invincium for it not to interfere with the radio signal. However..." he gestured at the walls of the ravine. "We're still under several hundred feet of rock. It's amazing that he managed to reach us at all. The only thing I can think of is that he might be using some kind of signal amplifier." He trailed off, deep in thought.

"The bigger question," Draagetsew said, "is what was he trying to tell us?"

Timothy opened his mouth to offer a suggestion when he was interrupted by a familiar rumbling sound, this time much louder than before. He spun around to see a massive earthworm, as tall as a semi truck and three times as long, covered in a shell of compacted dirt. It bore down on him, bending mushroom stalks and leaving behind a slimy trail in its wake. Timothy dove out of the beast's path, rolling to his feet and pulling out one of his shurikens.

To his surprise, however, the worm seemed to have no interest in attacking him, continuing to barrel through the forest. From his new vantage point, Timothy could see why. Close behind the worm ran a pack of moles, about the size of large dogs. They pursued the worm, slashing at it with their claws. The worm sped up, gradually beginning to put some distance between it and the moles.

The moles began to slow down, noticing the Guardians of Kawts for the first time. Slowly, they fanned out between the mushroom stalks, creeping around the group.

They're planning to attack us! Timothy realized with sudden clarity.

"Gearwire? I think we need to-" He cut off as one of the moles jumped on him from behind. Timothy twisted out from under it, swinging his staff into the mole's head as he did. The mole staggered backwards as the other moles charged forwards, and Quill dropped one of them with his stun rifle, even as Gearwire glued two of them to the floor.

The moles retreated a few yards, eyeing them warily. Timothy glanced around, searching for a way out. *Last time I got into a fight with a pack of wolves, they almost killed me! I only made it out because Snipps decided to lend me a hand.*

A pile of boulders caught his eye, and Timothy realized the canyon wall was only a hundred yards away. He looked over at Quill, and he knew his friend was thinking the same thing.

"You guys start climbing," he said, jerking his head toward the wall. "Quill and I will hold them off."

"You can't fight them off by yourselves!" Jewel protested.

Gearwire examined Timothy, then Quill. "Timothy's right," he said at last. "He and Quill can handle this."

Still, Jewel hesitated, and Timothy took his eyes off the gathering moles to look back at her. "Go!" he said. "Quill and I won't be able to get out until you are all out of the way."

"I can help you."

Timothy shook his head. "The fewer people in that final sprint, the better. Trust me." The moles charged, and Timothy ducked under one of them, hitting it out of the air with his staff. "Go!"

Reluctantly, Jewel followed the others to the other side of the cliff. Quill and Timothy stood back to back, Quill's stun rifle flashing like a sparkler as he picked off any moles that got too close for comfort. Timothy elected to stick with his staff, the agility ring enabling him to dodge the mole's claws and to counter with his own blows before they even realized he had moved. After a few minutes, Timothy realized with dread that the number of moles was steadily increasing.

They've called in reinforcements somehow, he realized with fear as the moles charged again.

Timothy's face hardened into grim determination as he batted another mole from its path.

If the others don't get up the cliff soon, we're not going to make it, he realized. Keeping his eyes on the moles, he said, "Quill? How far are they?"

Quill glanced back at the wall. "About half of them have made it up to the first ledge," he reported. "But I don't think it's going to be big enough to hold everyone at once." He turned his attention back to the fight, his stun rifle buzzing like an angry hornet as another ball of crackling electricity shot out of it. He fell silent for a moment, then said, "Hey, Tim? What do you think happens after people die?"

Timothy glanced back at him incredulously. "Really? You want to discuss this right now? We're trying not to die right now ourselves!"

"I'm *thinking about it* right now," Quill said. "I've been meaning to talk to you about it since the animal room."

"Can't this wait?" Timothy asked, sliding past the claws of a mole and shoving it to the side with the end of his staff.

"Not if we don't make it to the cliff."

Timothy gave an exasperated sigh. "I don't know," he said. "They're dead. Probably nothing?" He looked back at Quill. "Why?"

Quill opened his mouth to reply, but at that moment, a mole jumped on him from behind, sending his stun rifle skittering away across the floor. The mole slashed at Quill's body, and Quill brought his arms up to shield his head from the attack, the band on his arm glowing brightly. Timothy tried to reach his friend, but more moles poured into the gap between them, pouncing at Timothy.

Suddenly, a flash of blue caught Timothy's eye, and Jewel appeared beside him, encasing the nearest of the moles in crystal. Timothy ran over to Quill, knocking the moles off him and helping him to his feet.

"You said it was easier if there were fewer of us," Jewel said. "But you forgot I had that speed ring. You don't need to worry about me getting in your way during the escape."

"Thanks," Timothy said, swinging his staff in a semicircle in front of him. "How far up are they?"

"Only a few minutes away from where they need to be," Jewel said, encasing another mole in crystal.

"They'd better hurry," Timothy grunted. "I don't know how much longer we can keep this up."

Suddenly, as if reacting to his statement, the moles withdrew.

Quill hesitated for a second, then slowly lowered his stun rifle. "I'm glad that's over. I'm not sure how much longer we could have held out."

"I wouldn't be so sure," Timothy said, watching the moles intently. "I think they're regrouping. We won't stand a chance."

Quill raised his weapon wearily. "How far are the others?"

"Not quite far enough," Jewel replied, glancing back at the canyon wall. "But we might have to risk it, anyway. With luck, enough space will open up in the time it'll take you to get there."

Timothy nodded. "On three, then." He counted to three aloud, never once taking his eyes off the moles. When he reached three, the trio ran for the wall of the ravine, Jewel quickly outpacing both of them. The moles hesitated for a moment as they watched them flee. Then they tore off after them, refusing to let their prey escape.

"I wish we would have had a ring like that for The Race!" Quill said as they watched Jewel scramble up the wall.

"Save your breath," Timothy gasped, his eyes darting behind them to the moles.

They're right behind us, he realized. *This is going to be close.*

The moles were only a few yards behind them when Timothy and Quill reached the wall. They both scrambled up the rock face, using whatever handholds they could find. Draagetsew reached over the side and pulled them onto the ledge just as the moles arrived, their jaws snapping just inches from Timothy's feet.

Timothy exhaled heavily, relief flooding him.

"We made it," Quill said, grinning.

"We made it," Timothy agreed, allowing a smile to touch his own face.

"Once you two are rested, we'll need to keep moving," Suorotiart called from the next ledge up. "We still have a lot of ground to cover today."

Quill leaned back against the wall, beginning to laugh. After a moment, Timothy began to laugh as well. It took them a few minutes to catch their breath before they resumed their trek up the ravine.

* * *

"So what was that all about back there?" Timothy asked as he and Quill waited on a ledge for their chance to climb.

"What do you mean?"

"You asked me about what happens after death in the middle of a battle."

"Right," Quill said, looking embarrassed. "Forget I said anything. It's probably nothing, anyway."

Timothy raised an eyebrow, his curiosity piqued. "What's probably nothing?"

Quill hesitated. Finally, he said, "While I was unconscious, I saw something. A dream or a vision, or something. I don't know." He stopped. "You're going to think I'm crazy."

"What did you see, Quill? Why are you being so cagey about it?"

"I saw a bright light," Quill said. "And then suddenly, I was in a different place. It was the most beautiful thing I've ever seen. And there were a bunch of people there, but I only recognised one." He looked Timothy directly in the eyes. "He was one of Gearwire's old crew members that we saw back in that trap. Kind of a stocky guy, with red hair…"

"Henry," Timothy said. "You're saying that you saw Henry?"

Recognition flashed in Quill's eyes. "I wondered if that was him. I wasn't sure. I tried to go to him, but something prevented me from getting over there. Then this being made of light appeared and told me I had to go back. That's when I woke up."

"What are you saying, Quill? That you saw Heaven? If this is a joke, it isn't funny."

Hurt flickered across Quill's face. "I don't know what I saw, Tim. I was hoping you would. You have a lot more experience with this kind of stuff than I do."

Before Timothy could apologize, Suorotiart shouted down at them to climb up the rope. Quill turned away from him, taking the rope in his hand. Timothy was left alone on the ledge, Quill's words still swirling in his head.

Chapter 26

"I still think it's a mistake for both of you to be here right now," the Mysterious Man said, looking out at their companions. "At least one of you should have stayed back in Kawts."

"If there's any trouble, my apprentice will contact us. Charles is a capable officer," Volker said.

"It'll still take you a while to get back there," Howard pointed out, looking up from the signal amplifier he was tinkering with. "Even if you reuse that short-range teleporter you found in Dr. Maddium's quarters."

"So what's the situation?" Samuel asked, cutting off a response from Volker.

"We know the Council has a mole in the ruins," Idalbo said. "Tapfer and Loyola have been keeping a close eye on them for the last several days. We were hoping they might be able to figure out how they were communicating and if they had any hard copies of their correspondence hidden anywhere. A few days ago, they finally narrowed it down to one possible location."

"Adalbo's going to be leading a raid in the next couple of days," the Mysterious Man said.

"I just can't imagine that anyone in Gearwire's crew could be a traitor," Samuel said, shaking his head. "Granted, I never knew most of them well. But still - they've always struck me as the most loyal people I've ever met."

"Even loyal people can be deceived," the Mysterious Man said, his face darkening. "Or manipulated. No one's immune."

The Mysterious Man's words hung in the air, and Idalbo couldn't help but wonder how the Council could possibly have corrupted a member of Gearwire's crew.

The Mysterious Man has a point, he agreed, *But for the most part, their primary concern is the safety of Kawts. How could any of them think betraying Gearwire is what's best for Kawts?*

Unbidden, a memory flashed into his mind of their initial attempt to liberate Alpen.

Unless one of them decided to take Ethos up on his offer. Could Gearwire have agreed to betray Alpen to protect Kawts? Or could someone else have done the same thing?

His thoughts were suddenly interrupted by a shout from Howard.

"I've got something!" he cried, hastily adjusting some dials on the signal amplifier. "Gearwire! Gearwire, can you hear me?"

"We...... you...ard."

"Gearwire. This signal might give out at any moment, so I'm going to have to talk fast. Listen carefully, because I probably won't have time to repeat it. The Council has a mole in the ruins. One of you is a traitor. We don't know who yet. We'll try to contact you when we find the culprit, but in the meantime, be careful. Trust no one. Beware of-" Howard cut off suddenly, frantically spinning a series of dials on the amplifier.

"Drat! I lost them," he exclaimed irritably, rocking back on his heels.

"Do you think they got the message?" Samuel asked.

"I doubt it. Not all of it, at least. The signal was pretty bad. We can't count on the fact that they know what's going on. The best-case scenario is that they now suspect something is amiss. I'll try to contact them again, but I suspect that they're in too deep now. I'd need considerably better tools to make a better amplifier." He shook his head. "I'm surprised that we were able to get through at all. They must've been near the outside of the compound."

"I can see if Revenant has the supplies you need," Idalbo said. "How long do you think it would take to build a more powerful amplifier?"

Howard shook his head. "I don't know. Gearwire did most of the work with the radio beacons himself. I'm learning on the job."

"It's better than nothing," Volker said. "Keep trying."

* * *

Timothy sat down in the center of their camp that night, near where the rest of the Guardians of Kawts had gathered. He replayed the day's events in his mind, his thoughts finally settling on how Jewel had come to their rescue. He glanced up at her, sitting across the circle from him.

Jewel smiled when she saw him, and Timothy smiled in return, a warm feeling washing over him.

Quill might have been right, after all, he thought, remembering his friend's words after the narrowing hallway trap. *I think I do have feelings for Jewel.*

You should talk to her. See if she feels the same way.

Timothy shook his head. *No. We're in the middle of a trap-filled complex right now. The last thing either of us needs is to be worrying about that.*

If you wait for the perfect moment, you're never going to find it.

Timothy took a deep breath, trying to calm the butterflies in his stomach. He started to stand, but then Quill spoke.

"What do you think your dad was trying to tell us down there?" he asked Madison.

Timothy quickly sat back down, hoping that no one noticed his face reddening.

"I'm not sure," Madison said. "But whatever it was, it must have been important. He sounded pretty urgent."

"Did anyone else hear him mention moles?" Jewel said.

Timothy nodded. "And the moles attacked us right after that. Do you think that's what he was trying to warn us about?"

Crystal snorted. "There's no way he could know about the moles! They weren't even in the blueprint! And even if he did, how would he have known we would be in the ravine when he called?"

"It's possible that he recorded the message earlier and let it broadcast on repeat," Dr. Maddium said, rubbing his chin. "That way he could make sure we received it once we got far enough down."

"I still don't buy it," Crystal said, shaking her head. "No one knew about the moles! He had to have been talking about something else. Maybe we misheard him."

"We might never find out," Dr. Maddium said. "We missed most of the message. Trying to reconstruct his message from a few garbled words is only asking for trouble."

"All we know for sure is that we have to 'beware,'" Draagetsew said. "That's the only thing we can do right now, anyway. Just keep our eyes and ears open."

* * *

Timothy pulled himself over the edge of the cliff, slowly getting to his feet. In front of him was a large, wide-open room, the bright light in the ceiling illuminating the silvery walls. In the center of the room was a row of short cubicles, the walls coming up to only about waist-height.

"What is it this time?" Crystal asked irritably as the last of the Guardians of Kawts pulled themselves over the edge of the cliff.

Draagetsew whipped the map out of his pocket with a flourish. But before he could share what it said, a voice came out of the ceiling.

"Please make your way to the nearest cubicle," the voice instructed. "No more than one person per slot."

Timothy glanced over at Gearwire, but the rebel general offered no indications of what he was thinking.

"I don't like this," Crystal said. "Last time we faced a trap like this, we got separated for days. We only just found everyone again."

"If we don't do what the voice says, we won't get to the Weather Belt," Gearwire said, shaking his head. "I'm not any more excited about this than you are, but as long as we're in the compound, we have to play by its rules, not our own."

He stepped away from the group, making his way to the first of the cubicles.

"Please make your way to the nearest cubicle," the voice repeated. "No more than one person per slot."

With one last look at his friends, Timothy made his way over to the cubicles, taking a seat between Gearwire and Quill. Once everyone had been seated, narrow walls rose up between them, sealing them in. A small computer panel lit up in front of Timothy as the voice returned.

"Welcome to the Prisoner's Dilemma. In front of you, you will notice a red button and a green button."

Timothy looked down at the screen, seeing the buttons in question. The voice continued.

"Each player will be given the choice between pressing these two buttons. If all players select the red button, the walls will come down, and they will be allowed to proceed as usual. If one player selects the green button, however, that player will be taken through a shortcut to the Weather Belt's chamber, and the others will be deposited into an extremely dangerous trap. If more than one player selects green, they will first be detained for an entire day, and then allowed to proceed as usual. Choose wisely."

Timothy pinched the bridge of his nose, running through the voice's instructions again.

I'm really just deciding whether I want to betray the others, he thought. *And deciding whether I trust them not to betray me.*

He bit his lip, thinking the situation through. Finally, he sighed. "No one on Gearwire's crew is going to press green. And I don't think Draagetsew or Suorotiart will, either." He reached out and pressed the red button. Immediately, the temporary walls around him lowered down, revealing the others.

"Timothy! What did you press?" Gearwire asked.

"Red," Timothy said. "You?"

Gearwire nodded. "So far, that's been the consensus. How about you, Quill?" he said, seeing the dividers around Quill's cubicle coming down.

Quill shifted in his seat, chewing on his lip. "I might have sorta pressed green," he said, wincing. "I'm sorry! I panicked and got the colors mixed up!"

Before Gearwire could say anything, the voice returned.

"All the results are in," it said. "All of you have passed. Except one."

The floor opened up beneath Quill's feet, dumping him down a chute to a cold, dark room below. Timothy hesitated a moment, then jumped down after him. He could hear the others shouting above him as he slid down the chute, descending into the inky blackness. Then the chute ended, and he fell, sliding to a stop on the ice-cold floor below.

Slowly, Timothy got to his feet, already starting to shiver. He exhaled heavily as he looked around for Quill, his breath visible even in the darkness.

"Quill? Where are you?"

"I'm right here," Quill called from behind him.

Timothy turned around to see him, standing with his arms crossed close to his chest.

"Are you okay?"

"I'm fine," Quill said. "You didn't need to come down here after me. I brought this on myself."

"I'm not leaving you behind, Quill." He looked up at the chute overhead, which had sealed itself shut once more. "Let's find a way out of here."

Before we both freeze to death, he added silently, trying to ignore the sudden fear that perhaps there wasn't an exit at all.

"We can use our bedrolls as coats," Quill said. "If we're lucky, that will buy us enough time to find the exit."

Timothy nodded. "We'd better start walking."

* * *

"I'm really sorry about this, Tim," Quill said as they marched on through the vast, cold room. He pulled his blanket tighter around him. "I really messed up."

"It's fine," Timothy said. "It was an honest mistake. We'll make it through this."

"It's not just that," Quill said. "I know I've been getting on your nerves a bit the last few weeks. Because I couldn't understand what you've been through with Henry and the Council and all that. It must have driven you crazy to hear me be so excited to fight them."

Timothy said nothing, resisting the urge to tell Quill that he was exactly right.

"I just wanted to do something myself to fight the Council. Sometimes it feels like the most helpful thing I did for the rebellion was get captured to allow you to discover my fate." He swallowed.

"But I get it now. When Madison fell in the pit… I realized for the first time that I might lose someone I… well, care a lot about," he finished lamely. "But you already had. You lost Henry, and your brother, and you even lost me and Samuel for a while. No wonder it bothered you so much to hear me going on and on about fighting the Council."

"I'm sorry too," Timothy said. "I've maybe been a bit touchier about it than I should have been." He shook his head. "You had no way of knowing what you hadn't experienced. Especially when I refused to talk about it."

Quill sighed, his breath rising into the air. "I'm glad we've gotten that sorted out," he said with a smile. "If we're about to die down here, I'd rather we be on good terms."

Timothy chuckled, for the first time in a long time. "Come on," he said. "We'd better find our way out of here before the others get too far ahead of us."

* * *

"I think we're going in circles," Quill said, shivering.

Timothy stared at the vast emptiness around them. "You might be right. It's hard to tell without any landmarks." He sighed. "We might as well set up camp here for the night."

"Tim, if we stop for the night, we're not going to be going anywhere," Quill said. "We'll freeze to death before morning."

Timothy nodded slowly. "You're right. Good call." He stared off into the darkness for a moment longer, then resumed his desperate march.

* * *

Where on earth are the walls? Timothy wondered. *We've been down here for hours!*

He shuddered as another thought occurred to him. *What if there are no walls? What if this just goes on forever?*

Timothy shook his head, clearing his mind. *What am I thinking? Of course this place has walls. The cold must be starting to get to me. Although now that I think of it, maybe it isn't as cold as I thought it was. I stopped shivering a while ago.*

They continued their silent march through the darkened room, both of them focused solely on putting one foot in front of the other.

After they had been traveling for several hours longer, Quill suddenly stopped moving, sitting down on the ground.

"Let's face it, Tim," he said. "We're not going to get out of here. We might as well take a break."

"Quill - hey, listen to me," Timothy said. "We're going to make it. You said yourself that if we stop, we die, remember?"

"What's the point?" Quill said. "We don't even know for sure if there is an exit."

"We can't give up," Timothy said. "Remember why we're here in the first place. We can't let the Council win. Not after everything that's happened."

Quill stared at him blankly. "Tim, there is absolutely nothing we can do to get ourselves out of this mess. I'm just sorry that I got the both of us killed."

Turning away from Timothy, he laid down on the ground. For a moment, Timothy was tempted to join him. But the thought of what would happen to the rest of their team made him hesitate.

What would it do to Gearwire if we died down here? Or Jewel? Or the others?

Mustering every bit of willpower he had left, he reached down and pulled Quill to his feet.

"We're not giving up," Timothy said. "There's too much at stake here. We're going to keep trying to get out of here until we can't move anymore, you hear me?"

Quill didn't respond, staring into the distance over Timothy's shoulder. A puzzled frown crossed his face, and for a moment, Timothy thought he was on the verge of passing out.

"Tim, there's a light over there."

"A light?" Timothy repeated, his brain struggling to grasp this new information. "What do you mean, a light?"

Quill grabbed his shoulders, spinning him around.

"A light," he repeated, pointing off into the distance.

Timothy squinted into the darkness. Sure enough, there seemed to be a light flickering in the distance, although it was faint, as if from a faraway candle. He rubbed his eyes, certain that he was hallucinating. But when he opened his eyes again, the light remained.

"The door," he breathed, his hope returning. "We have a chance."

With a renewed determination, they set off towards the light. Neither spoke, focusing all their energy on reaching it.

They continued walking for another hour, the light never seeming to get any closer. Several times, Timothy worried that it was a mirage, but each time, he shoved the thoughts aside.

Even if it is, he thought, his determination renewed, *I'd rather die fighting.*

Yet as time stretched on, it became harder and harder to continue. Each step became a struggle. But just when Timothy was beginning to think that they would never make it, he saw the door itself. A smile broke out across his face as he pressed on towards it, throwing open the door and pulling Quill into the warm, bright room beyond.

Chapter 27

A bright light shone in Timothy's eyes, and he flinched, muttering something under his breath. He heard his name, then felt someone begin gently shaking him. Reluctantly, he opened his eyes to see Draagetsew standing over him, grinning like a madman.

"He's awake!" he bellowed, and Timothy winced.

"Yeah, I'm awake," he said, sitting up. He spotted Jewel standing a few feet away, and a warm feeling washed over him.

"How's Quill?" he asked, turning back toward Draagetsew.

"Quill's fine," Quill said from behind Timothy.

"Are you two both okay?" Jewel asked, coming over to them.

"I'm fine," Timothy said, swallowing. "It was a bit dicey there for a minute, but we made it."

"And all without getting frostbite," Dr. Maddium said. "At least, as far as I can tell."

"Good, good," Timothy said, nodding. He turned to Gearwire. "How did you find us?"

"Draagetsew's map," Gearwire said. "That blast of cold air was enough of a hint as to which trap you'd fallen into. We had to go a bit out of our way to get here, but there wasn't anything too serious. We arrived earlier this morning."

Timothy pulled himself to his feet. "We'd better keep moving, then," he said. "It sounds like we have a lot of time to make up."

"Not quite as much as you might think," Draagetsew said. "If everything goes according to plan, we're less than a week out from the Weather Belt room itself. We're in the home stretch."

"If everything goes according to plan," Dr. Maddium agreed. "Which it rarely does."

Even so, Timothy couldn't help but grin at Draagetsew's announcement.

We're so close to the Weather Belt. And so far, we've all survived.

"It'll take a lot more than a week if we stand around lollygagging," Suorotiart said. "Let's keep moving. Before the Council catches up to us." Without waiting for a reply, he turned and pushed open the door to the next trap.

There was a humming noise, and the lights in the room suddenly flickered to life, revealing a control panel mounted below a massive screen. The words "Welcome to the Control Center" danced across it. Timothy craned his neck upward as he entered the room, staring in awe at the vast, futuristic space.

As soon as the last member of the Guardians of Kawts entered the room, the door slid shut, vanishing into the wall. On the other side of the room, another door opened up, marked with a sun-shaped crest.

"We must be closer than I thought! That's the emblem of the Weather Belt!" Draagetsew said, dashing off towards it. The others followed him at a jog, glad to have a reprieve from the endless line of traps. Only Gearwire and Dr. Maddium seemed wary of the room.

Timothy saw their concerned expressions out of the corner of his eye and slowed to a walk. When they were halfway across the room, the lights began to flash red as a siren began to blare.

"Self-destruct sequence initiated," a computerized voice announced. "Detonation in five minutes."

Draagetsew skidded to a halt, his eyes widening. "If this place blows,

Alpen is doomed!"

"I'm not particularly keen on being blown to bits, myself," Suorotiart said. "But if we can get to the Weather Belt before that timer goes off, we might still have a shot."

"You don't understand," Draagetsew said, grabbing his advisor by the shoulders. "Blancstadt is a lot closer to the compound than it was when this place was built."

Something clicked in Timothy's brain, and suddenly, he understood. "Blancstadt might get caught in the blast."

"Or at the very least, the debris field," Dr. Maddium added. "The amount of power needed to destroy an invincium building could very well level this entire mountain."

"What have we done?" Draagetsew said. "We came here to save Alpen, not destroy it!"

"It's just another trap," Crystal said. "And if that's the case, there has to be a way to stop it," she added, sprinting over to the control panel. A dizzying array of buttons greeted her, most of them unlabeled. She licked her lips. "This may be a little above my paygrade," she said, turning back to face the group.

"Let me take a look," Dr. Maddium said, joining her at the panel. He inspected the buttons for a few seconds, then began to type, his fingers a blur. Timothy watched the screen as the red countdown clock was replaced by a complicated schematic.

Dr. Maddium looked up at the screen himself, studying the diagram. "Most of these buttons are decoys, I think," he said at last. "But I can't shut off the self-destruct sequence from here. It looks like there's a second control panel in a room below this one. Both need to be deactivated at roughly the same time in order to stop the countdown."

Draagetsew groaned. "We'll never find the room directly below us in time! And even if we could, it might take days to get there!"

"I think it's a little easier than that," the Golden Knight said. He pointed with his sword to a small metal panel in the floor by his feet. "This panel moves. I'd be willing to bet that it covers the access hatch."

"Four minutes remaining," the computerized voice came again.

"We have to go, now," Suorotiart said. "If this place blows with us inside it, we don't stand a chance. The Council will win."

"They'll win anyway if we let Blancstadt get blown up," Draagetsew said, a look of resignation on his face. He turned to Dr. Maddium. "What do you need us to do?"

Dr. Maddium nodded sharply. "Draagetsew, I'm going to need you and Suorotiart to come with me to the lower control panel. And Quill, we might end up needing your stun rifle."

Quill nodded and joined Dr. Maddium at the strange metal plate. Draagetsew slid the plate out of the way, revealing a rusty metal ladder stretching down through a ten-foot drop.

"Crystal, I'm going to need you to deactivate the control panel up here. All the buttons you'll need are in the right-hand corner. They all seem to be labeled correctly."

"Got it," Crystal replied, examining the buttons in question. "I think I can figure it out."

"Good. The countdown will only be deactivated if both control panels are turned off within a minute of each other." He paused to glance down the hole. "Give me two minutes to get to the lower control panel, then deactivate your end."

"Three minutes until self-destruct," the computer informed them.

"Good luck," Dr. Maddium said, then he disappeared down the ladder, followed by the mutants, Quill, and Madison.

Timothy counted the seconds in his head as the timer continued to tick towards zero. He glanced over at the twins. Jewel was pacing back and forth in front of the control panel. Crystal was fiddling with a small sphere of crystal, rolling it over her fingers. Gearwire alone seemed calm.

"Fifty-nine… sixty," Crystal muttered. "That's two minutes. She looked down at the keyboard in front of her and began to punch in the deactivation protocol, slowly at first, but faster and faster as the timer ticked closer to zero. With only seconds to spare, she jabbed the final button, freezing the clock at twelve seconds. The number flashed on the screen for several seconds before it was replaced by another message.

"Congratulations! You passed!"

A low grinding sound echoed through the room, and another door emerged from the wall, even as the original exit slid shut. The diagram on the screen was replaced by a video feed of a small room. A dozen missiles flew into the room, all detonating at once. A flash of light came from the other side of the control room, and Timothy knew without turning around that the missiles had been detonated in the room that claimed to have been the path to the Weather Belt.

Imagine if we had listened to Suorotiart, he thought with a shudder. *We'd have been blown to smithereens.*

A loud pounding from the floor broke him from his thoughts. Timothy's heart sank as he turned to face the source of the sound. Somehow, whether by accident or by design, the metal plate in the floor had gotten sealed shut, cutting Dr. Maddium and those who accompanied him off from the rest of the group.

Chapter 28

"Hey! Hey you! Stop that!"

"Help! There's been a breach at the southern gate!"

From his hiding place across the street from the castle, Adalbo listened to the guards' footsteps as they ran to help Tapfer and Loyola fend off the imaginary attack. He nodded to Inn beside him, then ran out in front of the castle. He unfurled his wings and flew into the air, filling the air with a soft buzzing sound. He landed on top of the wall and quickly dispatched the remaining pair of guards with blows from the hilt of his sword.

He flew down to the gate and unlocked it, and Inn soon joined him inside the castle walls. The tentacled mutant grinned. "Once Draagetsew gets back, I think he's going to have to up security a little," he said. "Being invaded four times in just a few months is not a great track record."

"Let's just focus on getting that information," Adalbo said. "We only have so long before the rest of the guards realize that Tapfer and Loyola tricked them."

Adalbo took off into the sky once more, scanning the windows for any sign of the Council. Once he was satisfied that there were no Councilmen in the immediate vicinity, he landed beside Inn.

"We're all clear," he reported. "For now, at least."

Inn nodded. "Then let's make this quick." The pair ran through the halls of the castle, making their way to the suite that Ethos had claimed for his own. The room was a mess, papers scattered all over the massive desk that sat in the corner. A coat tree lay on its side near the door, the sheath of Ethos' sword still tangled on one of the hooks.

"Looks like someone left in a hurry," Inn said with a chuckle. "I'm flattered that he thinks we're that much of a threat."

"It'll backfire if he decides this is worth vaporizing Blancstadt over," Adalbo said, walking over to the desk. "Let's just get the proof we need and get out."

He moved one of the papers slightly, trying to catch a glimpse of the page underneath. His blood ran cold as he realized he was looking at shorthand messages between the Council and the mole.

With a quick glance back at Inn, Adalbo slowly moved the page out of the way. Emblazoned on the bottom of the page was a golden gear emblem. The symbol of the Golden Knight.

* * *

"There's no use pounding on it," the Golden Knight said, stepping back from the floor panel. "It's sealed pretty tight. Unless they made this panel out of something other than invincium, they're stuck down there."

"We're not stuck, per se," Draagetsew's voice came from beneath the panel. "We can access one of the traps from here. It might take us a little extra time, but there's only a brief detour from here to the main control room. We can meet up with you there."

Gearwire nodded, absently stroking his beard. "It looks like that might be our only option," he said at last. "What's the fastest way to get to the main control room from where we are right now?"

There was silence for a while, and Timothy began to worry that something had happened to them. Then Draagetsew spoke again. "There should be a door to your left. There's a room full of loose stalactites and floor spikes. Beyond that is a laser web. And then there's a room full of heat-seeking machine guns."

"Sounds fun," Crystal muttered.

If Gearwire heard her, he gave no indication of it. "Wait for us outside the main control room," he said. "I suspect we'll need to enter together."

"Or we'll have it cleared before you even get there."

"No," Gearwire said, shaking his head. "It's far too dangerous. Wait until we get there before you go in."

There was silence for a moment.

"Draagetsew?" Gearwire asked. Silence.

"Draagetsew!" There was still no response, and he recoiled from the metal plate, his irritation plain on his face.

"We'd better keep moving," he said, turning towards the remaining half of the Guardians of Kawts. "If we want to catch up with them before they get to the control room, we'll have to hurry." He set off toward the open door, maintaining a brisk pace that the others struggled to match.

By the time Timothy caught up with him, Gearwire was already staring into the next room. Just as Draagetsew had said, the ceiling was covered in stalactites, casting strange triangular shadows all around the room. Gearwire bent down and brushed away some of the sand that covered the floor of the room. A rusty, four-spiked piece of metal appeared, and Gearwire picked it up.

"Caltrop," he said, turning back toward the others. "Ancient people used them to cripple enemy horses and infantry."

He tossed the caltrop back into the sand. "Our best shot at getting through unharmed is if I go first to find a path."

The Golden Knight shook his head. "Let me. I'm the one wearing indestructible armor."

"I appreciate that," Gearwire said. "But I need something other than Draagetsew's impulsiveness to think about right now." A wry smile crossed his face as he gestured to his robotic legs. "Besides, I think I can handle a spike in my foot."

"As you wish," the Golden Knight said, retreating to the back wall of the room.

Timothy watched Gearwire set off across the sand-covered floor, slowly and methodically ferreting out the location of each caltrop.

"I'm glad you found your way out of the cold room," Jewel said, breaking the silence that followed.

Timothy looked over at her. "Me too," he said with a laugh, trying to avoid the sudden butterflies in his stomach.

Jewel smiled. "We were really worried, you know." She shook her head. "I kept telling myself that if I had just been a little faster, I could have made it through the opening with you before it closed."

"Don't worry about it," Timothy said. "Everything turned out fine." A thought popped into his head, and he asked, "You guys didn't happen to see us come out of there, did you?"

Jewel frowned. "No. You and Quill were both passed out on the ground by the time we caught up with you. Why?"

"When we were in the room, we saw a light that led us to the exit," Timothy said. "I thought it was the doorway to the next room. But now that I think about it, the door was closed when we got there. Weird, right?"

"I have my theories," Jewel said hesitantly.

Timothy raised an eyebrow. "Yes?"

"We were all praying that God would show you the way out," Jewel said after a moment's hesitation.

"You think the light we saw was God?"

"Not exactly," Jewel said. "From God, maybe."

Unbidden, Timothy's mind went back to what Quill had told him about his dream.

"How do you know it wasn't just a part of the compound? Maybe it was programmed to lead us out after we'd been in there for a certain amount of time."

"It's certainly possible. But who says those two explanations are mutually exclusive?"

Timothy frowned, thinking over what Jewel had said. Before he could say anything more, the Golden Knight appeared behind him.

"Gearwire's across," he said. "Follow me, and step exactly where I do."

With that, he was gone, retracing Gearwire's path to the other side of the room. Timothy and Jewel exchanged glances. Timothy shrugged and set out after the Golden Knight.

There'll be plenty of time to finish this conversation later.

* * *

Quill yanked on the hatch, but it remained stubbornly closed. He tightened his grip on the handle and tried again, but to no avail.

"We're not going to be able to get back through there," Suorotiart said. "I suspect that was kind of the point of the trap."

"I should have stayed with them!" Quill said, slamming his palm into the panel.

"They're all fine," Dr. Maddium said. "But we'll need to keep moving if we want to reach the control room at the same time as they do."

"Before they get there," Draagetsew corrected. "We'll have it cleared by the time they arrive."

Dr. Maddium frowned, but he said nothing.

"What's the next trap?" Madison asked.

Draagetsew glanced down at the map, then flung his arms out, gesturing vaguely to the wall behind them. "Behold - the ultimate maze!"

He took a step backwards, and the tile sank into the floor, revealing a twisting corridor beyond. A grin spread across the face of Alpen's president. "After you."

Dr. Maddium nodded and stepped into the maze, keeping his left hand on the wall. Draagetsew followed him, trailed closely by Suorotiart. Madison and Quill brought up the rear, trailing a few yards behind.

For a long time, the pair walked in silence, each lost in their own thoughts. Finally, Quill said, "Madison? Can I ask you something?"

Madison turned to look at him. "What is it?"

"What do you think happens to people after they die?"

Madison was silent for a moment. "You go to Heaven to be with God," she said at last. "Or the other place," she finished, breaking eye contact for a second. "Why?"

Quill hesitated. *Maybe I'm making too much out of this,* he thought. *Tim seemed pretty sure there's nothing after death.*

But Madison disagrees.

Steeling himself, he took a deep breath. "When I was in a coma," he started, swallowing hard. "I... saw something."

Madison looked at him quizzically. "Like a dream?"

Quill shook his head. "It was different than that. I felt like I was coming out of my body. I saw Draagetsew giving me CPR. And then there was this really bright light. I followed it. Somehow, I felt completely at peace. I came through the light into the most amazing place I'd ever seen. Everything seemed almost... more real, if you know what I mean."

Madison shook her head slightly. "I can't say that I do."

Quill shrugged. "Anyway, Henry was there. And a few other people I didn't recognise. And then there was some sort of being made of light, telling me I had to go back. That's when I woke up."

Madison was silent, and Quill felt something sink inside him.

I knew I shouldn't have said anything. She probably thinks I'm crazy now.

"Wow," Madison said at last. "That's - I don't know what to say to that, Quill." She fell silent for a moment, gathering her thoughts. "I think you died, Quill. And I think you might have met God." A frown flickered across her face for a brief second. "I don't know how it happened, or why, but that's my best guess."

"What does it mean?" Quill asked.

Madison opened her mouth to reply, but Dr. Maddium suddenly came to a halt, standing at the edge of a large pool of water. "We'll have to finish this conversation later," she whispered, then jogged over to the others.

By the time Quill arrived, Draagetsew and Dr. Maddium were deep in discussion.

"It's the second part of the maze," Draagetsew said. "It weaves in and out of the water. Fortunately for us, the air pockets are marked out on the blueprint."

"At least, they marked where air pockets *used* to be," Suorotiart said. "We have no way of knowing if the air's even still breathable."

"If only Omor were here," Draagetsew said, shaking his head. "He'd be able to scout out these passages in no time."

"But since he's not, we'll have to figure this out ourselves," Dr. Maddium said, activating his battle armor. "I'll swim over to the first air pocket and check its composition." As his helmet slid into place, he added, "Draagetsew? Which way am I heading?"

Draagetsew studied the map. "Two lefts, a right, another left, and then straight up," he said.

"Got it," Dr. Maddium said, wading into the water. "If I'm not back in the next fifteen minutes, assume that the air isn't safe to breathe."

"Good luck," Draagetsew said. Dr. Maddium nodded in acknowledgment, then dove into the water.

Nearly twelve minutes passed before he returned, emerging from the water like some sort of aquatic robot. His helmet folded back, and he took a large gulp of air. "It's a little far," he reported, turning to look at the others. "But it's not impossible. The air is fresh - I suspect it's being pumped in from outside." He looked at Draagetsew. "There's a sizable ledge over there, too - we can take the maze one section at a time."

Draagetsew nodded, a grin stretching across his face. "We'll be at the main control room in no time!" he exclaimed.

"Put anything that shouldn't get wet in the Infini-case," Dr. Maddium said. "Then follow my lead." He opened the Infini-case and passed it around. Quill deposited his rifle inside, then passed it off to Madison. When the case returned to Dr. Maddium, he snapped it closed, his helmet reforming around his head. Then he dove into the water, the others close behind him.

Quill swam after Dr. Maddium, following the trail of bubbles he left behind. Before long, his lungs began to burn, screaming desperately for air. He fought to keep himself from gasping. The urge to breathe became unbearable, and a swarm of bubbles escaped from his mouth. Just as he thought he couldn't swim any further, Dr. Maddium suddenly turned upwards, breaking through the surface. Quill joined him a few seconds later, gasping for breath.

A gentle breeze rippled across the water, and Quill suddenly understood Dr. Maddium's suspicion that the air had been pumped in from outside. As Madison and Suorotiart popped up beside him, Quill swam for the ledge, pulling himself ashore.

As Dr. Maddium and Draagetsew plotted out the next part of their route, Madison climbed out of the water a few feet away from Quill. When she had caught her breath once more, she made her way over to him.

"Anyway, about your question from earlier - I can try my best to tell you what I think the answer is," she said. "But it might be a little bit of a long story."

A loud splash interrupted their conversation, and Quill half turned around to see Draagetsew swimming off deeper into the maze. He turned back to Madison. "I think we have time."

Madison nodded. "Okay. So basically, the entire universe and everything in it was created by a loving, eternal being called God…"

* * *

For most of the remainder of the day, the five of them made their way through the maze, pausing in each air pocket for a brief rest. During these rests, Madison did her best to explain the story of the Bible to Quill. Quill peppered her with questions all throughout her explanation, which Madison answered as well as she could.

By the time they reached the last ledge, Quill was deep in thought, mulling over everything she had said.

"I know it sounds crazy," Madison said. "But I've seen too much since joining Gearwire's crew not to believe it."

Quill nodded slowly. "I get what you mean. It seems unbelievable… but it has to be true. There's no way what I saw was a dream. And then there was my recovery. And what happened when Tim and I were in the cold room." He looked up at Madison. "I don't know how else to explain it." He sighed. "I wish Tim knew all that too. He tries to hide it, but Henry and Maurice's deaths are still weighing on him. If he could see-"

"Sorry to interrupt," Dr. Maddium called from the other side of the ledge. "But I'm moving on to the exit now. It's two lefts and then straight down. There's an airlock down there that you'll have to seal behind you before you can enter the next room."

"Thanks!" Madison called back. Dr. Maddium nodded, then jumped into the water. "We should probably get ready," she said, turning back towards Quill. "I know it's a lot to take in all at once. If you want to discuss this more later, I'd be happy to talk it through with you in more detail."

"I'd like that," Quill said, nodding.

With Madison's words repeating in his mind, Quill walked to the edge of the water and dove in. Madison was only a second behind him. Together, the pair swam for the exit, pulling the door shut just as they ran out of breath. The water began to drain out of the box, and they both gasped big lungfuls of air. The exit door slid open, and they stepped out into the master control room just in time to see Draagetsew get kicked across the room by a giant robot.

Dr. Maddium tossed the Infini-case toward them. "Get your weapons!" he shouted, his palms crackling with electricity. "We're going to need all the help we can get!"

Chapter 29

"I 'm going to need to borrow some of your gear," Gearwire said as they approached the door to the last trap between them and the control room.

"Aren't we kind of going to need it ourselves?" Crystal asked. "I'm not sure I like the idea of going into a room full of heat-seeking machine guns without every advantage I can get."

"If I'm successful, you won't need any of your gear at all," Gearwire said. "I plan to take out all the guns before you four go in."

"And what happens if you aren't successful?" the Golden Knight asked, his voice not betraying a hint of emotion.

"If I'm not able to take them out, we may not make it to the Weather Belt. I don't know any other way of getting through a room full of heat-seeking machine guns other than destroying them first."

"What do you need?" Timothy asked.

"I'm going to need to borrow all of your rings," Gearwire replied, loading his glue gun with a fresh hot glue cartridge. "And I'm going to need to borrow your shield," he told the Golden Knight.

For a moment, no one moved, each contemplating Gearwire's proposal. Then the Golden Knight shrugged and passed his shield to Gearwire, who quickly strapped it onto his own arm.

Gearwire inspected the shield, which was white with a golden gear emblem in the center. He gave the shield a shake, and it began to shift, creating several small windows along the rim and a quarter-sized hole in the center of the gear. A blue energy field spread out over the shield's surface, crackling with electric energy.

Timothy felt his jaw drop, and Gearwire smiled slightly at his reaction. "Dr. Maddium added a few bonus features to the shield when he built it," he explained. "In case I ever needed to borrow it."

Timothy closed his mouth and slipped the ring off his arm, handing it to Gearwire. Crystal and Jewel did the same, and Gearwire accepted them without a word. He slid the rings onto his own arm, then turned and faced the door. He closed his eyes, and for a moment, he didn't move. Then he kicked open the door and ran inside, revealing the guns mounted at random intervals along the walls.

Timothy watched in amazement as Gearwire slid under a stream of bullets, all three rings glowing brightly. He fired his glue gun through the center of the shield, melting one of the guns just before it fired. Even before his own shot landed, Gearwire was on the move again, deflecting bullets from two other guns as he fired off three quick shots of his own. He slammed the shield into one of the guns, leaping backwards over another attack as he did.

He became a blur of movement, dancing away from every attack as if the guns were firing in slow motion. The shield became like an extension of his own body, working in perfect tandem with his weapon to take out the guns. Less than a minute after he entered the trap, Gearwire stood alone in the center of the room, the guns on the walls smoking in various states of destruction.

Timothy stared at him, his mouth hanging open. *That was amazing! Quill would be freaking out right now if he saw this!*

Gearwire rolled his head around, wincing as it popped loudly. "I'm getting too old for this," he muttered, walking back to the others and returning their gear.

"How did you-" Timothy began. "That was-"

Gearwire smiled softly. "I've wielded the rings before," he said. "And I've had a lot of practice with my weapons." He looked around at the group. "Shall we continue?"

Timothy followed Gearwire through the room, looking around at the still-smoldering walls. When they were halfway across, a loud click echoed throughout the room.

"Look out!" Jewel shouted, tackling him to the floor. A pair of bullets whizzed overhead, fired from a sputtering gun on the opposite wall. As the gun struggled to readjust its angle, Crystal froze it in place, trapping it in a chunk of translucent blue crystal.

Jewel and Timothy quickly disentangled themselves, scrambling to their feet. As Timothy's breathing began to return to normal, he locked eyes with Jewel. For a moment, neither spoke as they both stared at each other.

"Thanks," Timothy said at last.

Jewel shrugged. "I was the closest person to you. Anyone else would have done the same thing."

Jewel fell silent again. Timothy opened his mouth to reply, but closed it again. They both stood in the hall in complete silence.

"Oh, will you two just kiss and get on with it?" Crystal asked from the opposite doorway, breaking the silence. "We have places to be." Timothy felt his face flush, and he stepped back from Jewel as if stung.

"That's not - I mean, we're not - *I'm* not-" Jewel protested, but Crystal rolled her eyes.

"Oh, come on, guys. We've all seen the way you two are when you're together. It's not exactly hard to tell."

"We're just friends," Timothy protested, trying to ignore the slight hurt he felt at Jewel's vehement reaction. "That's all."

Crystal snorted. "If you say so," she muttered, turning away from them once more.

"Hey, wait! Crystal!" Jewel shouted, jogging after her. Timothy followed, noting the glint of amusement in Gearwire's eyes.

But before he could say anything, a loud crash echoed through the room, followed by shouts of pain and surprise.

"They're already in the control room!" Gearwire shouted, kicking the door open as he drew his glue gun. Timothy forced himself to forget about Crystal's comment, charging into the room with his staff and a shuriken at the ready. He slowed to a stop as he entered, searching the complex array of computers and cameras for the source of the sounds.

Near the center of the room, one of the monitors toppled over, revealing Draagetsew grappling with a nine-foot-tall robotic security guard.

"Timothy! Duck!" Quill shouted. Timothy dropped to the ground, and a bolt of energy flew over his head, smacking into the torso of another security robot. The electricity crackled across its chest plate, but the robot kept coming, protected by invincium armor.

Timothy swung his staff at the robot's legs, sending it crashing to the floor. Before it could recover, Timothy plunged his shuriken into a gap in the robot's armor. The robot twitched once and then fell limp.

"Thanks!" Timothy said, yanking his weapon out of the robot's neck. He ran deeper into the room, trying to make it to Draagetsew. Out of the corner of his eye, he saw another security robot swipe at him with a long staff. At the last second, Timothy twisted out of the path of the weapon, the hairs on the back of his neck standing up as the electrified tip of the staff swung past him.

Timothy pivoted and jabbed a shuriken into the robot's leg. The robot took another step toward him, its leg now dangling limply. It swung its weapon again, and this time, Timothy blocked it with his own staff. For a moment, they were locked in place, neither willing to back down. Then the robot lifted its good leg and kicked Timothy in the chest, sending him flying through a computer monitor and crashing onto a desk beyond it.

Timothy gasped for air, wincing as the movement sent waves of pain through his ribs, still recovering from his fight with the robotic snake. Winded though he was, however, he staggered back to his feet, anticipating a follow-up attack from the robot. He limped back towards the battle, his boots crunching over the shards of glass from the broken monitor.

The robot he had been fighting now lay on its back, one leg buckled beneath it. It was struggling to stand, seemingly unaware that it was damaged. Timothy finished it off with another strike from one of his shurikens, recalling both weapons to his hand.

As he tried to catch his breath, he saw Draagetsew out of the corner of his eye, being held in the air by his throat by a larger-than-normal robot. He clawed at the robot's hand with all four of his arms, but to no avail. Timothy ran over to him, although he doubted how much help he would be. By the time he arrived, Draagetsew was already making strangled choking sounds, his battleaxe falling from his hands and clattering to the floor.

Timothy ran to it and picked it up, lurching forwards as he tried to carry it. Quickly, before it could slip out of his hands, he ran toward the robot, slinging the axe into the robot's hip joint. The robot turned towards Timothy, reaching for him with another massive hand. Timothy dove out of the way, the hand smashing into the ground a few feet from him.

"Incoming!" Dr. Maddium shouted from somewhere behind Timothy. Seconds later, two balls of crackling electricity slammed into the robot's chest, dissipating in seconds. Dr. Maddium flew past, firing two more blasts from his gauntlets as he did. The robot turned, batting at him with its free hand. Dr. Maddium zipped back out of range, then flew directly at the robot's face.

At the last second, he pulled up, firing a blast of electricity through a gap into the robot's chest cavity. The robot's eyes faded to black, and it released Draagetsew, toppling over seconds later. Madison ran over to the fallen mutant, half pulling and half tossing him out of harm's way just as the robot hit the ground.

"Gearwire wants us to regroup by the entrance," Dr. Maddium said, hovering down closer to them. "We'll be more effective in fighting these robots as a team," he said pointedly, giving Draagetsew a stern look before flying off.

"I guess I deserve that," Draagetsew gasped, massaging his neck. "We'd better go," he added, yanking his axe from the fallen robot's side. Wearily, the trio jogged back over to where they had come in, joining Gearwire and the others in a semicircle of a defensive line.

Gearwire had positioned himself in the center of the outer edge, his glue gun in his right hand and his sword in his left. The remaining robots slowly turned to face them. The two groups stared each other down, neither making a move. Then the robots surged forwards, crashing into the Guardian's of Kawts' formation with startling ferocity. The Guardians of Kawts fought back, but slowly, they were forced to give ground before the robot's onslaught. Even with the numbers of robots steadily dwindling, they still found themselves pressed up against the wall after only a few minutes.

"Heads up!" Madison shouted, suddenly lobbing several small grenades at the robot's torsos. Timothy shrank back as the projectiles flew overhead. Some of them slipped through gaps in the robots' armor, exploding them from the inside out. For a moment, the robots faltered, their formation disrupted. Before they could recover, Madison leapt forward, her electrified whips darting among the remaining robots and pulling their feet out from under them.

The Guardians of Kawts surged forwards, finishing the robots off before they had a chance to recover.

As the dust settled, Timothy recalled his weapons to his hands. A low rumbling sound suddenly echoed through the room. Timothy tensed, waiting. Before long, another robot appeared, several feet shorter than the others.

"Greetings!" the robot said, raising its hands in surrender. "I am J37769Q. I will be assisting you with the remainder of your journey to the Weather Belt."

Timothy stared at the robot, slack-jawed. For a long moment, the Guardians of Kawts were silent.

"You appear confused," the robot said. "Feel free to ask me anything you wish."

"Is this some sort of double-trap?" Quill said, raising an eyebrow. "We follow you and you lead us to our deaths?"

The robot tilted its head. "You humans have very strange ideas. Why would I do that?"

"Because we're in a massive death trap that seems to be full of robots that are trying to kill us."

The robot straightened up again. "I see. Yes, that would be a reasonable assumption under the circumstances."

"So… Why exactly did you say you were helping us?" Crystal asked.

"I have been programmed to assist any who reach this point to obtain the Weather Belt."

Crystal nodded skeptically. "Sure. And meanwhile, you've just been pulling the strings from this control room and trying to kill us? Forgive me if I don't exactly trust you."

"I have no control over this compound," the robot said. "The security drones that you so recently decommissioned were in charge of that. I was installed by the builders of the compound to assist anyone who reaches this point. My programming did not allow me to power on until all the security drones have ceased to be operational."

"We - we're going to need some time to discuss this," Gearwire stammered. "Some of us are a little distrustful of strange AI's.

Especially when they live in the middle of a trapped facility."

The robot blinked. "Yes. Your concern is most valid, General. I will be waiting by the other door for your decision."

The robot slowly walked to the other side of the room. Timothy watched it go, frozen in place. Only once the robot was out of sight did the Guardians of Kawts begin to move again, quickly forming into a huddle.

"I don't like it," Gearwire said. "There's something off about this whole situation." Timothy stared at his leader, surprised by the note of fear in his voice. Something about this robot had clearly rattled him.

"I think he might be telling the truth," Draagetsew said thoughtfully. "There are legends that tell of a guide that will be sent to guide the worthy to the Weather Belt."

"I'm not putting my trust in an AI I don't know based solely on the testimony of an old legend."

Dr. Maddium bit his lip, turning a light shade of pink. "Gearwire, I have a bit of a confession to make."

Gearwire raised an eyebrow.

"There's a… a very strong chance that I was the one who pro-grammed that robot."

"You built an AI? After everything we went through?" Gearwire shouted, a horrified look coming into his eyes. "Why!"

"While you were working on the fail-safe devices, I was working on a project of my own. I developed a code that could be used to restrict an AI's movements. Restrict its access to information, make it unable to interface with code directly, that sort of stuff. Lars and a few of the other architects of this place approached me and offered to help me test the code for a project they were working on. I think this is that robot."

"But why would you be tinkering with AI's in the first place?"

"You know as well as I do that not all AI's are evil, Gearwire," Dr. Maddium said. "Some of them had more goodness in them than most men. I was trying to create something that could help us restore the world. This program was my Kawts."

"That's hardly reassuring."

"Why don't we give our new friend here a little test?" Draagetsew suggested, trying to alleviate the tension between the Guardians of Kawts' senior members. "As far as I can tell, there's only one path to the Weather Belt's chamber from here. I say we quiz the robot on what traps are left and see if he's right. We haven't taken out the map since we entered the room. He won't know we have a way to fact-check him."

Gearwire was silent for a long while, his brow furrowed in concentration. Timothy looked back and forth from Gearwire to Dr. Maddium, waiting with bated breath. After what seemed like an eternity, Gearwire spoke.

"How confident are you in your code?"

"There's a sixfold security system. If the AI tries to override any part of it, the others will wipe the entire program."

"And you're sure this is yours?"

"Eighty percent. I could make sure by asking it a few security questions I built into the program."

Gearwire sighed. "Let's test it, then. But at the first sign of anything suspicious, we're getting rid of it in whatever way we have to."

Timothy eyed Gearwire warily, slightly uncomfortable with the vehement way he had opposed Dr. Maddium. Gearwire marched off to the other side of the room, trying to track down the robot.

"What was that all about?" Quill asked, looking just as stunned as Timothy felt.

Dr. Maddium sighed. "He doesn't trust anyone who hasn't already proven themselves to be trustworthy. Fighting the Council certainly hasn't helped that." He shook his head. "He'll be fine once he starts to trust this robot. There were a couple AI's in our original crew, and Gearwire was their biggest advocate. I suspect he's mostly feeling a bit betrayed. After the Robot War, there was a general agreement not to make any more intelligent robots to try to avoid a repeat of…" he trailed off as Gearwire returned, the robot a few steps behind him.

"Good to see you again, robot-man!" Draagetsew exclaimed cheerfully.

The robot emitted a clicking sound. "I am not 'robot-man'. I am J37769Q."

Draagetsew frowned. "That's no good," he said, shaking his head. "No one's going to remember that. We need to give you a nickname or something."

The robot clicked again. "Standing by to receive nickname."

Draagetsew screwed up his face in a mask of concentration. "J37769Q… How about… Jeff?"

"Nickname accepted," Jeff said. "Rebooting." His eyes faded to black, remaining that way for several seconds. A whirring noise came out of his chest, then his eyes lit up once more. "Greetings! I am J37769Q, also known as 'Jeff'. I will be assisting you with the remainder of your journey to the Weather Belt."

"Brilliant!" Draagetsew exclaimed, rubbing his hands together. "What do we have to do?"

Jeff buzzed, then clicked. "There are three traps remaining between our present location and the Weather Belt. There is a river of acid, the lair of the Guardian, and the Weather Belt chamber itself."

Draagetsew pulled the map out of his pocket and examined it. "Right on all three counts," he said. "Welcome to the team, Jeff," he said, extending his hand. Jeff bent down and took it, shaking it gently.

Standing a few feet away, Gearwire's frown deepened, suspicion in his eyes. "Let's set up camp here for the night," he said. He glanced at

Jeff. "And let's set a watch roster. This close to the Weather Belt, we have to be extra careful."

Timothy moved off to the side to begin setting up his tent, still uncomfortable about Gearwire's uncharacteristic hostility.

He does have a good reason to be skeptical, I suppose. But still, he's not normally this edgy. I think he's giving Councilman Ray a longer leash than this robot.

As the Guardians of Kawts set up their camp, a red light blinked on and off in the corner of the ceiling. Once again, the thing in the center of the complex had witnessed everything that had transpired.

Soon, it thought. *Very soon.*

Chapter 30

"Let's get going!" Draagetsew bellowed, banging his axe on the ground as he ran through the campsite. "If we get started soon, we might be able to reach the Weather Belt tonight!"

Timothy rolled out of his blankets with a yawn.

At least it's a more reasonable hour this time, he thought as he checked his watch, remembering the last time Draagetsew had woken them up.

"Affirmative," Jeff buzzed, following behind the burly mutant. "I have downloaded the security footage from your journey thus far onto my hard drive. Based on my analysis, it would not be difficult for you to reach the Weather Belt by the end of the day."

Gearwire arched an eyebrow toward Dr. Maddium, but the scientist shook his head.

It's fine, he mouthed.

A little over an hour later, their camp was packed up again, and they were ready to set off.

"The next trap is the acid river," Jeff began. As Draagetsew approached the door, he added, "Be careful. The compound's systems indicate that-"

Draagetsew threw the door open and stepped inside, yelping in surprise as the acid began to burn through his shoes. The Golden Knight yanked him back inside as Timothy stared at the 'river'. The acid filled the entire floor of the vast room, becoming a massive lake so large that it lapped against the doorframe.

"-the acid has gradually eaten away at the invincium, creating a much wider pool than originally intended," Jeff finished without so much as a moment's pause.

"That's not a river anymore," Crystal said, raising her eyebrows.

"It certainly isn't," Draagetsew agreed, shaking the last droplets of the acid off of what remained of his shoes. "We're going to need a boat."

"There are no boats in the vicinity," Jeff said. "Additionally, the acid is strong enough to dissolve almost anything weaker than invincium in a matter of minutes."

"Thanks, captain obvious," Crystal said. "We need to find some other way to get across."

"I will run a scan for available materials. Please stand by."

Jeff closed his eyes, suddenly becoming silent, except for a loud whirring coming from deep within him.

Timothy and Quill exchanged glances. Suorotiart walked up to the robot and waved his hand in front of his face. "Hello?" he said, knocking on his shoulder. Jeff did not respond, and Suorotiart turned back to the others. "That is, without a doubt, the most annoying robot I've ever met!"

"He's trying to be helpful," Madison said. "And he did try to warn Draagetsew about the acid at the door."

Suorotiart snorted. "A lot of good that does if it can't get a sentence out in time to do anything about it. I say we leave the invincium tin can here!"

An idea tugged at the corner of Timothy's mind, and he looked up at Suorotiart. "Could you repeat that?"

"We should leave the old hunk of metal behind," Suorotiart said. "It's more likely to get in the way than actually do anything useful."

Timothy frowned, his forehead furrowed in concentration. He began to pace the floor, a hint of an idea just out of reach. Suddenly, he stopped stock still, as if struck by a thunderbolt.

"The robots! Their shells are made of invincium! We can use them as a raft or something!"

"Brilliant!" Draagetsew exclaimed, thumping Timothy on the back. Timothy staggered forwards, eyeing Draagetsew warily.

"Everyone, drag as many of the robots over here as you can," Gearwire instructed. "I'll glue them together. Hopefully, the glue will last long enough to get us to the other side." As the others dispersed to look for parts, he turned to Timothy. "Good thinking," he said simply before vanishing into the maze of computer monitors.

It didn't take long before the Guardians of Kawts returned, dragging the fallen bodies of the robots behind them. Under Gearwire's direction, Draagetsew arranged them into a rough square shape. Then, with workmanlike precision, he glued the seams together, resulting in a single solid sheet.

"Now let's get this into the water!" Draagetsew exclaimed, rubbing his hands together gleefully.

"There's one slight problem with that," Dr. Maddium said. "Invincium is a lot more dense than most liquids. This raft won't float. It'll sink."

Timothy's heart sank.

So much for my bright idea, he thought. *I've just wasted everyone's time for nothing.*

"Inventory complete," Jeff said. "Resources available: fifty security drones, in various states of disrepair. Three-hundred and two intact computer monitors. Seventy three-"

"We don't need you to give us an inventory of the room!" Timothy shouted. "We just need you to come up with a way to get across this lake!"

Jeff whirred, then turned toward the raft. "It appears you have already constructed a raft of invincium parts. Use it to cross the lake."

"Invincium sinks," Suorotiart said.

Jeff emitted a clicking noise. "Only if there is enough liquid to sink in. Based on the schematic of the compound in my database, I calculate that the acid cannot be more than three feet deep at any given point."

He bent over to examine the edge of the raft, his robotic body twisted at an awkward angle. "Your raft appears to be exactly one and a half feet tall. Adding another identical layer would result in the desired depth."

"We could use those staves they were using to push ourselves along!" Jewel said, snapping her fingers. "They're made of invincium too, right?"

Jeff nodded stiffly, straightening up once more. "Affirmative."

"You heard the man," Draagetsew boomed. "Gather up some more robots and those fancy sticks of theirs!" Without waiting for a response, he ran off into the room in search of supplies. It took them nearly another hour and a half to finish their project, finally pushing it into the acid an hour before noon.

Timothy grabbed one of the makeshift oars and began to pole the raft across the bottom of the lake. Jewel stood on the other side of the raft, avoiding eye contact. Crystal's words from the previous day hung over them, fueling an almost tangible awkwardness between them.

Sooner or later, we're going to have to talk about it, Timothy thought, risking a glance at Jewel. He sighed inwardly.

I wish I could discuss it with Quill, he thought, but Quill had been deep in conversation with Madison ever since the raft had started off.

It took them most of the afternoon to cross the lake, scooting along at a snail's pace as the invincium scraped against the floor of the trap. It was evening when they finally reached the other side.

Timothy stepped off the raft into the next room, his weapons at the ready.

"Your caution is respected," Jeff said, following him. "But unnecessary. This is only a waiting room. Challenging the Guardian is a task not to be taken lightly. This room has been left trap-free as a place for challengers to prepare for the penultimate trial."

"Well, what do you say?" Draagetsew asked. "Should we take on one more trap today?"

"This Guardian is a robot?" Gearwire asked, his eyes narrowing.

"Affirmative," Jeff said. "It has been watching all the security footage since you entered the building. It has studied your strengths and weaknesses, particularly those you exhibited during the battles with the other robots."

"Did you make this robot, too?" Gearwire asked Dr. Maddium.

Dr. Maddium shook his head, looking profoundly uncomfortable. "I don't think so. But it's a little hard to tell without actually meeting it."

"The Guardian is not permitted to leave the battle chamber," Jeff continued, talking over Dr. Maddium's response as if reading from a script. "I may accompany you into the chamber and answer any questions you may have, but I am not permitted to assist you in battle. The Guardian is the most dangerous robot in the entire compound, and it is among the deadliest traps. Once you enter the chamber, the door will seal shut until the Guardian has been defeated."

Gearwire stroked his beard thoughtfully. "Does this robot have any weaknesses we should know about?"

"I am not permitted to disclose the Guardian's weaknesses. But if I could, it still would not be helpful, as it has no recorded weaknesses."

"Can you tell us about the robot's abilities?"

"I am not permitted to disclose the Guardian's abilities before you enter the chamber."

Gearwire sighed heavily, his blue eyes stormy. He was silent for a long time. Then he looked up at the others. "Why don't we have a vote?" he said at last. "All in favor of attacking the Guardian tonight, raise your hand."

"Let's do it," Draagetsew said, rolling his shoulders and cracking his neck.

"Is there any benefit to doing this tomorrow?" Dr. Maddium asked. "One way or another, we're going to have to face this mysterious death robot. We might as well do it while we're still on relatively normal rations."

Slowly, the other Guardians of Kawts began to raise their hands. Timothy looked around at the others and raised his hand as well.

Looks like this is it, he thought. *By the end of the day, we'll either be dead or within sight of the Weather Belt.*

"I guess that settles it, then," Gearwire said. "We're going."

He started toward the door, followed by Jeff and Draagetsew. Timothy started to follow, but Gearwire stopped him.

"No," he said. "You five need to stay here. It's too dangerous. You still have your whole lives ahead of you."

"You didn't protest when we fought the Council's army with you," Crystal said archly. "Or when we fought those other robots."

"And one of you almost died on both occasions. The chances that we'll defeat the Guardian without losing anyone are slim enough already."

"We're coming with you," Madison said. "We're all in this together. And besides, we all have one of those power rings. We can hold our own."

Gearwire said nothing for a long time, staring at each of them in turn. There was a faraway look in his eyes, and Timothy couldn't help but wonder what their leader was truly thinking about.

"Fine," Gearwire said at last. "Just don't die."

He turned back towards the door and pushed it open. The Guardians of Kawts followed him inside, and the door slid shut, merging seamlessly with the wall. Timothy stared up at the enormous sphere in the center of the room, floating several feet off the ground.

"I've been waiting for you," the sphere said in a level, almost musical voice as it unfolded into a massive robot, standing several stories tall.

Timothy stared at it in shock, all secret hopes of an easy victory quickly forgotten. As he stood there, frozen, the robot began its attack, swiping at them with a hand the size of a bus. Timothy dropped to the ground in the nick of time, the massive hand whooshing by just overhead.

"I've been watching you for quite some time," it continued, swiping at the Guardians of Kawts again just as they started to stand up once more.

Timothy threw himself to the ground again, his heart pounding.

It's just toying with us, he realized with a sickening sense of dread. *It could have killed us all by now if it was really trying.*

"I know all your strategies," the robot continued. "Your strengths… and your weaknesses." A sneer curled over the robot's metallic face as it let out a spine-tingling chuckle.

Gearwire's eyebrows shot up in alarm. "Where did your people find this robot!" he yelled, a panicked note creeping into his voice as he jumped out of the way of another backhand.

"How should I know?" Draagetsew shot back, turning his head to look at Gearwire. A massive metal hand crashed into him with a sickening crunch, and Draagetsew dropped limply to the ground, sliding across the floor.

Gearwire ran over to him, but the robot slammed one of its hands down in front of him, blocking his path. Gearwire scrambled backwards, eliciting another chuckle from the robot.

"What's wrong?" Timothy asked, throwing two futile shurikens at the massive robot.

"This is THE robot!" Gearwire shouted. "The one that started the Robot War!"

"My, you're a perceptive one, aren't you?" the robot said in its musical voice. "Those cursed freaks have imprisoned me here, weakened just enough to prevent me from escaping. But if you can tell who I am so easily, you must have known me from somewhere. So who, may I ask, are *you*?" The robot paused its attack, standing back up to its full height as it examined Gearwire.

"You," it growled, its amused sneer hardening into a look of pure hatred. "I know you very well indeed. It will be my pleasure to eliminate you once and for all, General." As it said the last word, it launched its palm at Gearwire, who jumped out of the way, avoiding the blow by mere millimeters. The robot's palm crashed into the wall, shaking the entire room.

The robot reared back for another attack, when suddenly, it recoiled. It looked down to see the Golden Knight standing beneath it, his sword buried in a gap in the armor on the robot's foot. The robot casually flicked out one of its massive hands, landing a glancing blow on the Golden Knight's shield, which he had been wearing on his broken arm. The Golden Knight gasped in pain and crumpled to the floor, his face pale. The robot chuckled again.

It tried to return its focus back to Gearwire, but it was instead struck by a massive blast of energy. It turned to see Dr. Maddium fly past its face, his palms crackling with electricity. The robot swiped at him, but he flew out of the way, launching another bolt at the robot as he did.

Timothy slowly backed away from the battle. *This isn't going to work,* he realized. *We can't defeat this thing with a frontal assault. And we're rapidly running out of time to come up with a plan.*

Out of the corner of his eye, he caught a glimpse of Jeff, standing like a statue in front of the door. Something the robot had said earlier flew into his mind, and Timothy ran over to him. Jeff turned his head to look at Timothy as he approached.

"Greetings, Timothy," he said. "How may I assist you?"

"You said something earlier about how the Guardian wasn't allowed to leave this chamber," he said breathlessly. "What did you mean by that?"

"The Guardian is a highly dangerous and intelligent robot who also is among the most malevolent ever created," Jeff replied. "The builders knew that installing a safeguard code would not be enough to prevent it from escaping. They created a physical safeguard to prevent it from leaving this room."

"How?"

"The walls of the chamber are laced with filaments of wires that are connected to a processor buried deep beneath the mountain. If these wires are severed, the processor will send a remote signal to a small explosive device embedded in the Guardian's hard drive."

"So what you're saying is, if the walls are broken, the robot is destroyed?"

"Affirmative," Jeff replied. "As long as the system is still operational."

Timothy glanced back towards the battlefield, an idea taking root in his mind. "Can you check? Quickly, please."

"Running diagnostic," Jeff replied, his eyes sliding shut.

Timothy tapped his foot up and down as he watched the battle continue. A blue blur, which he assumed to be Jewel, ran circles around the robot's feet, encasing them in layers of crystal. The robot stamped his feet, shattering the crystal into millions of tiny fragments. Jewel tripped over a chunk of one of the fragments, sprawling out across the floor.

"A little faster please, Jeff!" Timothy said, watching with horror as the robot raised a foot to stomp on her.

"Diagnostic complete," Jeff said. "The system is operating at 100% capaci-"

Timothy bolted away from the robot, throwing his sharpest shuriken at the Guardian's face with all his might. The shuriken glanced off one of the lenses of the Guardian's eyes, leaving behind a long scratch. The robot turned to search for him, its foot slamming to the ground mere inches from Jewel's face. It swung its other foot at Timothy, and Timothy slid under it, his heart pounding. The robot reared back for another attack, but Gearwire blasted it in the face with a cartridge of glue, temporarily blinding it.

Timothy ran towards Jewel, quickly helping her to her feet.

"I have an idea how we can beat this thing," he said. "At least, I hope I do. But I'm going to need all five of Marathon's rings."

"What are you planning?" Jewel asked.

"We're going to help the Guardian break out of here." He looked around the room, spotting Quill kneeling in the corner with his stun rifle. He jogged toward him, Jewel right behind him.

"What do you mean, help the Guardian break free?" Jewel asked. "Just think of all the damage it would cause if it was running loose!"

"If the walls of this chamber break, the robot dies," Timothy said, turning to face her. "It's a fail-safe system the designers of the ruins built into this room to prevent the Guardian from escaping."

Understanding spread across Jewel's face. "And you need all five rings to help break the walls?"

"Not exactly," Timothy replied. "Just trust me." He turned to Quill. "Quill! I have a plan to defeat the Guardian. But I need all the rings."

Quill nodded and slid the ring off his arm. "Here you go, Tim. Good luck."

Timothy forced himself to smile as he slipped the ring onto his own arm. "I'll go get the others," Jewel said, taking off with lightning speed. Less than thirty seconds later, she returned, holding the remaining three rings.

Timothy slipped them on with an anxious sigh, double-checking to make sure they were in the right order for what he had planned. Then he took off toward the robot, marveling at how fast he could move.

As he neared the Guardian, he slowed to a stop. He took one of his shurikens in his hand and threw it at the robot's face again. This time, with the aid of the strength ring, the shuriken managed to penetrate the robot's eye, lodging itself in the center of the lens. The robot turned to face him, lashing out with a massive hand. Timothy exhaled heavily as he watched the hand hurtle towards him, every fiber of his being yelling at him to get out of the way. As the hand drew nearer, he gritted his teeth, bracing himself for impact.

The hand slammed into his armor, knocking the wind out of him. The blue ring shone like a star, and Timothy knew that if not for the added durability granted by it, he would have been killed outright, even with his armor.

As the robot started to lift its hand once more, Timothy grabbed onto one of its fingers, clinging to it for dear life. As the ground disappeared below him, he removed two of the rings from his own arm and slid them onto the Guardian's little finger. Then he ran up the Guardian's arm and down its back, the speed ring allowing him to run all the way down without falling off. As the ground approached, he leapt clear, rolling onto the ground to absorb the impact.

He got to his feet slowly, still winded by the robot's attack. "Suorotiart!" he shouted, wiping off blood from a cut on his forehead. "I need your help!"

Suorotiart flew down beside him, abandoning his hiding place in the upper corner of the room. "Yes?" he asked tiredly.

"I need you to deliver a message to Dr. Maddium," Timothy said. "It's very important. Tell him to get the Guardian to attack the wall."

Suorotiart gave him a strange look. "In what universe is that a good thing?"

Timothy gave him an exasperated sigh. "Just do it. Trust me."

Suorotiart glared at him, then flew off, meeting up with Dr. Maddium in midair. Timothy licked his lips as he watched their discussion. He saw Suorotiart point towards him, and Dr. Maddium leaned to the side, making eye contact with him. Timothy nodded, silently begging him to listen. Finally, after what seemed like hours, Dr. Maddium nodded and flew off, positioning himself directly in front of the robot's face.

Dr. Maddium flitted around like a hummingbird, leading the robot closer to the wall. When the robot was within attacking distance, Dr. Maddium stopped, staring at his gloves as if trying to fix a malfunction. The robot laughed and threw a punch at him. At the last second, Dr. Maddium flew under it, the punch slamming into the wall and leaving behind a massive dent. On the robot's finger, a blue and red light glowed fiercely. The robot stared at its hands in amazement. Then its expression hardened, and it threw another punch at Dr. Maddium, even harder and faster than the last. Dr. Maddium jerked to the side, blown out of the way by the sudden rush of air. The robot's fist slammed into the wall again, and this time, a small hole appeared.

Timothy watched with horror as the robot geared up for another attack.

Jeff must have been wrong, he thought, his heart sinking. *Or maybe the hole isn't big enough yet. Or maybe-*

Suddenly, a loud popping sound echoed through the chamber, and the robot's eyes faded to black. It toppled over, landing in a heap at the base of the wall.

A dazed grin broke out across Timothy's face.

We did it, he thought, relief washing over him. *We did it.*

Chapter 31

As soon as the robot had been defeated, the remaining Guardians of Kawts set about tending to their injuries. Draagetsew and the Golden Knight were carried over to the center of the room, where Dr. Maddium could examine them. Timothy walked over to the fallen robot and removed the rings from its massive fingers, returning them to their rightful owners. Jeff was standing over their wounded friends when he returned.

"I believe I can be of assistance," Jeff said, half turning to face Dr. Maddium. "I have access to a large medical database."

Dr. Maddium nodded. "Do what you need to do."

Jeff looked down at the Golden Knight. "Running biometric scan." The now-familiar whirring noise returned, and after several seconds, Jeff looked up once more. "Scan complete. Patient has a severely broken arm. Recommended treatment: reset the bone and wrap it tightly. Patient should avoid using said arm for at least eight weeks. The patient also appears to be in shock. Recommended to keep the patient warm and stationary until a further analysis can be completed."

Jeff produced a buzzing sound and turned towards Draagetsew. "Commencing biometric scan on patient beta." He buzzed again, then emitted a sharp click. "Patient beta has severe contusions and moderate internal bleeding. Factoring in the accelerating healing ability of the people of Alpen, the patient should rest for the next two to four days."

"Do what he says," Gearwire said, nodding to Dr. Maddium. Then he turned and began setting up his tent. Timothy followed suit, helping to set up their camp for the night.

* * *

Three days after their fight with the Guardian, Timothy was again woken up in the middle of the night.

It's just the Golden Knight talking in his sleep again, he told himself. *Go back to bed.* He rolled over and tried to sleep, but the voice continued, rising in intensity.

"Yes. Early tomorrow morning," the voice hissed. "Be here. I'm sick of this place. And I'm sick of pretending to like that good-for-nothing fool of a president." There was a pause, and Timothy's eyes widened as the man's words began to sink in. "Don't forget our agreement." There was another pause. "Relax. You'll get what you want, and I'll get what I want. Just make sure you're here tomorrow. Yes. I'll see you then."

Timothy poked his head out of his tent, looking around to see if he could spot the speaker. He heard a rustle of fabric, but he saw no one. Grabbing his staff from beside his pillow, he stepped out of his tent. Slowly, he scanned the camp, eyes narrowed. No one. Moving silently, he crossed over to Jeff, who was standing still as a statue in the middle of their camp.

"Jeff," he whispered. "Did you hear that?"

The robot opened his eyes. "Greetings, Timothy. What do you need?"

"Did you hear that?" Timothy repeated.

"Hear what?" Jeff asked, his head swiveling nearly one hundred and eighty degrees.

"Just now. Someone was talking."

"I have no record of such an event. I am programmed to enter sleep mode at night, during which time my audio sensors only pick up certain predetermined sounds."

Timothy frowned. "Well, thanks anyway." He walked slowly back to his tent, making sure the tent flaps were tightly secured. His mind was running in circles, trying to make sense of what he had just heard.

Okay. What do I know for sure? he thought, his heart pounding. He shook his head, forcing himself to stay calm. *Uh... I know that someone is planning something for tomorrow when we retrieve the Weather Belt.*

And that someone probably knows that I overheard their conversation, he realized with a sudden stab of fear. *If I fall asleep, I might wake up to a knife in my chest.*

Timothy set his staff down on the ground, quietly slipping into his armor as he continued to puzzle over their situation. His eyes widened as realization hit him.

This must be what Howard was trying to warn us about! He didn't mean 'mole' the animal! He meant 'mole' as in double agent! Someone is planning to turn the Weather Belt over to the Council!

They must have some sort of signal amplifier on them if they can contact the Council from all the way in here. But it couldn't be too large, or I would have noticed it by now. They would have had to have been working for the Council since the very beginning!

"Come on. Think, Timothy!" he muttered to himself, wracking his brains for the identity of the traitor. "You know that voice!"

He squeezed his eyes shut. *Who is it? Who might have a motive for betraying us to the Council?*

* * *

When Draagetsew woke everyone up early the next morning, Timothy was already awake. He hadn't slept a wink since he had overheard the traitor's plan, unsuccessfully trying to place the voice.

"I say we get the Weather Belt first, and then have breakfast and pack up camp," Draagetsew said to Gearwire and Dr. Maddium. "We're so close! I can practically taste it!"

Timothy eyed the mutant president suspiciously.

Could Draagetsew be the traitor? He wondered. Then he shook his head, dismissing the thought. *No. Whoever it is really seems to hate Draagetsew. And the voice doesn't match either. If it had been Draagetsew, he would have woken up the entire camp.*

Gearwire exchanged a look with Dr. Maddium. Then he looked back at Draagetsew. "Why not?" he said wearily. "I suppose it makes no difference if we eat breakfast with the Weather Belt or without it. It might actually be better for planning purposes."

"So what have we got today, Jeff?" Draagetsew asked. "What's the final trap?"

Jeff clicked. "The Weather Belt and its blueprints are located on top of a pedestal in the center of the room, surrounded by an electrified moat. The stepping stones to the central island are made of metal, thus making it ill-advised to step on them. The Weather Belt also produces a constant stream of strong wind within the chamber."

"Let's have a look!" Draagetsew said, easing open the door.

The room was just as Jeff had described it, although his utilitarian explanation hardly did it justice. Between the intricately decorated marble pillar in the center to the small waves that lapped against the edge of the moat, the trap was remarkably picturesque.

"That actually looks pretty relaxing," Quill observed. "Are you sure there's really a trap in there?"

"Affirmative," Jeff said. He removed a small bolt from a hidden pouch and tossed it into the moat. There was a loud crackling sound, and Timothy could see sparks leaping up from the water.

"Point taken," Quill said, nodding nervously.

"How are we supposed to get across if we can't touch the water or the stepping stones?" Madison asked.

"Easy," Suorotiart answered, an incredulous smile breaking out across his face. "I'll just fly over there and grab the Weather Belt."

Draagetsew let out a booming laugh and slapped Suorotiart on the back. "Brilliant! Why didn't I think of that? Bring us home!"

"Wish me luck," Suorotiart said as he flew off, swaying erratically in the wind.

Something clicked in Timothy's brain as Suorotiart spoke. "Stop him!" he shouted, pushing past the other Guardians of Kawts in an attempt to catch Suorotiart before he flew out of reach. Suorotiart flew higher, evading capture.

Gearwire's eyes darted to Jeff, then back to Timothy. "What's wrong?" he asked, his face a mixture of concern and suspicion.

"Suorotiart's the traitor!" Timothy exclaimed. Gearwire raised an eyebrow. "Howard was trying to warn us about a mole among us! A spy for the Council. It's Suorotiart!"

"Impossible!" Draagetsew exclaimed. "How dare you insult Alpen's second-in-command like…" he trailed off, realization dawning on him. "He was the one who arranged all this, wasn't he? He was the one who suggested we come here in the first place."

He turned to face his rapidly disappearing countryman. "Come back here, Suorotiart, you rat!"

Gearwire whipped out his glue gun and carefully aimed it at Suorotiart. His finger tightened on the trigger, but he hesitated, his hand frozen in the air.

"Give me that," Draagetsew said, snatching the gun from Gearwire's hand and pointing it at Suorotiart. But in the short time it took for Draagetsew to take control of the weapon, Suorotiart had already reached the pedestal. He landed on the platform, curling his fingers underneath the Weather Belt. Then, with a jerk, he pried it free.

As he held it aloft triumphantly, a massive blast of energy shot from the device, smashing a hole through both the ceiling and the outer dome. Gearwire's radio roared to life, no longer blocked by the invincium walls of the ruins. It was beeping in a steady pattern. An S.O.S. signal.

Through the hole in the ceiling, Gearwire's ship slowly descended. When it was only a few yards above Suorotiart, the door slid open and someone threw down a rope. Ethos climbed out of the ship, taking the Weather Belt from Suorotiart. As he buckled it around his waist, Dr. Maddium's eyes widened in sudden fear. His eyes darted to Gearwire's radio, then he reached inside his lab coat and vanished.

Out of the corner of his eye, Timothy watched Dr. Maddium blink out of existence, coming to the same conclusion half a second later. He bolted for their campsite just as Ethos unleashed a blast of electricity from the Weather Belt. The blast rippled through the room, dropping everyone in its path. Timothy had just reached the nearest of the tents when the blast hit him. The world faded to black, and he slumped to the floor, unconscious.

* * *

"We need to get out of here!" Inn shouted, barging into the back room where Adalbo and the other Kriegerhelden were planning their next move.

Adalbo quickly took his feet off of the table, sitting bolt upright. "What's going on?"

"It's the Council, more likely than not. There's a huge squadron of royal guards gathering outside the café as we speak!"

Adalbo frowned. "I thought you said they didn't know where your café was?"

"Well, they've figured it out now!" Inn said. "You need to get out of here!" he added, shooing Adalbo toward the back door.

"If you guys are staying to fight them, so am I," Adalbo said. "We're in this together."

"You're the one they're looking for," Tapfer said. "Our best bet is to bluff."

"Come out with your hands up!" A voice ordered from inside the café. Inn's eyes darted one way, then another. He dragged Adalbo over to the oven and stuffed him inside.

"Don't worry. We haven't turned it on yet for the day," he said as Adalbo tried to protest. "Stay here until they've left," he added in a frantic whisper. "No matter what happens, you need to stay here until the Council is gone."

"I can't let you guys do this," Adalbo said, trying to climb out.

"This is our fight just as much as yours," Inn said. "And besides, someone has to warn Idalbo and the others." With one last glance at the door, Inn closed the oven and followed the others out of the kitchen, his hands raised above his head.

"What seems to be the problem, officer?" Inn's muffled voice asked from the other room. "I was just making up a pot of coffee and some muffins. Why don't you join us?"

"You know why we're here, Nagninnur," another voice replied. "All of you are under arrest for aiding and abetting an enemy of the state. Not to mention your own treason."

"I'm not the treasonous one here, Deyeneek," Inn said. "You and I both know that."

"Where's Adalbo, Nagninnur?"

"Come a little closer and I'll show you!"

The sounds of a scuffle reached Adalbo's ears, followed a few seconds later by a sharp pop. There was a heavy thud as Inn hit the ground.

Adalbo started to push open the door to the stove when Seililyad appeared in the kitchen, slipping through the back door. Gently, she pushed the oven door closed again.

"Stay here," she whispered, getting a kettle down from the cupboard and filling it with a brownish liquid from a flask she had hidden in her apron. "It's going to get a little warm in there. Sorry about that." She reached up and turned on the burner, then turned to leave.

"Seililyad?" Adalbo whispered.

Seililyad turned to face him.

"I'm sorry."

Seililyad smiled sadly and slipped back out the door, leaving Adalbo alone in the oven with a kettle boiling above him.

"Search the premises," he heard Deyeneek shout from the other room. He heard the tromping of feet and knew that he had only a few minutes before they would find his hiding place.

A bell chimed, and Adalbo heard Seililyad's voice. "Hey, dad. Sorry I'm late. I couldn't get..." she trailed off, and Adalbo knew she was taking in the mess in the café.

And Inn's body, he added grimly, hoping against hope that his friend was still alive.

"What happened here?" she asked, her voice trembling.

"Your father and his compatriots have been arrested for treason, ma'am," one of the soldiers said. "And for harboring a dangerous criminal. He was resisting arrest. I don't think it's too serious," he said, trying to reassure her.

Seililyad said something in response, but Adalbo couldn't hear it, her words drowned out by the squeal of the kettle above him. Before long, a thick black smoke began to rise out of it, triggering the smoke alarm.

As the alarm blared, Adalbo could just barely hear the soldier's shouts of confusion. Seililyad ran into the kitchen, followed closely by two soldiers. "He must've been making some coffee when you showed up," she said, frantically adjusting a dial on the stove. She picked up the pot and threw it in the sink, running cold water over it.

But the damage had already been done, and the café's sprinkler system whirred to life, dousing everyone inside. The soldiers ran back towards the front door, and Seililyad followed, pausing in the doorway to nod to Adalbo. As soon as they were out of sight, Adalbo climbed out of the oven and slipped out the back door, his sword in his hand as he ran back to their temporary base of operations.

As he ran, he caught a glimpse of a platoon of mutants marching in the same direction, led by Councilman Karr. As he approached the border, he slipped past the guards and continued on to the ramshackle house, running up the stairs three at a time.

He threw open the door, stopping short as the others looked up at him in surprise.

"The Council," he gasped. "They're coming with an army!"

"Idalbo! Get Omor and the others out!" The Mysterious Man shouted. "We found a cave in the foothills when we were looking for a permanent base a while back. We can hide out there until we can figure out what's going on."

Howard pulled the radio out of the amplifier, punching in a series of buttons. "I'm setting this up to send an S.O.S. on repeat to Gearwire's radio," he said, hiding it beneath the floorboard. "We'll be down to just one radio from now on."

"What's going on?" Omor asked, appearing at the top of the stairs.

"We're evacuating. The Council's on their way here."

Omor's eyes grew wide, and he vanished back upstairs, emerging a couple of seconds later with the quill Idalbo had given him while he was in the Council's prison. The rest of his troupe scrambled over each other in their haste to evacuate the building. When the last of them made it out, the Mysterious Man led them over the nearest ridge, vanishing from sight just as the Council's troops appeared on the horizon.

Chapter 32

Timothy's eyes flew open, and he looked around in a panic, ready to fight off any of the Council's minions who showed themselves. He breathed a sigh of relief when he realized he was back in his tent.

It was all just a bad dream, he thought, laughing at his fear. He crawled out of the tent. Immediately, his heart sank.

I wasn't dreaming, he realized as he walked closer to the Weather Belt room. Sunlight streamed in through the hole in the ceiling, gently illuminating the final trap. Timothy spun in a slow circle. *Everyone's gone*, he realized. *The Council must have captured them.*

Something clicked behind him, and Timothy spun around, a shuriken in his hand.

"Greetings," Jeff said, light pouring from his eyes like twin flashlights. He swiveled his head upwards to face the hole. "Your friends have been taken by Suorotiart and the men in the ship. They took the Weather Belt with them."

"Did you see what happened to Dr. Maddium?"

"He vanished from my radar shortly before the energy blast was released. His current whereabouts are unknown."

Timothy sighed, trying to collect his thoughts. "The Council has the Weather Belt and the rest of the Guardians of Kawts. Dr. Maddium is missing in action, and I'm stuck in the center of a death trap all by myself."

"You are not all by yourself," Jeff said. "Now that the Weather Belt has been removed, my original protocol has been completed. I am free to choose a new mission." He looked directly at Timothy. "Your commander was one of the finest warriors and generals of the Robot War. It is clear that Suorotiart and his compatriots are pursuing malevolent aims. I will help you escape from the compound and reunite with your compatriots."

Timothy shook his head. "We barely made it through those traps going forwards with all of us helping. How are the two of us supposed to get past all of those traps again in reverse? Especially since I'm almost out of food."

"The Weather Belt was the power source for the compound," Jeff said. "Now that it is gone, all the traps will be deactivated." Jeff began to whir loudly. "Additionally," he said, "We do not have to travel all the way. There is an exit point roughly three days' travel from here."

Timothy took one last lingering look at the hole in the ceiling, then turned to face Jeff. "Let's get going, then. We have a long walk ahead of us."

* * *

Two days later, Timothy looked up at the ruined maze, swaying with exhaustion. He hadn't stopped to rest since he had woken up in the final trap, and the lack of sleep was beginning to take its toll on him.

"The exit point is only a little beyond this maze," Jeff announced.

"How much longer?" Timothy asked.

Jeff whirred and buzzed as he calculated the answer. "One day at most, unless you get lost in the maze."

"Great. I'm just going to rest here for a minute."

"Entering sleep mode." Jeff closed his eyes, plunging them into almost total darkness. Timothy leaned up against one of the walls, trying desperately to fall asleep. He heard the swish of fabric from behind him, and he opened his eyes again.

"Jeff?" he whispered. "Is that you?"

Jeff opened his eyes again, illuminating the room once more. "Is what me?"

Before Timothy could answer, a dark shape dropped from the ceiling. In the light of Jeff's eyes, Timothy could make out the shape of a hairy mutant, dressed in a hooded cloak.

"W-who are you?" he asked.

The mutant turned towards him, as if noticing him for the first time. He nodded deeply, a friendly smile on his face. "Swehpen Echse, at your service," he said. "But you can call me Penn." He squinted at Timothy. "And who, might I ask, are you?"

"Timothy Hawthorne," Timothy said. "How did you get in here?"

"I could ask the same about you," Penn said. "I didn't think anyone else had gotten this far into the compound."

Something clicked in Timothy's brain. "You're the one who tried to get the Weather Belt hundreds of years ago! The one Draagetsew was always talking about!"

Penn raised an eyebrow. "Hundreds of years ago? How long was I stuck in that statue room?"

"You have been in suspended animation at least one hundred and thirty-four years, by my calculations," Jeff said with a click. He turned toward Penn. "Greetings. I am J37769Q, also referred to as 'Jeff.' I was created to guide those who seek the Weather Belt through the last three challenges."

Penn pinched the bridge of his nose. "You're going to have to start from the beginning. "What did I miss?"

Taking a deep breath, Timothy explained to Penn everything that had happened, starting with his own involvement with the rebels and leading up to when Suorotiart had stolen the Weather Belt.

Penn's face darkened when he heard the story. "He sounds just like his predecessor. Or would it be his predecessor's predecessor? Whoever it is! Seeking to use the Weather Belt to further his own aims. And this Golden Knight you mentioned - he doesn't wear the symbol of a golden gear, by any chance?"

Timothy nodded. "On his shield."

"Well, that settles it," Penn said. "I'm coming with you. Any friend of my old partner is a friend of mine. Which way out, robot?"

"The exit point is in the trap before the Medusa Hall," Jeff said.

Penn snapped his fingers. "Of course! The ejection room! Let's go!" he exclaimed, climbing over the nearest wall of the maze.

Timothy remained where he was, watching the place where Penn had disappeared. After a few seconds, Penn's head popped up over the top of the wall. "Right!" he said, climbing down again. "I forgot! You're not a mutant." He paused for a moment, frowning in concentration. Finally, he said, "Here. Climb up on my back. I'll carry you over."

Timothy did as he was directed, but the sight of Jeff standing on the ground made him pause. "What about Jeff?"

"I will follow you," Jeff said, walking over to the wall and then up it, sticking out parallel to the floor. "My feet are equipped with the climbing technology engineered by Dr. Rachel Wilson before the Great Heroes War."

"That settles that question, I guess," Penn said with a shrug. He looked back up at the wall. "Here we go!"

* * *

With Penn's help, it only took them a few hours to reach the exit point. Timothy swallowed hard as he stared at the floor. He took a deep breath, then stepped out onto a trapped tile.

For a moment, it seemed as if nothing had happened. Then, without warning, it dropped away from the others, swooshing down a narrow tube. Timothy gave a shout of surprise as he clung to the edge of the tile, trying desperately to keep it from flipping over. Soon, his ears began to pop, and he held his breath in an ineffectual attempt to relieve the pain.

He had been sliding for several minutes when he suddenly saw a speck of light in the distance, growing larger with every passing second. Before he could properly brace himself, he shot out of the tube onto the side of the mountain, losing his grip on the tile and rolling onto the ground. He exhaled heavily and shakily got to his feet.

"Wonderful day, isn't it?" a voice asked. Timothy turned around to see Dr. Maddium standing beside a campfire.

"How did you get here?" Timothy asked, starting to laugh in spite of himself.

"I knew that if anyone managed to escape, they would make their way to the nearest exit," he said. "After the Council left, I came looking for the place where the exit comes out of the mountain."

"But how did you even get out of the ruins?" Timothy asked.

"I used my pocket teleporter to transport myself to a safe distance outside the compound."

"You mean we could have just teleported into the center of the ruins this whole time?"

Dr. Maddium shook his head. "Remember how the invincium walls blocked out the radio signals? Parts of the transmission got lost en route. Now imagine that you are being transported through space via a similar technique."

Timothy's eyes widened. "I see," he said. "That's a pretty good reason."

Dr. Maddium nodded. "That, and the handheld teleporter can only go short distances. I would have been teleporting blindly into traps without a way to inspect them first."

Before he could say anything further, Jeff whizzed out of the pipe, spiraling through the air like one of Timothy's shurikens and crashing in a heap on the ground. Slowly, he hauled himself upright. "Greetings," he said, turning to face Dr. Maddium. "We have been-"

He cut off suddenly as Penn flew out of the pipe as well, nearly colliding with Jeff's head. He rolled clear of the tile he had been riding, standing up and looking around.

His eyes finally settled on the little group, and he wandered over. "Penn, this is Dr. Maddium," Timothy said after an awkward pause. "Dr. Maddium, this is -"

"Swehpen Echse," Dr. Maddium finished, extending his hand. "I've heard a good deal about you."

"Likewise," Penn said, taking Dr. Maddium's hand. For a moment, they stood there, studying each other.

Finally, Dr. Maddium stepped back. "We've got a long way to go if we want to meet up with the others," he said, and Timothy felt hope surge within him.

"They escaped?"

Dr. Maddium winced. "Sorry. I meant the group we left at our temporary HQ. There's been no sign of the rest of the team since the Council flew off. Seililyad's been keeping an eye on the Council's movements, but it's getting harder and harder to move around town undetected." He walked over to his tent and began to take it down. "They're waiting for us in a cave in the foothills. Howard sent me the coordinates last night."

"Do you think they're okay?" Timothy asked. Dr. Maddium stopped what he was doing and turned back to face him, concern written across his face.

"I hope so," he said. "But the Council has always been vindictive. And now they have even more reason to hate us. Unless we act soon, I very much doubt that everyone will make it out alive."

A somber feeling settled over the camp at Dr. Maddium's proclamation. "We'd better get going, then." Penn said. "I don't care what century we're in. No one overthrows Alpen on my watch without a fight."

Chapter 33

Quill flinched as he heard the door swing open. Two Councilmen tossed Gearwire into the cell, laughing as he landed limply in a heap on the floor. Quill waited until the Councilmen had retreated from view once more before he crept up to his fallen leader. Gearwire's breathing was ragged, his face a mask of blood streaming from a severely broken nose. With Madison's help, he tried his best to slow the bleeding. The twins came up just as they were finishing, setting Gearwire's nose in a sheath of crystal.

Gearwire nodded in thanks, then slipped into unconsciousness. Jewel smiled sadly, then vanished back into the recesses of the cell, where she and Crystal were attempting to treat a tentacled mutant suffering from a gunshot wound. After a moment, Madison stood and followed. Quill stared at Gearwire's battered form. For the first time since he had allied himself with Gearwire against the Council, he began to worry that they might lose.

It's all up to Timothy and Dr. Maddium now, he thought, slowly getting to his feet.

* * *

"We've been hiding out here ever since," Seililyad said, finishing the tour of the tiny cave that now housed the last remnant of the Guardians of Kawts and the Kriegerhelden.

"Are the others still alive?" Timothy asked.

Seililyad hesitated, then nodded. "As far as we know. From what your friends have said about the Council, my guess is that they're planning to use them as bait for the rest of us."

"A fair assessment," Dr. Maddium agreed. "So, what do we have to work with?"

"We have three swordsmen with two swords between them, an archer, a security officer, a scientist without any equipment, an unofficial member of the Kriegerhelden without a weapon, and about a dozen actors. And now that you're here, we also have a scientist with a mech suit, a ninja, a folk hero, and an unarmed robot."

Dr. Maddium grunted in acknowledgement. "That's not much," he agreed. "This isn't going to be easy."

"What do you suggest we do?" Samuel asked.

"The way I see it, there are three things we have to do," Dr. Maddium said, ticking each one off on his fingers. "First. We must make sure that those of us who can fight are properly armed. Second. We must try to covertly recruit as many of Alpen's citizens to our cause as we can. And third, we have to prevent the Council from using both the Weather Belt and the evaporation cannon."

"That's a pretty tall order," Howard said, running his fingers through his hair.

"Howard's right," the Mysterious Man said. "We couldn't prevent the Council from doing that even when we were at full strength. We don't stand a chance with only nine of us."

"We'll have to cross that bridge when we get to it," Dr. Maddium said. "For now, we just need to focus on the first two." He turned to Omor. "Any luck on convincing your friends to join us?"

Omor shook his head. "They'll fight if their lives depend on it. But they aren't warriors. They won't last long against the Council, with or without their superweapons."

"I don't think we actually need a citizen's revolt, anyway," Seililyad said. "Alpen just finished a war. There are still plenty of former soldiers stationed in and around Blancstadt who would fight with us if we could get word to them."

"The only problem is, we don't have any way of getting word to them," the Mysterious Man said.

"I could do it," Seililyad said. "The Council doesn't know I'm part of the Kriegerhelden. I never officially joined."

"But Suorotiart will still know," Adalbo said, putting his hand on her arm. "And he'll tell the Council."

"I don't think so," Seililyad said. "I was there when they arrested the others. Either Suorotiart doesn't remember, or he doesn't think I'm enough of a threat to worry about."

"It's too much of a risk," Adalbo protested. "It could be a trap!"

Seililyad shook her head. "Right now, anything could be a trap. But if we want to have any chance of defeating the Council, I need to do this."

Adalbo was silent for a moment, then nodded. "Just be careful."

"In the meantime," Dr. Maddium said, "we need to figure out how to get weapons for the rest of us."

"I think I have an idea on that front," Idalbo said, plucking a quill from his back. "If we affixed a handle to one of these, we would have a passable rapier."

The Mysterious Man took the quill from Idalbo and inspected it. "It's rather flimsy for a sword," he said. "You wouldn't really be able to take a direct hit with it. But it might do in a pinch."

"Which is exactly where we are," Penn reminded him. "But what are we going to do about our friend Jeff here?"

"I am not programmed with a fighting database," Jeff said. "Such upgrades would be difficult to accomplish under the present circumstances."

"Jeff, I think you're going to help us most in the planning stages," Dr. Maddium said. "We're going to need your statistical analysis." He looked around at the others. "Let's start there and see how things develop. Meeting adjourned."

The remaining Guardians of Kawts and Kriegerhelden dispersed back to their tasks, but Timothy remained at the table, staring off into space.

I hope Jewel and Quill and the others are alright.

"Is everything okay, Timothy?" Samuel asked, putting a hand on his shoulder.

Timothy started. "What? No, it's nothing."

Samuel just stared at him, clearly seeing through his lie. Timothy sighed.

"I'm just worried about the others," he said at last. "Who knows what the Council is doing to them?"

"It's not a pleasant thing to contemplate," Samuel agreed. "But all we can do for them right now is continue to pray."

"Yeah," Timothy said after a moment's hesitation. "I guess you're right. It's out of all our hands."

Samuel smiled gently. "Things will work out for the best," he said. "Even if it doesn't seem like it at the moment." Then he turned and walked deeper into the cave, leaving Timothy alone with his thoughts.

* * *

"I'm afraid I have bad news," Seililyad reported when she returned to the cave a few days later. "The Council has made it known that they will be executing their prisoners tomorrow night."

"We can just do the same thing we did last time," Omor said. "We'll pick up some more suits from Revenant's."

Idalbo shook his head. "Revenant only made a few suits. There wouldn't be enough for everyone."

"And the execution is going to be private," Seililyad said. "They haven't even told the palace guards where it's going to be."

"So we have to break them out of the jail directly," Penn said. "A little trickier of a task, to be sure, but not impossible."

The Mysterious Man shook his head. "This has 'trap' written all over it," he muttered.

"It probably is," Dr. Maddium said. "But it's a risk we have to take. We don't stand a chance without the others' help. If we want any chance of defeating the Council, we're going to need everyone."

"But we might not need all of us to rescue the others," Timothy said. "I have an idea. It's a gamble, but I think it might be our best shot."

* * *

As the sun peeked out over the horizon, the remaining members of the Guardians of Kawts crept into position around the jail. Timothy lay flat on his stomach, scanning the area for anything amiss. He glanced up at the sun, estimating the time.

If Seililyad's information was correct, they'll start moving the prisoners any minute now.

Below him, the door to the prison swung open, and guards began to march out. "Now!" Timothy shouted. The Guardians of Kawts and the Kriegerhelden rose from their hiding spots and charged down the slope to the jail, pushing past the startled guards to get inside.

Timothy skidded to a halt as he entered the building. Just inside the door stood not Gearwire and the others, but the Council and a fleet of attack drones.

Timothy spun towards the door, only to find it sealed shut, guarded by Councilman Wade.

"Chain them up," Ethos said. "And confiscate their weapons." The Council moved among the remaining Guardians of Kawts, disarming them.

It looks like the Mysterious Man was right, Timothy thought as one of the Councilmen forced his arms behind his back. *This was a trap.*

The shuriken sewn into his shirt pressed up against his skin, narrowly avoiding drawing blood. Timothy ignored the pain, hoping that no one would notice.

I don't know if you're listening right now, God. But if you are, we could really use your help.

Chapter 34

A drawn-out creaking sound filled the air, and Timothy opened his eyes. He lay there in the darkness, listening. He heard footsteps approaching, then stopping in front of the cell where he and the rest of the Guardians of Kawts were imprisoned. There was a jingling of keys, and then another creak as the door swung open.

"Timothy?" a familiar voice whispered.

Aksell.

He quickly sat up, reaching instinctively for his staff before remembering it had been taken. "I'm over here," he whispered back.

Aksell's eyes darted around the cell nervously, then he stepped inside, walking quickly over to Timothy. He reached down and unlocked Timothy's handcuffs. Timothy looked up at him gratefully, rubbing his sore wrists.

"Come on," Aksell whispered, turning back towards the door. "The guards are busy right now. If you go now, you can escape!"

"Why are you doing this?" Timothy asked quietly, scanning his friend's face for any signs of deception.

"I couldn't let my dad kill you. Anarchist or not, you're still my friend. You saved my life once. Now I'm returning the favor." He glanced from side to side. "But you have to hurry. There's a horse waiting at the edge of town. Take it and ride far away from here."

"What about the others?" Timothy asked, standing. "What about Samuel and Quill?"

Grief flashed across Aksell's face. He shook his head. "They're already dead, Tim. You know that."

"No. They're still alive," Timothy said. "They were turned into Blanks. They're in this cell with me right now."

"That's - impossible," Aksell said. "Quill lost The Race and Samuel was executed for treason. That's what Ethos said."

"Ethos isn't the person he seems to be," Timothy said. "That's what got Quill and Samuel and I into this mess in the first place. We discovered the truth."

Aksell turned away from him. "Are you coming or not?" he asked finally. "The guards will be back soon."

"I can't leave without the others," Timothy said, more confidently than he felt. He turned toward the wall. There was silence for a while, then he heard the main door creaking shut. Timothy exhaled, trying to calm his shaky nerves and hoping he hadn't just made a grave mistake. He stood up and gently pulled the cell door shut, hearing the click as the lock engaged.

He left his handcuffs draped loosely around his wrists, looking around the room. Already, an idea was forming in his head, one last throw of the dice that might tip the odds in their favor.

Or it will kill us all, he thought grimly.

Then again, we're dead men already if I do nothing.

* * *

Aksell lay on his bed and stared up at the ceiling, too conflicted to sleep. As he pondered Timothy's words, a memory bubbled to the surface.

He was only seven years old then. His mother was dying of the deadly virus that had been sweeping through Kawts. Despite the danger, Ethos had allowed Aksell to see her one last time.

Edeline had already been severely weakened by the disease, but still, her face lit up when Aksell had entered the room. She had propped herself up on one elbow and called him over. For nearly half an hour, they had simply talked to each other, although Aksell no longer remembered what about. But he did remember the last thing she told him, when Ethos appeared in the doorway to signal the end of the visit.

She put her hand on Aksell's shoulder and looked into his eyes. "I'm going to go away soon, Aksell," she said. "Hopefully, I'll see you again someday. But in the meantime, I want to tell you something very important." Aksell nodded.

"Never stop searching for the truth. It is the only thing that can set you free." She opened her mouth as if she was going to say more, but at that moment, she broke into a coughing fit. Aksell was quickly ushered out of the room, replaced by a white-coated doctor. It was the last time he had seen his mother alive.

Now, as her words joined Timothy's in his mind, he couldn't help but wonder if she had been trying to warn him about Ethos. But just as quickly as he had the thought, he dismissed it.

You're spending too much time with anarchists, he thought, shaking his head. He rolled over and pulled his blankets higher.

But sleep continued to elude him.

* * *

Early the next morning, the Council arrived at the prison, herding the Guardians of Kawts to a hill just outside of town. On one end of the hill sat the evaporation cannon that Ethos had used to conquer Blancstadt. On the other side was a guillotine.

"Kneel," Ethos commanded. No one moved, and Timothy stared Ethos down, hoping that no one realized how anxious he was. Ethos nodded to the other Councilmen, and they forced the Guardians of Kawts to the ground. Timothy flinched as Councilman Alexis shoved him to his knees. Part of him was tempted to strike back, but he quickly quelled the impulse.

No. I can't let them know I'm free before it's time.

Suorotiart marched out in front of the prisoners, his head held high as he carried the Weather Belt to Ethos.

"Kill me if you like, Suorotiart!" Draagetsew growled, struggling with his handcuffs. "But don't doom Alpen to the Council's rule."

Suorotiart glared at him. "You've been calling the shots for far too long," he sneered. "It's time Alpen had a real leader. Someone who will turn them into a great and glorious empire! Now that we have the Weather Belt, no one can stop us from becoming the greatest nation on earth!"

"Very well said, Suorotiart," Ethos said, taking the Weather Belt from him. "Only, you forgot to mention one little detail. 'We' don't have the Weather Belt. I do."

He nodded to the Councilmen standing on either side of Suorotiart. With a mile-long grin on his face, Karr stepped forward and forced Suorotiart to the ground, pinning his arms behind his back with practiced efficiency.

"You really should have known better," Ethos said, clucking his tongue. "Didn't Milkop and his merry band of miscreants warn you I am not to be trusted?" He buckled the Weather Belt around his waist. He sighed, a smile spreading across his face. "It's been a while since

I've felt this much raw power!" he said, a strange light coming into his eyes. "We'll be unstoppable!"

Overhead, storm clouds began to gather. The wind picked up, and bolts of lightning flashed to the ground, heedless of whatever lay in their path. Soon, the hill was pockmarked with smoking craters. One blast even struck the evaporation cannon, and it exploded, leaving behind only a gaping crater that rapidly grew into a deep cavern.

"You have no idea how many years I've been waiting to do this," Ethos said as the lightning slowed. "To have the great General Quawz helpless at my feet. It was no easy task to convince you to go after this for me," he said, admiring the Weather Belt. "But everyone played their parts perfectly."

"I can't believe we fell for Ray's act!" Samuel groaned, and Aksell's head snapped toward the sound. His eyes widened when he realized who had spoken. "I was so sure he was telling the truth!"

"But that's the best part!" Ethos exclaimed, unable to contain his glee. "He was. Or at least, he thought he was. We knew he'd turn traitor, so we told him exactly what we wanted you to know. We hoped you'd capture him, eventually. Between that and Suorotiart's influence with Draagetsew, we were confident you'd try to get the Weather Belt sooner or later. Though I must say, Milkop, I was a little concerned by how adamantly you opposed this idea at first. Tell me, how does it feel to know that you were right?"

Gearwire met Ethos' gaze, one eye swollen nearly shut.

"And as for your backup plan," Ethos continued, "the so-called 'Kriegerhelden?' Suorotiart told us who you were and where you were meeting from day one!"

A crack of thunder echoed across the mountains, and Ethos fingered the handle of his sword. Now," he said, a wicked grin spreading across his face. "Who will be the first to die?" he asked, looking at his captives.

He pointed at Draagetsew. "How about you?" he said. "The one who so unwittingly arranged his own downfall? Or what about you?" he sneered, pointing to Gearwire. "The man who has been the bane of my existence for decades. Or you." He pointed to Volker. "The traitor who didn't know which side his bread was buttered on." He scanned the line of prisoners, a manic look in his eye. His gaze finally came to rest on Quill. "You," he breathed. "You caused all this. If you hadn't meddled in things that weren't your concern, we'd all still be living happily in Kawts. You should have listened to me when I warned you to mind your own business. Yes... I think you'll be the first."

Two Council members grabbed Quill's arms and hauled him to his feet. "Hey!" Quill protested, squirming in their grip. "I wouldn't have gotten involved in the first place if you guys weren't terrorists!"

"Silence!" Ethos shouted, slapping him across the face.

Timothy heard his gasp of pain and fingered the shuriken hidden in his sleeve. He glanced over at the Councilmen who guarded the rest of the prisoners, but they were still watchful. Timothy bit his lip, hoping his opportunity would come before it was too late.

The Councilmen forced Quill into the guillotine, then stepped back, awaiting Ethos' orders.

Ethos turned to Aksell. "He's all yours, son," Ethos said. "Kill him and take your place on the Council."

"No," Askell said, stepping between Ethos and Quill. "I'm not doing it."

"You must!" Ethos said. "You are a Deogol! Our family has ruled Kawts for hundreds of years! It is your destiny to sit on the Council!"

"No," Aksell repeated, fire blazing in his eyes.

Ethos made a strangled sputtering noise, unable to even form a complete thought. Councilman Wade subtly stepped back a step, eyeing his leader warily.

He's lost it! Timothy realized as Ethos began to shout at Aksell. *He's gone completely mad!* The Councilman next to him shifted nervously, and Timothy glanced around again.

And if he keeps this up, I'm going to have just the opening I need, he added, the ghost of a smile touching his face despite his concern for Quill.

"We'll discuss this later!" Ethos snarled at Aksell. *"I'll* kill him." He picked up an axe from the ground and started towards Quill.

Aksell charged at him, tackling him to the ground. Ethos dropped the axe, trying to pry Aksell off of him. For a moment, no one moved. Then a roar echoed from the hills as Seililyad and Penn led a small army down into the valley. Timothy let his handcuffs drop from his wrists, running to the nearest tree and breaking off a sizable branch.

He swung it experimentally, testing the weight.

Not bad, he thought. *A little unbalanced, but not bad.* He slipped the shuriken from his sleeve, throwing it with all his might toward Councilman Darren. The Councilman reared back in shock, and Gearwire took advantage of the opportunity, head-butting him in the stomach and stealing his sword.

Dr. Maddium slipped a high-powered laser pointer from his sock and aimed it at his chains, burning through them in only a few seconds. As his lab coat transformed into his battle armor, he flew up into the air, landing beside the twins and severing their chains before moving on.

Near the chasm formed by the evaporation cannon, Timothy caught a glimpse of Aksell and Ethos wrestling over the Weather Belt. A swishing sound caught Timothy's attention, and he dropped to the ground. Councilman Alexis' sword collided with the tree behind him and stuck there, biting deep into the wood. As he tried to yank it free, Timothy thrust the branch at him, hitting him square in the chest and knocking him over. Alexis was back on his feet in an instant, and Timothy swung the branch again.

Alexis swayed back out of the way and grabbed the end of the branch, jerking it out of Timothy's grasp. Timothy withdrew the shuriken hidden in his other sleeve and charged at the Councilman, gripping the weapon like a tiny knife. He threw an uppercut punch at the Councilman, and was rewarded by the appearance of a gash on Alexis' chin. Alexis kicked Timothy in the chest, and he gasped in pain, his shuriken falling from his hand as he fell to his knees.

Alexis grinned and advanced on Timothy, pausing for a moment to withdraw his sword from the tree. But when he turned around, Timothy was nowhere to be seen. The Councilman looked around suspiciously, suddenly wary.

Timothy crept up closer to him, moving soundlessly through the grass. He reached over to pick up a stick from the ground - a little smaller than his staff, but thick and sturdy nonetheless.

Alexis suddenly turned to one side, hearing the movement.

So much for surprise.

Timothy jumped up from his hiding place and swung the stick at Alexis' head with all his might.

Caught by surprise by the unexpected attack, Alexis was too slow to bring his sword up to block the blow. The stick hit him in the face, breaking his nose and making his eyes roll back in his head. As he slumped to the ground, Timothy picked up his fallen weapons, scanning the battle for an opportunity to be helpful. Over by the chasm, Ethos seemed to have gained the upper hand, throwing Aksell off of him and sending him flying into a nearby boulder.

With a malicious grin, he stood up and withdrew a small rectangular device from his pocket. "Milkop Quawz! I have a deal for you!" The fighting raged on, and Ethos tried again. This time, Gearwire stepped forwards.

"What do you want, Ethos?"

"A cease-fire while we negotiate would be appreciated," Ethos said.

"Hold your fire," Gearwire said. "But don't take your eyes off of the

Council!" He turned back to face Ethos. "What is it?"

"I have in my hand a device that will summon the Orgwar to my aid. You and I both know that Earth would stand no chance against them. If you release my men and let us go free, I will surrender this communicator to you."

Gearwire fell silent, and Timothy could tell that he was wrestling with Ethos' offer.

"Time is ticking," Ethos said, tilting the box back and forth. "Five… four… three… two-" Out of the corner of his eye, Timothy saw Aksell pull himself into a sitting position, drawing a strange pistol from his belt - the very same one he had used on Timothy in the Battle of Kawts. He fired it at Ethos, and the head Councilman froze in place, his finger resting on the activation button of his device.

Before he could recover, Gearwire snatched the device from his hand and tossed it to the side. Draagetsew grabbed Ethos and roughly pinned his arms behind his back as Seililyad's soldiers did the same to the rest of the Councilmen.

"Let's get these usurpers locked up," Draagetsew said, marching Ethos toward the castle.

Aksell slowly got to his feet, his hands shaking. Timothy ran down to him, joined a few seconds later by Quill.

"That was amazing!" Quill exclaimed. "I knew you had it in you!"

"I… You're still alive," Aksell said.

"We have a lot to catch up on," Timothy said, breaking into a smile.

"Do any of you know what happened to the Weather Belt?" Dr. Maddium interrupted, coming up to the group.

"It fell into the chasm while I was fighting my dad," Aksell said. "I don't think we're going to be able to fish it out anytime soon."

"We'll worry about retrieving the Weather Belt later, Thomas," Gearwire said wearily. "We're the only ones who know where it is right now, anyway. Let's just bring the Council back to Blancstadt and then get some rest."

"You go ahead," Dr. Maddium said, picking up Ethos' communicator from where it had fallen. "I'll be along soon."

Gearwire nodded and led the way back to Blancstadt, the Council-men in tow.

Epilogue

"I can't thank you enough for what you've done for Alpen," the feathered mutant said, looking back and forth between Quill and Timothy. He had introduced himself as a member of Alpen's Congress, recently released from the castle dungeons.

"I didn't really do all that much," Quill said, shaking his head. He gestured toward Timothy. "Timothy was the one who came up with the plan that helped us turn the tables on the Council."

Timothy bit his lip, suddenly uncomfortable. "The only reason my plan worked at all was because we got lucky," he said. "And because there were so many recently discharged soldiers still in Blancstadt. It was Alpen's own armies that really turned the tide."

"Well, whoever's ultimately responsible, I know that you two still played an important role," the Congressman said with a kindly smile. His attention drifted to something over Timothy's shoulder, and he added, "Excuse me for a moment. I have to go talk to President Draagetsew about something."

The Congressman hurried off across the banquet hall, leaving Timothy and Quill alone for the moment.

"This is beginning to feel like Kawts all over again," Quill said with a smirk, and Timothy couldn't help but agree.

"I'd rather be thanked by random strangers than risk getting brainwashed by the Council," Timothy said. "It seems like a fair trade to me."

"Food's ready!" Draagetsew bellowed, cutting through the chatter. "Everyone, take a seat!"

Slowly, the Guardians of Kawts and the surviving Alpenite Congressmen made their way to the table. Spread out before them were a variety of dishes that Timothy had never seen before, ranging from what looked to be white asparagus to thin, breaded slices of meat.

They began to eat, but their meal was soon interrupted by the sound of the door slamming open. Timothy turned to find the source of the sound and saw Dr. Maddium standing in the doorway. His hair and lab coat were more disheveled than usual, looking as if he had just run all the way from the site of the last battle with the Council.

As Timothy watched, the time-traveling scientist made his way over to Gearwire and said something to him that Timothy couldn't quite make out.

Gearwire's eyes widened, and he said, "Are you sure?"

Dr. Maddium nodded. What he said next was heard by everybody, despite his attempt to stay quiet.

"We have only sixty hours until the Orgwar arrive."

Author's Note

If you've enjoyed this story, please consider leaving an honest review on whatever platform you purchased this book from. It really goes a long way toward my ability to continue to release new titles in a timely fashion. And remember, if you haven't already, sign up for my e-newsletter at weston-fields.com to receive a free digital copy of "The Smugglers"!

Acknowledgements

This book would not be what it is today without the help and input of so many people who gave me support and advice throughout the process.

I would first like to thank my sister, Natalie, for reading through the early manuscripts for me on multiple occasions and allowing me to talk at her about the story when I got stuck. A special thank-you is also due to my mother for helping me iron out some of the remaining wrinkles in the story, and to Dr. Smit, for providing invaluable advice on Quill's conversion scene.

A few more rounds of bonus thank-yous: Dad, for letting me name my main character after him; Natalie and Elizabeth, for allowing me to use the characters of Crystal, Jewel, and Madison in this story. I hope I did them justice.

Last, but certainly not least, I would like to thank God for giving me the abilities and the resources to complete this project and for providing such an amazing world for me to gain inspiration from.

About the Author

Weston Fields is a student at Calvin University, where he studies religion, philosophy, writing, and ministry leadership. When not considering adding yet another minor to his degree, he can be found working at the library or working on his latest book.

You can connect with me on:

🌐 https://weston-fields.com

Subscribe to my newsletter:

✉ https://tinyurl.com/WFieldsnewsletter

Also by Weston Fields

The Guardians of Kawts

Everything is not as it seems in Kawts. It's been nearly a year since Quill lost The Race, leaving his best friend Timothy with a mysterious wooden box and a host of unanswered questions. Although Timothy has tried to move on from his friend's death, the unusual circumstances of Quill's last days continue to haunt him. When Timothy is caught up in the middle of a raid on the Kawts Library, he realizes that there is more going on in Kawts than meets the eye.

www.ingramcontent.com/pod-product-compliance
Lightning Source LLC
Chambersburg PA
CBHW020739310726

48969CB00002B/337